Praise for *The Brink*

"*Awakened* goes international, and the terror sky-rockets. *The Brink* is proof that sometimes the most horrible creatures lurk closer than you think. Powerful and horrifying. Curse you, Murray and Wearmouth, for keeping me awake so late."

—Brad Meltzer, #1 bestselling author of *The Escape Artist*

"It's monsters. It's horror. It's danger and shocks and scream-out-loud surprises! And mainly, it's FUN. A tense and haunting thriller. Don't miss out."

—R. L. Stine, #1 bestselling author of the Goosebumps and Fear Street series

"Murray and Wearmouth's latest, *The Brink*, is a white-knuckled rollercoaster. This novel is chock-full of everything I love: strange creatures, a world teetering on the edge, and heroes who I'd want at my side during any firefight. This isn't just a story hopped on steroids—but one injected with nitrous and blazing on all cylinders. Give me more!"

—James Rollins, #1 *New York Times* bestseller of *Crucible*

Praise for *Awakened*

"This book is no joke. Get ready to not sleep tonight. *Awakened* does exactly what it advertises. Scary-amazing fun."

—Brad Meltzer, #1 bestselling author of *The Escape Artist*

"Murray and coauthor Wearmouth . . . sculpt a briskly moving narrative that includes a plethora of short-burst action sequences and pacing fit for a Brad Meltzer novel. Along the way, they plant the seeds for sequels and craft a tight, pulse-pounding story that practically cries out for a film adaptation."

—*Booklist*

"*Awakened* is a tautly written, brilliantly unexpected thriller from authorial duo James S. Murray and Darren Wearmouth. . . . *Awakened* hits the high notes of Douglas Preston and Lincoln Child's *Relic* and Scott Snyder's *The Wake* . . . but its scope actually extends much further."   —*Kirkus Reviews*

"*Awakened* is a good old-fashioned monster story with devious new twists. Creepy and disturbing in all the right ways!"

—Jonathan Maberry, *New York Times* bestselling author of *Glimpse* and *V-Wars*

"A great book with both science fiction and horror elements, along with some mystery. I highly recommend this."   —*Sci-Fi Movie Page*

THE

Also by James S. Murray
and Darren Wearmouth

AWAKENED

JAMES S. MURRAY AND DARREN WEARMOUTH

THE BRINK

AN AWAKENED NOVEL

HARPER Voyager

An Imprint of HarperCollinsPublishers

THE BRINK. Copyright © 2019 by James S. Murray. All rights reserved. Printed in the United States of America. No part of this book may be used or reproduced in any manner whatsoever without written permission except in the case of brief quotations embodied in critical articles and reviews. For information, address HarperCollins Publishers, 195 Broadway, New York, NY 10007.

First Harper Voyager premium printing: March 2020
First Harper Voyager hardcover printing: June 2019

Print Edition ISBN: 978-0-06-286897-8
Digital Edition ISBN: 978-0-06-286898-5

Cover design by Richard L. Aquan
Cover photography by Larry Rostant

Harper Voyager and the Harper Voyager logo are trademarks of HarperCollins Publishers in the United States of America and other countries.

HarperCollins is a registered trademark of HarperCollins Publishers in the United States of America and other countries.

20 21 22 23 24   QGM   10 9 8 7 6 5 4 3 2 1

THE BRINK

CHAPTER ONE

Mark set down two wine glasses on his kitchen counter. So far, the fourth date had gone perfectly. After three months of living in London, he had finally found a British girl who liked his Boston accent. He liked hers, too. He had taken Imogen out for a lovely dinner. They had laughed at each other's jokes. Two twentysomethings having a good time. They had walked back to the warmth of his basement apartment on Westbourne Park Road and watched some Netflix. He wanted to watch a scary movie, like *The Descent* or John Carpenter's *The Thing*. Nothing like a good horror flick to make the heart race faster and help break the touch barrier. But she insisted they watch a popular hidden camera show starring these four guys from New York. As an aspiring stand-up comedian, he had to admit—the show was funny.

It was getting late, almost midnight. He guessed she was staying over for the first time, but so far it had gone unsaid. Mark uncorked a second vintage bottle of Chianti, letting out the rich aroma, and poured two generous measures. He wanted to impress her. She worked for an investment bank in Canary Wharf, and despite her protestations, he could tell she had class. Old money with the type of cut-glass English accent reserved for those in high society.

He wanted things to be perfect.

Unfortunately, a faint, sulfurous odor knocked away the scent of the wine, as if somebody had struck a match or something was burning. Mark frowned as he visually inspected the kitchen's electrical ports and appliances. Everything appeared fine. He had taken the garbage out, so it wasn't that, either. Perhaps, he considered, the source was of a romantic nature. Imogen making the next move. He craned his head from the kitchen alcove to check if she had lit a candle.

The TV screen bathed the dark room in a monochrome glow. In this light, Imogen looked even more like Charlize Theron, lounging on the leather couch in her purple dress. She looked stunning.

But no lit candles.

"Do you smell that?" he asked.

"Smell what?"

"I dunno. Burning?"

She shrugged. "It only stinks of you in here."

Mark smiled at her joke. He inhaled through his nostrils, trying to track the smell. He could still detect it. Only slightly, but it was there, lingering in the air. Maybe Imogen was being polite by denying its existence. He had gotten a great rate on this basement apartment, especially given how old the building was, but he was now beginning to regret it. Technically, his studio apartment was actually in the converted sub-basement, below the basement itself. There was no way it could be legal, but it was so very cheap. The lack of natural light was tough to deal with at times, but at moments like this, he wanted the place as dark and cozy as possible.

A new episode began playing on the TV. ". . . *among four lifelong friends who compete to embarrass each other* . . ."

"Do you want to watch another one?" he asked.

Imogen rose from the couch. Her hand caressed his. "Nah. Let's go to bed . . ."

His heart raced even faster. He grabbed the TV remote control and switched it off. The room transformed to near darkness, and she led him to the bed.

A lamp on the bedside table provided soft lighting. The comforter was folded in half on the lower end of the bed. Crisp white sheets and pillows covered the rest. He had arranged it immaculately in the hope of this moment.

Mark spun to face her.

She had slipped off her dress and was wearing fancy black lingerie.

His heart skipped a beat. He moved toward her and reached out his hand to caress her face.

Here goes nothing . . .

The strange smell forgotten, he focused on the alluring subtle floral scent of Imogen's perfume, which had driven him crazy all evening. He closed his eyes and leaned in to kiss her.

Her soft lips made contact with his, for the first time. The moment felt electric, exhilarating. She bit his lip lightly, and they both opened their eyes, smiling.

They fell back onto the bed, intertwined in each other's arms. She pulled off his shirt. He nuzzled into her neck, kissing every inch of her skin there. She was easily the sexiest girl he'd ever kissed.

He drew the comforter up over them, and their bodies moved in rhythm.

Then the sound from the TV blurted in the room.

"*. . . among four lifelong friends who compete to embarrass each other . . .*"

They froze, peering into each other's eyes, and giggled.

"Sorry," he said.

He reached out from under the covers and fumbled with the remote on the nightstand, hitting what he thought felt like the power button.

The sound stopped.

Silence returned to the room.

He dove back into her neck, nibbling softly. Her breathing quickened as he made his way slowly down to her chest. He lifted the straps of her lingerie off her shoulders. Imogen peered into his eyes and gave him a seductive grin.

"*. . . among four lifelong friends who compete to embarrass each other . . .*"

The TV was even louder this time, making them both jump in fright under the covers.

"Oh, for fuck's sake," he said, confused. "I'm sorry."

"Haha, it's okay. It *is* my favorite TV show."

He grabbed the remote and sat up to face the TV. This time, he'd do it right.

"What the hell?" he asked.

She sat up to look.

The room remained in near darkness.

Nothing played on the TV screen.

The two lay there in silence for a moment, baffled by the experience.

". . . AMONG FOUR LIFELONG FRIENDS WHO COMPETE TO EMBARRASS EACH OTHER . . ."

The words again, even louder. The identical line as the previous two times, like it was being repeated over and over on a loop. But that was impossible, because the TV was off. Unless the damned thing had broken, and that was the last thing he needed on a tight budget.

He tracked the sound downward. It wasn't coming from the TV.

In fact . . . the sound had come from underneath the bed.

How could that be?

Somebody had to be playing a cruel trick on him. Nothing else made sense. Whoever it was, their timing was awful.

He peered over the side of the bed to investigate. It was too dark, though, and he couldn't see anything. He *could* smell sulfur again, stronger this time, and he was now firmly convinced one of his friends had somehow sabotaged his date. Furious, he leaned over to grab his cell to light underneath his bed, when he heard, behind him, the sounds of ripping fabric and an odd gurgle. He spun back to face Imogen—

A serrated black spike erupted out of her stomach, a few inches below her bra. She let out an ear-splitting scream. She wrapped her hands around it, and the sight of the wriggling appendage made it seem as if she were controlling the thing that had burst through her torso. Blood pooled around her body and soaked into the white sheets as she stared at him with fear, confusion, and agony in her eyes.

Mark scrambled off the mattress, wide-eyed, consumed with her terror, which was mirrored on his own face.

Something clasped around his ankle.

He looked down.

Before he could move or think, scaly black hands with razor-sharp claws squeezed harder. He gasped at the feeling of his shin being crushed. He tried to kick free, but the tightness of the grip only increased. Above his anguished roar, he heard his bones crack.

The claws sliced through his ankle, severing his foot in the blink of an eye. He screamed in agony as he collapsed face-first onto the bed, his eyes blinking away the blood that had come out of Imogen.

His stump sprayed blood over the floor of his miserable little apartment.

The black spike thrust through the bed between them, like a flexible spear. It carved through the mattress, splitting it in two, and punctured Imogen's rib cage, impaling her with its serrated edge once more.

She tried to gasp, but there was so little life left in her that she didn't have the energy—or the air in her lungs—to scream.

Her odd silence unnerved Mark.

The tail withdrew from her body. A moment later, it thrust through her mouth, turning her subdued cry to a brief gargle. Dark purple blood streamed from the side of her mouth onto the pillow. Her head rolled to the side and she stared at Mark through dead eyes.

"*NO!!!*" he yelled.

As if in response, a massive creature exploded out of the center of the bed. Black and muscular, the scant light from the lamp seemed to be absorbed by its obsidian skin. Its tail wafted from side to side, spattering drops of Imogen's blood from its tip across the bedroom walls. It punched her corpse to one side, the force so strong it threw her across the room, a deep depression knocked into her blood-soaked sternum. Her limp body battered against his set of drawers.

Mark attempted to scramble back, but the creature's foot pressed him downward, forcing the air from his lungs. His torso crushed against the remote, hitting the power button. Light blasted out from the TV set.

The creature towered over him, thick strings of saliva dangling from three rows of dagger-like teeth. The overwhelming smell of sulfur burned Mark's nostrils now.

The creature reached down and lifted him by his jaw.

Claws plunged into his neck.

Sprays of his blood joined Imogen's on the walls.

His vision fogged. He attempted a bubbling breath.

The creature twisted his head to the side.

Mark's neck cracked.

His body went limp.

The last thing he saw was the outline of the vicious creature, silhouetted by the bright white light of the TV, as all life quickly drained from his body.

CHAPTER TWO

The Red Army's artillery shells whistled through smoke-filled sky and exploded around the shrapnel-scarred Reichstag building. The stench of cordite and death clogged the air. Colonel Otto Van Ness crouched by the side of the Führerbunker's emergency exit in the chancellery garden, Luger pistol in hand, and peered at the shattered remains of his beautiful city.

The dream was over.

Otto removed his black peaked cap and wiped the sweat from his brow. He had risen from the bunker to witness the final twitches of the Third Reich's corpse. He wanted it seared into his mind so he'd never forget how it all ended.

Some brave souls still fought on at the central zone's defensive ring.

That was suicide.

Reports inside the bunker had stated Soviet troops

were already fanning through Berlin's streets in over-whelming numbers. The increasingly loud crackle of gunfire confirmed they'd be here in minutes—if that—ready to capture the Führer and subject him to a public show trial and execution.

One way or another, that wasn't happening.

It was decision time.

Otto blanked out the sounds of his city in its death throes and focused on the Führer's survival. Every-one talked about Göring, Himmler, and Goebbels, but Van Ness—perhaps because of his anonymity—was truly Hitler's right-hand man. The voice from the shadows whispering advice to the Führer. It was Van Ness' job to anticipate all possibilities and plan for the worst.

Which was exactly what this moment was.

And Van Ness was prepared. His escape plan cen-tered around the Führerbunker, the deepest human-made subterranean complex in history. So deep, in fact, that his latest excavation had exposed a massive cavern, containing the dusty black claw of a pre-historic predator—perhaps from a mighty dinosaur that had once ruled the plains of Europe. It was an exciting find, but even more exciting was knowing those caves could lead Herr Hitler safely out of the city.

Otto had ordered workers to build a false wall to conceal the cavern and construct a set of stairs leading to the antechamber in the Führer's bunker accommodations. Nobody beyond his closest team members knew it even existed . . . and he'd had most of those men sent to fight off the Russians in the streets of Berlin.

Suicide, he thought with a grim smile.

A shell burst to his right, close to the public parkland of the Tiergarten.

A blood-curdling scream rose above the cacophony of explosions and gunfire. Otto scanned the rubble-strewn road for the injured soldier. Something about a single person suffering cut through him deeper than the collective noise of total war. It was as if his cruelty could be tempered by individual pleas.

He hated the feeling of weakness.

A cool spring breeze cleared the acrid smoke.

Three members of the Hitler Youth lay dead, their bodies spread behind a howitzer in grisly twisted shapes. The sole survivor of the gun crew had lost a leg. Tears streamed down his blackened face and he reached out a quivering hand. The boy tried to raise himself. He coughed out a spray of blood.

Part of war is playing God with people's lives, for better or for worse.

He hated this intimate reminder of the Third Reich's failings. With a sneer, Otto aimed his gun and fired.

The boy's brains spattered the howitzer's barrel and he slumped against its wheel. The Fatherland had lost another son, added to the millions who had already sacrificed themselves in a noble yet failed cause.

Another explosion ripped through the air.

Closer.

Small fragments of debris rained down on him. The Russians were finding their range, and this death by a thousand cuts would soon be over.

Otto had seen enough. He needed to get the Führer out.

He also wanted to live.

Hitler sealed off in the bunker was like keeping
a wasp in a jar. His anger would only increase with
every piece of bad news, pushing him toward . . .

"No," he growled.

Not suicide.

They had to get away and regroup. Argentina perhaps, or Chile.

Otto scrambled to his feet, dusted down his uniform, holstered his Luger, and headed through the
entrance of the Führerbunker. This place was supposed to be his crowning glory, a haven for the upper echelons of the regime. Now they were trapped
like rats in the bilge of a once great ship. His jack-
boots pounded the steps as he descended toward the
main complex.

The nervous, sweat-stained faces of the soldiers
told him they had come to the same grim conclusion: Berlin had finally fallen. From here, it was
every man for himself, though no self-respecting
German would disobey orders and flee. That was
for the French and the Italians.

"Close the bulkhead doors," Otto ordered.

An explosion boomed overhead, causing the lights
to flicker. A few of the soldiers ducked and glanced
toward the ceiling.

Otto shoved a junior officer and bellowed in his
face. "Nothing is getting through four meters of
concrete, you fool. Run to the upper bunker and
order them to close the doors!"

Another set of stairs led deeper down. Otto strode

along the corridor, past rooms on either side containing generators, telephone switchboards, and Eva Braun's private quarters.

None of the senior officers met his glare while he advanced. The whole place stunk of despair. Their faces made it clear that they knew this place was nothing more than a mortuary waiting for its inhabitants to die. He shook his head as he passed the empty map room and reached the door leading to the Führer's accommodations.

Hitler's personal adjutant, Major Günsche, and his private valet, Lieutenant Colonel Linge, blocked his path.

"Out of my way," Otto snapped.

Linge bowed his head. "It's over."

"What?"

"The Führer is about to pass from this life to the next."

"You fools—get out of my way!"

Otto attempted to squeeze between them.

Günsche threw a stiff arm across his chest. "I cannot allow you to disturb his final moments. The Führer gave the order for no one to enter."

"Is that a fact?"

"Yes, that's a fact."

Otto grabbed Günsche by the lapels and thrust his forehead toward the younger man's nose. It connected with a satisfying thud.

Günsche slumped in his grip. Otto threw the moaning idiot against the wall, even as he took the man's Luger from its holster. He turned toward Linge and raised the gun at the remaining gutless obstacle in his path.

"*Nein*—" Linge shouted.

The bullet tore through the valet's throat. The officer crumbled to the ground.

He spun and shot Günsche in the head. Then he dropped the gun on the floor, slipped through the door, and locked it behind him.

The silence in the empty living room concerned him. Nobody sat in the luxurious chairs, and the painting of Frederick the Great had been ripped off the wall and stomped upon. However, the bookcase he had used to conceal the secret hatch remained in place.

Otto tentatively moved toward the study, fearing the worst. He pushed the door and it creaked open.

The scent of bitter almonds wafted out.

Cyanide.

Eva Braun lay contorted on the near end of the couch, mouth wide open and dead eyes staring at the ceiling.

The door opened wider, and relief washed over him.

Hitler sat hunched on the far end of the couch, still in uniform, his greasy dark hair slapped against his forehead, and he clutched a gold-plated pistol in his shaking hand. He raised his bloodshot eyes toward the doorway.

Otto stepped toward him. "My F—"

"Get out, Van Ness."

"Sir, I've got a plan to save you."

"You imbecile!" Hitler screamed. "Can't you see it's over?!"

Hitler glanced at Eva, then down at his pistol. Otto hated seeing the once proud man look defeated, on the brink of taking his own life.

It couldn't end like this.

History would judge Hitler a coward. And a man of his vision and strength . . .

No. I won't let it end like this. There's still so much to do.

"It's not over yet. My Führer, below this bunker—right below our feet—is a cavern that extends under all of Berlin. There's a secret entrance next door to a room of supplies, and a false wall where we can begin our escape."

"And then what? Hide underground like a cockroach? No, I will not."

"The caverns go deep and far. Kilometers. We'll find a way out once we clear Berlin."

Hitler's icy stare made Van Ness freeze. It had made many men freeze and often signaled their final moment. "Don't you see it's over?" he repeated. "We've been defeated."

"My Führer. As long as you're alive, as long as I am by your side, the Third Reich—and your vision for the new world order—has not been defeated."

Hitler rotated the pistol in his hand. He was on the edge, that much was clear.

"My Führer . . . do not allow your dream to die. Not here, not in this place. The Third Reich *will* rise again, rise from that cavern below, rise for future generations of our children and our children's children."

Hitler slowly lowered the pistol just as another explosion rocked the bunker.

"We need to act fast," Otto said. "Follow me."

He strode back into the living room and thankfully the Führer's footsteps followed. He thrust his shoulder against the bookcase. It scraped to the left, revealing a circular steel hatch. Once he had snapped open the fastening mechanism, he unlocked the door to the quarters and found a group of four soldiers.

"The Führer is leaving," Otto stated matter-of-factly. "The four of you are with us. Let's go."

They didn't even glance at the bodies on the floor and obeyed his command without question. As they stepped inside, they saw Hitler and executed perfect salutes.

Only the most loyal were allowed to serve in the Führerbunker.

Van Ness hauled open the hatch, grabbed a lantern from a ledge, fired it up, and climbed through the circular gap into the narrow shaft. The lantern's glow brightened the carved rock walls on all sides. Otto descended, treading carefully. The wooden steps creaked beneath his boots.

Hitler followed immediately behind. As they neared the bottom of the fifty-foot stairwell, the last soldier slammed the hatch shut, cutting out the artificial light. From here, they were on their own.

Otto entered the tennis court–sized chamber and swept his lantern from left to right, bathing the walls in a warm orange hue. He breathed a sigh of relief. The place was exactly how he had left it. Boxes of dried food. A stack of twenty-liter containers holding water and fuel. Rifles. Grenades. Fake papers. Flashlights. Everything they required for this eventuality.

The rest of the group entered the chamber.

"There's no time to waste," Otto said. "Grab an

entrenching tool. We need to break through the far wall into the cavern below."

They grabbed six collapsible spades and jogged to the far end of the chamber. One of the soldiers raised a spade over his head, preparing to strike. But instead, an ominous thud came from *behind* the wall.

The plaster fractured.

Hitler recoiled to the middle of the chamber, and the guards quickly dropped their tools and readied their weapons.

Something crashed against the opposite side of the wall again. This time, much harder. Chunks of plaster broke free and skidded across the ground.

"What the hell?" Otto said.

"Is this a trap, Van Ness?" Hitler asked through clenched teeth. "You traitor!"

Two soldiers turned to Van Ness and aimed their rifles toward him, while the other two covered the wall.

In his fear, he was still proud of how perfect these warriors of the Fatherland were.

But then another crash echoed around the chamber, and all the attention was back on the wall. Otto placed the lantern on the supply boxes. He drew his Luger and took up a firing position behind the steel containers. His heart hammered against his chest while he waited for the inevitable attack.

Perhaps the Russians found the cavern and are attacking from the other side. Yet, how could they have found it so quickly?

It made no sense.

The chamber shuddered. A six-foot section of the

wall collapsed inward. Otto aimed at the dark gap, ready to cut down the first Red Army soldier.

A moment of silence followed.

He tensed. Gunfire would soon swamp the chamber.

But still no weapons discharged. No grenades rolled in. No blasts from a flamethrower turned the room into a broiler. Instead, a gentle, acrid breeze blew through the gap.

What the hell is happening?

A piercing shriek filled the air, like nothing he had ever heard before. The ungodly sound sent a shiver down Otto's spine, and he was about to cover his ears when he bolted upright at what appeared before him.

A massive figure burst into the chamber, bigger than any man he knew. A giant. He tried to track it in his sights, but it raced across the ground at an unbelievable speed and possessed a darkness that the oil lantern couldn't possibly penetrate.

Unlike Van Ness, the soldiers were elite and didn't choke under pressure. They fired in unison as the figure closed in.

Their muzzle flashes briefly lit the room.

Otto, if possible, felt even more frozen at the sight.

A black creature, with a long, serrated tail and talons on the ends of its four arms, towered over the soldiers. The shots to its body had little effect. It roared at them, exposing three rows of razor-sharp teeth, and lifted its tail to strike.

A creature was all Otto could think about. There was no other word for it, just as there was no thought that could move him to action. His mind just kept screaming *creature creature creature*, and the horror of it glued him to the spot like nothing ever before.

He had shivered while under fire in a crumbling house in Stalingrad. He had toured Auschwitz. He had seen the gas trucks. He had even survived the trenches of the Great War.

Nothing compared to this.

Hitler screamed, and he stumbled backward into boxes of rations.

The creature's tail whipped through the air and carved through the four soldiers like they weren't even there, slicing their torsos clean in two. Body parts collapsed in a soggy heap. Blood spattered the stone in all directions.

Otto fired at the creature's scaly back.

Nothing.

He fired again.

No effect.

It was futile. Terrifying. Incomprehensible.

The creature leaped forward and grabbed Hitler's head. Its talons sunk into his face as it lifted him off the ground in an instant.

The Führer screamed again. He looked so small in comparison to this predator of the deep. Insignificant, even, as blood was squeezed from his jaw.

Otto repeatedly fired until the Luger's magazine ran dry.

The bullets continued to have no effect.

The creature stood there, crushing Hitler's head, harder and harder. One of his eyes popped out of its socket and hung against his cheek. Blood poured from his face and stained the ground beneath his dangling boots. His legs twitched in the air.

"Van Ness!" Hitler cried out, his voice raspy.

The creature leaned closer to the Führer's face and perfectly mimicked the gravelly sound of Hitler's voice.

"Van Ness!"

A moment later, Hitler's skull collapsed under the pressure. The last words the most powerful man in the world had screamed were Otto's name.

They were also very likely the last words Van Ness would ever hear.

Blood sprayed the ceiling. It dripped from the creature's claws. The whole place now looked like a gruesome slaughterhouse.

The creature threw Hitler's limp body against the carved rock wall, then turned toward the supply boxes. Otto had imagined his death a thousand times. On the end of a rope. At the hands of a firing squad. In a burning building. Trapped in a tank.

Never like this.

He backed against the wall and reached into his holster for a fresh magazine.

But something stopped the creature from advancing. It prowled in the shadows, staying out of his lantern's glare. Snarling. Letting out guttural wheezes. Staring at him through its lifeless eyes, which were more intimidating than any Allied weapon.

Another creature thrust itself through the gap in the wall, and, like the other, it wouldn't come near him . . .

No, not me. The light.

Otto grabbed a flashlight from a supply box,

switched it on, and focused the powerful beam on the creatures.

Both roared—*in pain?*—before racing back into the dark cavern. Van Ness let out a shuddering breath, his legs buckled in shock, and his back slid down the cool stone wall. They would surely come for him again.

The flashlight could only last so long.

Minutes ticked by and the creatures did not return. But the sound of hundreds—thousands—of distant shrieks from the cavern below betrayed their continued presence.

An hour passed.

Then two.

He had nowhere to go. Escaping through the cavern below wasn't an option. Going back into the bunker meant certain death as well.

While he waited for events to dictate his destiny, a realization struck him: the world suddenly faced an enemy even more sinister than the Russians. And even as the thought frightened him, his ever-scheming mind led him to ask himself:

How can I turn these creatures to my advantage . . . if I survive?

Otto believed wholeheartedly in the Nazi vision of a homogeneous society, despite the world not yet being ready to take this next evolutionary step. The impure had fought against them, and it seemed—for now—they had halted the march of progress. But here, in this cavern, he had witnessed a new, powerful force. And if he could control that force . . .

This discovery changed everything.

And only he knew about it.

He started looking around for a new way out, plans already forming in his brilliant, devious mind.

I will find an escape. *And the Third Reich will rise again.*

I will rise again.

CHAPTER THREE

Lightning split the dark Parisian sky.

Albert Van Ness navigated his wheelchair toward a framed photograph of his father, Otto, on the office wall. He knew the world right now stood on the cusp of a great precipice, just like his father had always predicted. A moment that would define the ultimate survival of a species. Much like when a giant asteroid slammed into the Yucatán Peninsula sixty-five million years ago and wiped out the dinosaurs, but this time the threat was coming from below, and it was coming for humanity.

Van Ness stopped in front of the photograph of his father. Every detail stood out. A sharp SS uniform. An armband with the swastika. An iron cross hanging around his neck. Chest proudly puffed out. The creator of the Foundation for Human Advancement and a true visionary . . . though also a man who had not lived to witness his dream become a reality.

It's okay, Father. Your reality is about to happen.

The creatures were evolving rapidly to tolerate higher levels of oxygen. Their rise to the surface was inevitable. The planet no longer had a choice.

Van Ness had reasoned the day would come when the Foundation would need to take more direct control over governments, but he did not think it would be so soon. The events in New York had changed that.

Thankfully, he had left nothing to chance.

He glanced at the flat-screen monitor on the wall. The tiny red circles on the global map indicated the Foundation's live operations. So many creatures' nests, spread across the entire world. New ones had appeared on a monthly basis since the botched mission under the Hudson River. In fact, that damned city appeared to have acted as a catalyst. Australia, India, Thailand, Oman, Argentina. Under major cities, capitals. The locations had an eerie coordination about them as they sprung up around the globe, like the creatures were preparing for war. He wondered if they had realized the time had come for a death match, where there could be only one winner.

Maybe.

His eyes narrowed when he focused on the United States of America.

It had several live nests growing, and one in particular—under San Francisco—was potentially what he had always been looking for. It was vast, according to initial reports, perhaps twice the size of the one below New York City. Van Ness had long suspected that he would know the true nature of the creatures only once his team had discovered their main lair—if there was one. He had a feeling this one in the Bay Area was it.

But there was still so much to learn about them.

They were an intelligent species—more so than humans—yet their purpose and motivations remained unclear in his mind. He wanted to investigate, but the new administration in America was a hindrance to finding out if San Francisco really was "creature ground zero." There was only one way to find out, and that meant he needed unlimited resources for the upcoming fight. With time running out for humanity, he couldn't afford to wait any longer.

The governments of the world no longer mattered except for their ability to give him what was necessary to save—and advance—the human cause.

"Shield mode," Van Ness snapped.

The office's voice activation system responded with an affirmative beep. Then the wall-to-ceiling window, twenty stories above the Parc du Champ de Mars, changed from transparent to gunmetal gray.

Darkness momentarily swamped the room before the overhead spotlights blazed down to restore the light. None of the array of international spooks who watched him from various vantage points on the city skyline needed to see this quiet moment of reflection.

The calm before the storm, he thought.

Van Ness reached across the table and poured himself a finger of Jameson. The smooth, sweet whiskey warmed the back of his throat, and he exhaled in satisfaction. It wasn't the most expensive bottle in his office—there were a few rare Scotches and a Pappy twenty-three-year-old in the sideboard—but the taste of this particular drink always brought back memories. Whiskey was his father's favorite, and they had shared a bottle of Jameson forty-five years ago in a villa on the Amalfi Coast after destroying a small nest beneath Naples.

He smiled to himself, picturing their heated political debates on the deck overlooking the sparkling Mediterranean. They were best friends as well as father and son, and even during times of levity, they had strategized.

Sadness momentarily engulfed him.

All of those years Otto had spent building the organization. Grooming Albert to take over. Teaching him the Foundation's doctrine. And the old man wouldn't be here to appreciate that their goals were about to be realized.

Van Ness poured another glass and washed it around his mouth.

This one's for you, Father.

It was cruel, really, watching such a powerful man wither away. Otto had spent four decades successfully fighting creatures and bringing most governments in line, only to be beaten by a disease. He remembered the old man staring up from his death-bed through bloodshot eyes, wincing in agony, muttering about revenge.

His final words were "Don't let our dream die," before Albert had suffocated him with a pillow to end both of their suffering.

Like father, like son.

Van Ness had never completely bought into his father's idea of revenge against the World War II

Allies. It had always felt spite-fueled and counter-productive to the Foundation's primary aim of protecting the world from the creatures. But as Van Ness grew older, and he learned the truth of how his mother had died, he clearly saw how his father was right about these supposed democratic nations. They were the real war criminals. It wasn't just bitterness; it was a cold, hard fact. To save the world, certain countries had to be brought to their knees.

I'll finish them, starting with Washington and London.

Van Ness checked his watch. He hated being late for meetings and his next was in five minutes. A couple of deep breaths brought him back to the cool, calm, and collected man his employees knew. He rotated his chair toward the mahogany bookcase and keyed in a code on his armrest.

A door-shaped section of the bookcase eased out with a pneumatic hiss and rolled to the side, revealing a brightly lit corridor. The labs and rooms on either side lay in darkness, empty. This part of the operation had moved to the newest area of the Foundation's complex. Hatching the master plan required extra protection, a safe space to deal with national leaders without fear of any reprisals.

A fortress from which Van Ness could save the world.

Van Ness drove forward.

The wheels squeaked against the polished corridor, and the quiet purr from the chair's engine echoed around the walls. He reached an elevator, got in, and hit the button to take him to the basement parking garage. The elevator smoothly descended through the center of the building, like the tip of a creature's tail spearing through a person's head and gliding effortlessly through their body. That had been the signature move his team had observed.

Within seconds the elevator bumped to a gentle halt, and the doors parted to a dull, football-field-sized parking lot. Cars packed the spaces.

At the far end, two guards, dressed in black coveralls with rifles at the ready, stood at either side of a concrete bunker, thick enough to shield against any conventional or nuclear attack. The massive central blast door opened with a mechanical grind as he wheeled closer, sliding from right to left to reveal an all-glass elevator that was twice the size of a typical one found in office buildings.

Van Ness entered. Seconds later, the door closed and the elevator began its smooth descent, plunging rapidly beneath Paris in a transparent shaft that had a slight blue tinge. After fifty feet, the carved rock wall opened out into a vast underground cavern. This moment always stunned any guest: the sheer scale of the prehistoric cavern, and the clear elevator plummeting downward into the abyss. Fifty huge, shining globes, mounted from the ceiling and from the outcrops, pumped enormous amounts of light on the hundreds of small cave entrances that were typical of how the creatures constructed their nests. The new complex let the creatures know who was the real apex predator on the planet.

Van Ness peered through the glass of the elevator at what he had built: the most cutting-edge complex in the world. A spectacular, domed operations center, like half a bubble built right into the cavern. It was made from the same ten-inch-thick graphene glass as the elevator shaft and sat right in the heart of a creatures' nest. Van Ness' version of the Cheyenne Mountain facility, though his was a thousand times bigger and nearly a mile below Paris.

Two stone corridors ran from the operations center to labs and testing areas for newly developed weapons. Other rooms contained supplies and dorms and machinery to keep the place running. The Foundation could survive down here for years if required. With what he was planning, it was an entirely possible outcome.

Van Ness leaned toward the wall-mounted control pad and hit the external speaker button. Faint shrieks filled the car. Hundreds of them. A sound that would strike fear into any person, but not him. Not here where he was in complete control.

To him, it was one of the sweetest sounds in the world.

The elevator slowed as it reached the operations center, which had the same faint blue tinge. He loved the hue. Twenty members of his staff, all dressed casually in light cotton shirts and dark blue trousers, sat in front of workstations that ran around the circumference of the center.

Allen Edwards, Van Ness' trusted number two, glanced up from the central command table as the car halted at the edge of the cool, air-conditioned area. Edwards had lost a lot of weight and most of his remaining hair over the past year. He appeared stick thin in his beige suit—painfully so—and he didn't have any known sicknesses. Van Ness didn't believe his claim of shedding those pounds through jogging. Edwards was loyal to his core, but the disaster in New York and its stress had clearly changed the man. It was a situation that required monitoring. Nobody understood the Foundation's activities as well as his number two. He needed him, though not to the point of him becoming a liability.

Ten large screens were suspended around the dome at regular intervals. Van Ness studied them while he wheeled to the central command table. They displayed maps of the Foundation's global presence, video footage from live operations, streams of public data being searched for anything creature- or Foundation-related, and feeds from cameras attached to the dome's four laser turrets.

One of the live cameras moved across the cavern, and one of the lasers rotated toward a small cave. A heartbeat later, it fired, slicing two red beams across the cavern into the darkness. None of the staff members reacted, and they continued with their work, having become numb to this almost continual occurrence.

Edwards acknowledged his arrival with a thin smile. "Good morning, Albert."

Van Ness peered at one of the big screens, which displayed a two-mile stretch of countryside and forest. "Do we still have him tracked?"

Edwards nodded. "Yes, he's in the forest. Everything is going to plan."

"Excellent." *Because now it begins.* "The former mayor of New York will not be a problem for much longer . . ."

CHAPTER FOUR

Raindrops pelted down, splashing into the puddles of the forest trail. Tom Cafferty's running shoes pounded the dirt. A biting wind cut through his drenched T-shirt, but he drove on, sucking in deep breaths.

These moments alone allowed him time to think about the next steps in taking down Albert Van Ness and the Foundation, to formulate decisive plans that would finally end the German's global reign of tyranny.

Exercise had also become an essential part of his routine. It had made him physically and mentally sharper. Fit body, fit mind. Blowing off steam, unlike the Z Train–obsessed mayor who had turned to booze and had caused everyone around him to suffer while he selfishly pursued his dream. This time his wife, Ellen, was an equal partner on their quest. And the two other people in his inner circle were as equally committed to seeing this through, whatever the cost.

Cafferty broke out of the forest and hit a narrow country lane. Hertfordshire's lush green fields surrounded both sides, separated by hedgerows and fences. He quickened his stride, pushing himself against the driving rain, pushing himself to the limit. He knew he had to do that in every aspect of his life if he was to achieve his aim.

A crow burst from the branch of a naked oak tree. It cawed as it flew overhead. Fast. Black. Shrill. It immediately evoked images of creatures in Cafferty's mind.

When the first one erupted out of the Jersey City subway tunnel . . .

Attacking the survivors on the train . . .

Facing them down in the nest . . .

Thousands swarming David North as he fought to the bitter end . . .

Cafferty pushed those memories to the back of his mind. Only the future was manageable. He had told himself to let go, again and again. But he couldn't. This was his new obsession, and it was only partly a revenge mission for the likes of North, Arnolds, and Spear. Dealing with the Foundation meant dealing with two types of creatures: Van Ness and the subterranean ones. Globally exposing them. He just hoped the world was ready to deal with that.

He was confident, though, that it didn't have a choice.

A small white cottage with a thatched roof came into view at the bottom of a shallow valley. Cafferty's lungs were near bursting and his legs ached, though he maintained his speed. The house was in an ideal, discreet location for the team: within striking distance of Paris, but not too close. Diego

Munoz, the team's tech guru, had already arrived for the briefing and had parked his silver van next to Ellen's Audi Q5.

Cafferty slowed to a walk as he neared. He rested his hands on his hips and took a minute to catch his breath. All the physical aches felt good.

Today was a big day, though. An afternoon meeting in London would potentially define the team's future. Since President Reynolds had disappeared nearly a year ago, the funding for his team was running out. Reynolds' newly sworn in successor, President Brogan, was yet to be convinced about the danger presented by Van Ness.

This cash flow problem had created a mental ache for the last few months. Running helped ease his anxiety, but it didn't wipe away his concern. He needed to make the UK's leading politician understand the importance of exactly what he faced on the other side of the English Channel. He needed a powerful partner. It frustrated him how most national governments either toed Van Ness' line or didn't take the threat seriously. Thankfully, Prime Minister Simpson had agreed to a meeting away from Downing Street, for obvious reasons. He didn't want any of Van Ness' team seeing him entertaining a man who was actively pursuing the Foundation.

The whine of a motorbike approached from a distance, Sarah Bowcut's usual way of announcing her arrival. A former NYPD SWAT team member, she appeared more badass than ever.

Cafferty checked his watch. It was just before ten in the morning, the planned time for their briefing.

He carried out a final few stretches, then entered the cottage. The mouthwatering scents of cooking bacon and brewing coffee hit him, making his stomach growl.

Munoz sat inside the cramped living room on the leather couch. He faced the cast-iron Victorian fireplace, looking every bit his usual self. Headphones planted against his ears while he focused on his laptop. Terrible T-shirt. This one had Darth Vader in a disco. Cafferty leaned against the doorway.

"What's up, Tom?" Munoz said without peering up.

"Ready for this afternoon?"

"You bet."

Cafferty gave him an appreciative nod, then continued along the hallway. The former head of the New York City MTA command center had done some great work over the past year. His van had everything they needed for surveillance and target acquisition, but even better, he had subcontracted the right people to allow them to reverse engineer the laser he had recovered while saving President Reynolds. The other laser had been requisitioned by DARPA.

Ellen stood by the stove in the farmhouse-style kitchen. She was dressed in sweatpants and a baggy T-shirt and had her hair in a loose bun. Her relaxed outfit reminded Cafferty that this was a long way from their spacious apartment in Manhattan. He knew she missed her previous lifestyle, but it was leaving their toddler, David, with her parents in West Virginia that had been a lot harder. There was so much they were still coming to grips with, from both before and after the Z Train opening, but one thing was clear: they were both committed to each other and the mission. They could have the life they wanted after they'd seen this through. Neither of them wanted little David dragged into a world of creatures and human monsters.

Neither of them wanted him growing up in a world where the Foundation even existed.

She flashed him a smile. "You're getting quicker, Tom."

Cafferty went to wrap his arms around her. The disaster in New York had brought them closer than ever before. It hadn't healed everything, but he no longer looked at Ellen and saw the shared baggage of the last few years. The affairs. The drinking. The silent treatment. He now viewed her with all that stripped away. As the person who had initially stolen his heart.

Theirs was a bond forged in the darkness below the earth, and their love—and, more important, their respect—for each other was stronger than ever.

Ellen stepped away. "You can keep your sweaty paws off me, mister."

"Not even a kiss?"

Through the kitchen window, Bowcut's motorbike crunched over the gravel and came to a halt by the side of the van. She tugged off her helmet and nodded at Cafferty.

"Grab a shower, then we'll eat," Ellen said. "We don't need you stinking up the kitchen."

Cafferty let out a mock deep sigh, then headed for the bathroom. As he closed the door, though, that sigh became a shortness of breath. Because ever since that day in New York, the shower always brought back memories of other people's blood falling from his body and swirling around his feet. Blackness rimmed the edge of his vision . . .

And then he was back in control.

That was something he'd managed to be able to do only recently: to put behind him the day-to-day reminders of the horror he'd witnessed. As with everything now, Ellen had helped, just as he helped her with the nightmares she'd lived through. The PTSD wasn't gone—not by a long shot—but it was something he could put away now and not let overwhelm him.

He took his shower and was dressed and back out in ten minutes. Munoz, Ellen, and Bowcut, who had her hair in a tight ponytail and was wearing jeans and a SWAT T-shirt, all sat around the kitchen table.

Bowcut had spent the last year tracking the Foundation's movements from Paris to various places around the globe. Its numbers were growing every month, and it appeared the Foundation was ramping up for something. She had worked on flipping a few of the staff, but the result had often been the same— that person would vanish off the face of the earth without any leads. All searches led to dead ends.

And, they assumed, the person was probably as equally dead.

"How you doing, Tom?" Bowcut asked.

"Not bad, all things considered. I'll be feeling a lot better if this afternoon goes well." Cafferty pulled out the spare chair with a scrape and took a seat. "Ready to go?"

"Yeah, we're good, but we need to proceed with caution."

"Caution?" Cafferty grabbed some toast and spooned on some scrambled egg. "Don't we proceed with caution for everything?"

"I mean extra caution. I've tracked some of the Foundation guys back to London. Things are heating up in the capital."

"Any idea what they're planning?" Ellen asked.

Bowcut nodded, then spread a schematic of the London Underground on the table. "I've seen them slipping through the entrance of a disused Underground station, disguised as workers. Some carrying heavy equipment. We might be looking at an engineered version of New York."

"Did you get pictorial evidence? Or anything else that we can use as leverage with the prime minister?"

"Of course. The photos are already uploaded to our secure server. But we need to go in tonight if they're planning something imminent."

"And that might be the case," Munoz added. "I hacked into their shipping manifests last night. They use the shell company Everglade Line for their business. Plenty of stuff goes around the world, but a lot has gone to the U.S. and UK recently. And I mean *a lot.*"

"Any hints as to what it might be?" Cafferty asked.

Munoz shrugged. "It's down as 'technology.' That's all I know. It's reasonable to assume they're paying people off at the customs checks."

"So that's why we need to go in tonight," Bowcut said. "If they're creating an artificial breach, we need to stop it before creatures flood the tunnels."

"Thank God the creatures can't breathe oxygen . . . right?" Munoz said, half believing his words.

Cafferty's thoughts drifted back to the creatures in the New York subway, slowly growing more tolerant of higher levels of O_2 and less dependent on their methane-filled nests. He forked scrambled egg into his mouth. Ellen had done his just the way he liked it, with some milk and sharp cheddar, seasoned with salt and pepper. He savored the taste for a moment before getting back to the task at hand. "Okay, sounds like we've got little choice. Let's strategize on our way to the meeting."

The team finished brunch in silence. Cafferty knew today would tell him if they had a shot at carrying on the fight in a structured way, or if they would be forced into more drastic action through lack of support. He also realized the consequences of the latter weren't worth considering. Yet.

THE FOUNDATION AGENT LOWERED HER PARABOLIC MICROphone back inside her covered trench. At last, after two weeks of surveilling the cottage, she had gotten some tangible information from these deluded New Yorkers. She had initially come in the dead of night, dug the hole, then laid a ground sheet over it. Once covered by fallen leaves, leaving only a thin slit to observe, her position was almost invisible to the naked eye. And now it had paid off.

She typed in a message on her secure data-burst radio:

Command, this is UK Four. Prepare for a transmission.

Edwards would be on this fast. That's the way he worked, and she liked that. Her arctic-condition sleeping bag had kept her warm at night, but the weather in England was a damp cold, rather than dry, and it chilled her to the bone.

Command:

Copy, send over.

UK Four:

Attached is a recording from the cottage. Tom Cafferty, Ellen Cafferty, Diego Munoz, and Sarah Bowcut in conversation.

She transmitted the burst. While waiting for a reply, she stared through the scope of her sniper rifle at the kitchen window. It was entirely possible that the kill order might come, which she had no qualms executing, as long as it got her out of this damned ditch.

Minutes later, the reply came.

Good work, UK Four. Your work there is done. Wait for them to leave, then head back to London to await further orders.

UK Four:

Roger, out.

She continued to observe for the next half an hour, willing the targets to leave the cottage. Eventually they did, Cafferty in a suit and his wife in business dress, the other two in casual clothing. They looked pleased with themselves, but she guessed they were in for a nasty surprise once in the capital.

CHAPTER FIVE

H is body shivered. Pain screamed in his head. His fingers and toes felt like blocks of ice. He swallowed hard to wet his parched throat. Every limb ached like he had the worst bout of the flu. Former (though he couldn't really be certain if that was true or not) president Reynolds' eyes flickered open, but everything was a blur. His back rested against a cold metal chair that had been bolted to the ground; his wrists and ankles were manacled to the arms and legs of the chair.

He gasped out a breath that fogged in the frigid air.

His mind raced to remember how in the hell he had ended up in this situation. The events came to him slowly. Leaving Camp David for a jog in the wooded hills of the Catoctin National Park along with five of his security detail. He thought it was overkill at the time. But the Z Train incident had taught him to take nothing for granted. So he thought he was safe.

He was wrong.

It happened in that clearing.

My God.

They had followed a trail through woodland. It was all pretty routine. Then rounds hissed through the air. Hundreds of them fired from suppressed weapons. The security detail went down fast, each man writhing as multiple shots tore through his body. The ambush had left Reynolds as the lone survivor, crouching behind a rock.

That was when the first dart embedded in his neck. The second dug into his shoulder. The third into his back. He attempted to run, but power had drained from his body. A heavy feeling quickly swamped him and he had slumped to his knees.

Reynolds shuddered as he relived his capture, and right now, he was at the mercy of someone.

But who? he asked himself. His memory was still hazy, so he replayed the attack in his mind to search for any clues. And the questions that he came upon most often were these:

Who would most benefit from kidnapping the president of the United States? Who would have the resources and audacity to pull off such an operation? Why would they risk it?

He shook his head in an attempt to clear it. More images slowly crystalized in his mind. Masked attackers had strapped him to the back of an ATV. He struggled with the memory now, because he had lost consciousness after that. Only small snapshots remained. Being in the back of a van when a doctor injected him with something. Sitting strapped to a seat in a small jet and getting the needle treatment again. Being rolled across a small airport's tarmac, Hannibal Lecter–style. A hospital room with monitors all around him. They were all blurs, all without much detail.

Then he recalled a face.

Albert Van Ness.

The man looking down at him, peering with the same kind of relish as a snake looking into a bird's nest.

Reynolds growled as he struggled against his restraints. He blinked hard, attempted to focus on his surroundings once again. Gradually, his vision cleared, and he gazed down at himself. They had dressed him in orange coveralls like the prisoners at Guantánamo Bay. His arms and legs were thinner. This made him wonder how long it had been since his capture, and what exactly they had put him through.

Are they starving me?

Keeping me alive for blackmail?

Where am I?

Reynolds searched for any visible markings to tell him where the Foundation had taken him. Company logos. Written language. *Anything* recognizable. But there was nothing.

His chair sat in the middle of a huge, empty warehouse on a smooth black floor. Rubber, perhaps, but he wasn't sure. Whatever the material, it looked like it had been fitted in sections, and he was on a large circular one, roughly twenty yards across. All the walls were pristine white and appeared to be made of glass. Behind the left one, it sounded like a basketball was being tossed around—an odd sound for a warehouse. At the far end of the area was a single door.

Reynolds peered at the ceiling.

Two massive mechanical arms extended from either end and met in the middle, as if it could be opened like a bascule bridge. The whole place confused him. It seemed extravagant for a simple warehouse, but he had no idea about its purpose. Nothing gave away his possible location, though it had to be somewhere remote; otherwise someone would have noticed him.

Right?

Reynolds' teeth started to chatter. He hunched, let out a breath through gritted teeth. It didn't matter if they were attempting to starve him. The cold would take him first if they kept him here for much longer. His toes were ice white, matching the temperature. All the hairs on his arms and legs stood at attention.

As if on cue, the door at the far end flew open. Two guards wheeled in a large portable monitor and headed over to his chair. Their footsteps echoed inside the vast space, and neither of them acknowledged him when they spun the screen to face Reynolds. He tried talking to them, but it only came out as the grunts of a man with no saliva. They ignored him anyway.

A small HD webcam was attached to the top of the screen, so he assumed he was going to talk to somebody. He was fairly certain who that somebody would be. One of the men hit the power button; the other carried a cup of water to him and held it toward his lips.

Reynolds twisted his head to the side. Rasping, he somehow got out, "I'm not drinking more of your drugs."

"It's water," the man said mechanically.

"Screw you."

The guard simply shrugged and then joined his colleague at the side of the monitor. He made direct eye contact with Reynolds as he slowly poured the contents of the cup onto the floor. It spilled across the ground and washed against his shivering toes.

Assholes . . .

A blue pinhead light on the HD camera winked on.

A meeting room flashed onto the screen. Albert Van Ness sat at the head of the table in his wheelchair, elbows on the desk and hands steepled. The dark blue suit neatly fitted his frail body, and his black tie had been fastened in an immaculate knot. The man next to him looked gaunt and tired, the top button of his shirt unfastened. Loose tie. He seemed like a two-pack-a-day smoker who had vodka for breakfast.

Is that Edwards?

"Good morning, former president Reynolds," Van Ness said.

Hearing himself greeted as "former" confirmed Reynolds' suspicion that he'd been a prisoner for quite some time. It also pissed him off.

"This is my colleague, Mr. Edwards," Van Ness continued. "I'll keep this brief because time is of the essence. Humanity is facing its greatest challenge. One that might lead to our species' downfall. The Foundation for Human Advancement has prepared as best as we could, but unfortunately the coming apocalypse has arrived faster than even I anticipated. To that end, we require immediate resources."

He leaned forward.

"And that's where you come in."

Reynolds simply glared at the screen. He remembered being led from the command center in New York City by the treasonous Agent Samuels, Van Ness' inside man on his Secret Service security detail. They had planned the president's death that day, but with the help of Diego Munoz, he had survived. Barely. There was no way he intended to help this terrorist hiding behind a supposedly benevolent organization.

"How long have I been a prisoner?" Reynolds asked, his throat raw.

"Ah. Yes. How rude of me," Van Ness replied. "You deserve some answers. We've kept you in a medically induced coma for eleven months, give or take. You've been kept alive because I knew a day would come when you'd be useful. And here we are."

Nearly a year. Reynolds could not believe it. He momentarily wondered what had happened in the world since his drugging.

Those thoughts quickly dissipated.

"Useful?" Reynolds spat, his cold breath continuing to cloud the air between himself and the screen. "What do you expect me to do for you?"

Edwards turned to Van Ness. "Perhaps we should raise the temperature and give him a hot meal. Make him a bit more comfortable."

"You seem to be forgetting I was in the Marines." Reynolds let out a bitter laugh. "Cut the bullshit. Tell me what you want."

Van Ness gave a sage nod. "We intend to trade

you for money. You will act as negotiator directly with President Brogan."

A modicum of satisfaction ran through Reynolds' shivering body. Brogan was aware of the Foundation. She had acted as a confidante when he went through the process of weeding out anyone in the administration with ties to Van Ness' organization, and Reynolds knew America was in safe and steady hands—assuming the Foundation hadn't turned her, too.

"The smugness on your face is unbecoming, Mr. President," Van Ness continued. "You of all people know how real the threat is. How dangerous these creatures are. We'll all perish if they are not stopped. I'll be frank with you, John . . . May I call you John?"

"You can call me whatever you'd like, asshole. It won't help."

"In that case, let's stick with former Mr. President," Van Ness replied. He turned to face Edwards. "It has a nice defeated ring to it, don't you think?"

Reynolds filled with anger but tried to remain defiant. "We both know the United States does not negotiate with terrorists."

"Terrorist?" Van Ness grinned. "I'm humanity's savior. Your protector. And a humble one at that—I won't make you thank me."

Reynolds used all of his strength to hold back his rage. He also attempted to stop his body from convulsing from the cold. If they were going to kill him, fine, but he wasn't acting as Van Ness' pawn. Not today, not ever. He'd been through too much in his life to pathetically appear worldwide on a hostage video, parroting outrageous demands. If he was going to die, he was going to face it like a man.

"All I require is two percent. Surely you can make that happen, former Mr. President."

"Two percent of what?" Reynolds asked.

"Why, of everything, of course. Two percent of the United States' gross domestic product."

Reynolds quickly did the math and nearly choked on the outrageous demand. "Two percent. You want four hundred billion dollars?"

"A year. To start. But, of course, we will renegotiate next year. Economies are going to take a tumble, especially yours."

"It's a small price to pay for the ongoing survival of our species," Edwards added. "Think of it like an insurance policy."

Reynolds broke into laughter at the ridiculousness of the statement. He laughed hard. He laughed maniacally at the screen, enjoying the look of annoyance on the faces of the two men. "You're insane," he said.

"Am I?" Van Ness replied. "Maybe. Maybe. But the United States will pay, and you'll make sure of it."

"To hell I will," Reynolds shouted in defiance. He stared into the camera and slowly repeated his earlier statement. "The United States does *not* negotiate with terrorists."

"Perhaps . . . perhaps not. But here isn't the time for this discussion. For now, you'll relay our request or face the consequences."

Reynolds shrugged. "Go ahead and kill me. I won't do it."

"Oh, John. *I* am not going to kill you. It's not what *I* do to you that matters here. Not what I do to you at all."

The oddness of the response unnerved him.

As did the look of triumph on the old man's face.

Van Ness hit a button on his wheelchair arm. "Farewell, former Mr. President. Look to your left and let us know when you change your mind."

The video feed cut abruptly.

The guards wheeled the monitor back toward the distant doorway, leaving him alone once again in the freezing cold.

Reynolds peered at the left wall, where he had previously heard those odd sounds. The middle section of it changed from white to transparent, revealing blood spatters and smears on the glass. Beyond it, in what looked like a bland prison cell, a creature gripped a man's naked body in its claws. The corpse had multiple slashes across the chest, half of his face had been ripped off, and he was missing an arm. The creature threw the mangled man against the rear wall, bounded up to him, and thrashed its tail against his back, slicing his spine in half.

Bile rose in Reynolds' throat. His pulse quickened as he watched the creature continue to throw the man around like a rag doll.

Then the creature noticed the section of now transparent wall. It approached, staring toward Reynolds through its soulless black eyes. The sight instantly brought back nightmares of escaping through the Jersey maintenance tunnel almost two years ago. Already hypothermic, he was still chilled to his core to be face-to-face with one of these monsters again.

The creature howled. It threw itself against the glass, but the wall held. That didn't stop it from repeatedly attacking in an attempt to reach Reynolds.

He thought he heard a fracture, like ice cracking in a whiskey glass. It reminded him of when the creatures had attacked the command center blast door. If they got through that, this material seemed much less of a problem. It left him with a simple decision. He could either take the cowardly way out and negotiate for Van Ness, which he knew was doomed to failure and would likely lead to his death regardless, or he could face being torn to shreds by sharp claws, teeth, and tail.

On balance, he preferred the second option.

Death before dishonor.

"Semper fi."

CHAPTER SIX

Cafferty, Ellen, and Munoz waited in the back of the van, surrounded by various surveillance devices and screens. Bowcut sat behind the wheel, driving them to their meeting through the thick London traffic. The prime minister had changed the location of the meeting to the De Jong Group building, which ruined the team's previous reconnaissance and exfiltration plans, though Cafferty was in no position to argue. He needed this to happen wherever it took place.

Ellen checked her watch. "Ten minutes, Sarah. How's it looking?"

"We'll be there in five."

Cafferty returned his focus to a diagram of the building on one of Munoz's screens. "So tell me about the De Jong Group."

"They specialize in diamonds. Mining, trading, retail, you name it."

"Any links to the Foundation?"

Munoz shook his head. "I'd have flushed it out by now. The prime minister's brother works there, though, so that might explain it. He wants this meeting off the radar, and him visiting there isn't out of the realm of possibility for prying eyes."

"What about the building?" Ellen asked.

Munoz pointed his pen at the screen. "It's got one of the only heliports in the City of London. I'm guessing that's how Simpson might arrive. The service entrance is on a back street. They've allocated us a parking space twenty yards away from it. There's a central elevator, six floors, stairs, a fire escape stairwell, and a front entrance through reception."

"Not ideal, but okay."

"We'll monitor from outside and give you your best escape route if the shit hits the fan. And I've been watching for any tails on us—we're not being followed. Don't worry. It's all good."

Good wasn't a word Cafferty would use to describe his thoughts. He wondered about the last-minute location switch. Maybe it was his paranoia getting the better of him, but in his experience, anything substantial that appeared straightforward always had a catch. And that catch often had a nasty sting. That was the case in all walks of life.

It also meant they were going into a building virtually blind. Yes, Munoz had just given them the overall layout, but it frustrated him to the point of anxiety that he wouldn't have the exits and contingency plans thoroughly ingrained in his mind before entering the building. After the New York subway tunnel attack, the idea of being trapped somewhere was a fear as palpable as the creatures themselves.

The low-grade panic wasn't helped by the fact that he was certain the Foundation was watching them. It had to be. The question in his mind was why Van Ness had let him come this far without a direct challenge. The team had expected one and had been ready with their prototype weapons, but nothing had transpired. This all added up to twist his stomach in knots.

Ellen, likely sensing this, rested a hand on the shoulder of his suit jacket. "It'll be fine, honey. When the prime minister hears what we have to say, he'll be on board."

"It's not him I'm worried about."

"We've been through this a thousand times. Van Ness' cronies won't want to unnecessarily expose themselves. Their whole modus operandi is secrecy."

"I still don't like it."

"We've got your back," Bowcut said.

"Don't worry, Tom," Munoz added. "This will all work out, and the four of us will be on a train to my favorite city in the world in no time."

"What city is that?" Ellen replied.

"Amsterdam . . . I have family there."

"Sure you do." Ellen gave him a wink.

"We're here," Bowcut said. She brought the van to a halt and ripped up the hand brake.

Munoz used a joystick on a console that was packed with switches and dials. The tiny camera on the van's roof spun and displayed external images on one of the screens. Only a few people walked up and down the street. Nobody looked suspicious to Cafferty. Then again, he reasoned, why would they go out of their way to stand out? For all he knew, the kid with the jeans halfway down his ass might be waiting to report on their arrival.

Ellen opened the rear doors, letting in the cool winter air. She stepped out and straightened her business suit. Cafferty followed. He gave Munoz a single firm nod before closing the door. He trusted only the three people with him—Ellen, Bowcut, and Munoz. Beyond that, everyone was open to question. Van Ness' reach was far and wide. They all knew that after the New York disaster, but had also been reminded of it during the last six months, when previous friends had transformed into enemies for no apparent reason.

That was until Diego had hacked into their bank accounts and found transactions from various offshore accounts. Traitors.

Settling those particular scores was for another day, though. For now, Cafferty turned his attention to the De Jong Group building and the man inside who might truly be able to help him, the prime minister of the UK. It appeared exactly how Munoz had described. Six floors constructed of reinforced concrete with ten rain-spattered windows on each level. Painted ivory to match the Edwardian buildings surrounding it.

A blond woman holding a clipboard waited by a set of double doors. She smiled as the Caffertys approached. "Welcome to the De Jong Group," she said. "If you'd like to follow me to the conference room."

Cafferty and Ellen exchanged pleasantries, then followed her through a sparkling marble corridor to an elevator. Within a minute they had ascended to a single room on the top floor. Windows on two sides offered stunning views of St. James and Green Park, where tourists packed the paths beside the lake toward Buckingham Palace. The heliport lay on the other side.

Ellen walked around a large rectangular table and flipped open her laptop beside the projector's connection point. Cafferty poured himself some water to quench his thirst. This opportunity was their first meeting with a G7 leader outside of the United States. Sooner or later, someone had to take the threat of Van Ness and the creatures seriously.

Somebody has to, or this has all been for nothing.

A distant buzz broke his reverie. In the gray sky, an average-looking helicopter thumped toward the De Jong building, rapidly closing in. It was hardly *Marine One*, though he understood that they did things slightly different here with their lead politician. Many MPs even took the train to work, with no security detail whatsoever.

"Looks like they're here," he said. He had been concerned that the prime minister might not take this meeting seriously.

"I never doubted it." Ellen brought up their presentation on the projector. "We're all set. Remember, let me do most of the talking."

"I know, I know—"

"Tom, I mean it. You know how you can get carried away."

The sound of the blades interrupted any response he might have had as the chopper banked over the park and came to a hovering stop above the heliport before descending. As soon as the skids hit the painted yellow *H*, the side door rolled open. Two of the prime minister's protection detail—heavyset men in bland navy suits—jumped out and scanned the immediate area. Shortly after, the prime minister headed out with two of his staff.

The same woman who had welcomed the Caffertys walked out to meet the UK delegation, and she ushered them inside. They carried in with them the strong smell of cologne. It reminded Tom of the eye-watering meetings in Washington, where midrange fragrances would fight for supremacy. He didn't miss that life at all. But he could stomach it here if it furthered his team's mission.

The two bruisers entered the room first and pulled open a countersurveillance kit, scanning the room for bugs of any kind. One spoke into his cuff. "It's clean in here."

A wave of paranoia hit Cafferty again. Was Albert Van Ness listening? Munoz had made him aware of Samuels' treachery in the New York emergency docking station. It wouldn't be beyond Van Ness to have a man deep inside the UK security team if he had managed it in America.

Prime Minister Simpson approached. He looked younger in the flesh, with a side part in his brown hair and a beaming smile. "Ellen and Tom, it's great to finally meet you."

"Likewise," Ellen said while shaking his hand.

Cafferty gave Simpson's hand a firm squeeze. "We've got important work to do, Prime Minister."

Simpson's smile dropped. He backed away to the far side of the table and sat between his two staffers. One was a man with gray hair and stern features.

The other was a woman in a royal-blue business suit who looked equally as harsh.

Cafferty hoped the distance wasn't symbolic. The UK delegation couldn't have chosen a position farther away, and now they faced each other from opposite ends of the large table.

"Allow me to introduce my private secretaries," Simpson said. "Stef Barratt and Ben McSeveny." Both gave a curt nod. "You can trust them implicitly."

"Of course. Thank you for taking the time to meet us," Ellen replied. "We realize you're potentially compromising yourself by being here, and we're glad you came."

An uneasy expression spread across the prime minister's face. He repositioned himself in his chair. Cafferty understood the man had taken a great personal risk and was potentially putting his country on a collision course with the Foundation. But somebody had to take a stand, and Great Britain was renowned for its sense of fair play and lack of corruption. A fighter against tyranny.

In other words, the perfect European partner.

"Let us be blunt," Ellen said across the table. "The Foundation for Human Advancement's threat has already reached your shores."

Simpson raised an inquiring eyebrow. "How do you know this?"

"Because we've got evidence. However, we'll come to that soon enough. It'll be useful if you first tell us what you know about Van Ness and the Foundation."

The prime minister shifted uncomfortably in his chair. "I think it's better if you talk first."

Cafferty had seen this look before. Fear. The prime minister was scared.

"You saw what happened in New York a year and a half ago, Mr. Prime Minister," Ellen continued. "Tom and I were right in the middle of it. All thanks to Albert Van Ness. The man orchestrated the events of that day, with no regard for the loss of human life."

The prime minister remained tight-lipped. He likely shared the same reservations about their talk being in complete privacy, despite his team finding no bugs or hidden cameras.

"Sir, it would be easier if we were open about this," Cafferty said. "The only person with something to hide is Albert Van Ness."

Ellen pinched his leg. The warning. The "Shut the hell up, Tom."

The prime minister glanced at his aides, who nodded at him. He explained, "The United Kingdom has been asked for a significant contribution from the Foundation. That's all I'm at liberty to say."

"Asked, or did he demand it?"

"It was a request. With certain conditions attached for noncompliance."

"So a demand." Ellen groaned under her breath. "He is extorting you and all world governments for money. He punishes those who don't comply, usually with violence. This *must* end, sir."

Ellen's words filled Cafferty with a sense of pride. She was using all her skills from her old job in public relations to keep her composure and speak compellingly, and it was at least getting the prime minister to open up.

Simpson cleared his throat. "I was briefed after winning the last election that I'd have to deal with Van Ness and his supposed creatures—"

"I can assure you they exist," Ellen said. "And thousands of them might be right under this city."

"Are you serious?" the prime minister asked.

The steely look in Cafferty's eyes appeared to answer the question.

Simpson should have known they hadn't come here to fool around.

"We've tracked the Foundation from Paris to London," Ellen said. "We know they're mounting some kind of operation here, a substantial one at that. We're here to help and give you all the information you need."

"And I assume you want something in exchange?" Barratt asked with her high-class British accent. The type that could make any person outside of the upper echelons of society feel inferior.

"Our aim is to stop the Foundation and expose the creatures to the world so that we can stop them," Ellen continued. "We can do that as partners, with your help. Not extortion. And not with complete disregard for collateral damage. Van Ness will burn London to the ground if it serves his agenda—or if you don't pay."

Ellen's words appeared to resonate with the prime minister. He leaned forward more attentively. She flicked to the next slide, showing the Foundation's global operations the team had identified, and the twenty thousand casualties associated with each covered-up "natural disaster."

"I'm sure you've seen these on the news," she said. "What will the excuse be for London? A gas explosion? A terrorist attack? Perhaps a release of a deadly toxin by the Russians? Whatever happens, Prime Minister, it'll be on your watch. But you *can* prevent this."

"And mark my words," Cafferty added, unable to stay quiet any longer. "If you don't play ball with Van Ness or his apparatchiks, you'll go the same way as John Reynolds, Prime Minister. This can no longer continue—you must stand up and fight with us."

The prime minister slowly nodded. "So tell me what you're doing."

"We've reverse engineered some of the Foundation's technology, specifically high-intensity strobe lights and their laser weaponry. As Ellen and I can directly attest to, they work," Cafferty said, his mind drifting to cutting the creatures in half in those claustrophobic NYC subway tunnels. "Our prototypes are ready to go."

"So what do you propose?" Simpson asked.

"We're launching an operation to see what the Foundation is planning and would like your assistance."

"And when you find out?"

"Then we decide how to stop them," Ellen replied. "Together. As partners."

Simpson shook his head, more like he was pulling himself together than in disbelief. He held a hushed conversation with his aides. Cafferty glanced across to Ellen. She returned his look of concern.

Eventually, Prime Minister Simpson locked eyes

with Ellen and Tom. "Mr. and Mrs. Cafferty. The British government is *in*."

MUNOZ HAD PICKED UP INCREASED RADIO ACTIVITY IN THE immediate vicinity. He scanned through his radio receivers and picked up several spikes from encrypted traffic. That meant either more law enforcement in the area—though he could hear no sirens—or something else.

"Sarah," he said, "something isn't right. We're getting a lot of secure chatter."

Bowcut twisted in her seat to face him. "How much?"

"Four or five conversations in the immediate area."

"Stay here and keep an eye on things. I'm going on patrol."

Bowcut unfastened her seat belt, grabbed her Glock from the glove box, and slipped it inside her coat. The local laws meant she was risking a heavy response if she publicly drew her weapon. But the risk of the Foundation trumped any doubts. Bowcut and the team had already accepted they may get shot, and possibly made, but they had been pushed into this territory by everyone else's apathy, fear, or lack of knowledge.

Bowcut exited the vehicle and started her sweep of the street.

A white van turned the corner and headed toward the De Jong building. Black tinted windows. Traveling fast. Too fast for a typical London street. Munoz tracked its movement with his vehicle's external camera. It roared past Bowcut, leaving her stranded at the far end of the street. Then it slowed as it neared and turned onto the opposite pavement.

"Sarah," he said. "Are you seeing this?"

"*How could I not see it?*" she replied through his earpiece. "*How many IT services vehicles have tinted windows and jump sidewalks?*"

The van reversed hard. Its wheels spun, gained traction, and it powered toward the De Jong service entrance.

Several pedestrians darted out of the way. One of them shouted an insult.

Munoz aimed the camera to the rear of the van.

The doors battered open in an unnaturally fast way, as if somebody had rammed them internally with brutal force.

Something leaped out in a blur and crashed through the service entrance's glass doors at an unnerving speed, leaving a big hole in the shattered remains.

In daylight.

Whatever or whoever it was turned for the basement stairs.

It can't be.

Aboveground.

Black. Rapid. Powerful.

Munoz swallowed hard. It reminded him of being in the command center, when he had first seen the footage of the creature in the still photos. That memory was seared into his mind. He knew creature traits when he saw them.

It couldn't be anything else.

He raised the radio. "Tom, Ellen—something is coming for you. Something bad. *Right now.*"

Neither tapped their earpiece to acknowledge.

"Tom, Ellen, are you hearing me?"

Again, no response.

Munoz spun to face his signal monitor and his eyes widened. Somebody was transmitting a signal on the same frequency, deliberately jamming their communications.

And something *inhuman* was inside the building.

CHAPTER SEVEN

afferty's earpiece crackled. He strained to listen but couldn't make out the faint voice behind the static. It was likely a technical fault or interference picked up from the prime minister's security detail. Whatever the reason, he decided to stay focused on the present and on the meeting, which had taken a positive turn.

"We'll lend our support to your mission and to your team," Simpson said.

Ellen and Tom locked hands under the table. Both had sweaty palms. Both knew what was at stake. Outside, it was almost like the world had understood the importance of the decision, because as the prime minister had spoken in their support, shafts of sunlight broke through moody clouds and radiated down onto parts of the city. This was exactly what the team needed to achieve success.

"But there are certain conditions to this partnership," the prime minister explained. "First, we'll attach a liaison officer from the Secret Intelligence

Service to your group. Everything between us remains top secret but also transparent."

"Agreed," Ellen said.

"Second, if things are exactly like you say, we'll be taking over in the UK once we create our own weaponry to counter the threat."

She nodded in agreement again. "Our aim is to share the technology we've acquired and everything we've learned about the Foundation, so you can defend yourselves."

"Excellent. Then we have ourselves a deal."

Relief washed away the months of stress. They had finally made solid progress. Once a G7 national government took the threat seriously and acted without the Foundation's support or consent to actually fight the creatures, it was game over for Albert Van Ness. His monopoly would fall, and the world could turn its attention to eradicating the threat, instead of being cowed by it.

"So, tell me about this operation you're planning," the prime minister said.

The sound of the chopper's rotors winding up interrupted him.

"You're not leaving us already?" Ellen joked.

Simpson looked quizzically at one of his security detail. "We're going to need more time here. Let the pilot know."

The agent spoke into his cuff, twice, though he didn't appear to be getting any response. He turned and headed out the double doors to the sunlit heliport.

The chopper's rotor blades sliced through the air

at an increasing speed and rapidly spun to a blur. It was primed to take off, that much was clear, but why?

Cafferty twisted in his chair to watch the agent approach the cockpit. An alarm went off in his head, though he told himself to stop being cynical about everything in the world that he couldn't directly control. That was Van Ness territory.

The agent ducked as he jogged under the blades. The rotor wash flapped his jacket away from his body, and his tie snapped over his shoulder. He approached the pilot's open window and hunched down.

"So, about your operation . . ." Simpson said.

Back outside, a red cloud exploded from the back of the agent's head, immediately followed by the report of a gunshot. He lifelessly collapsed to the ground as if somebody had turned him off with a switch.

"What the h—" Cafferty gasped.

The shooting had paralyzed him. He watched openmouthed as the pilot switched his aim to the conference room.

The surviving agent grabbed Simpson and wrestled him to the ground.

Ellen grabbed Tom's shoulder and they both dropped to the carpet. He tensed while he waited for the inevitable rounds to hiss through the air.

Five shots rang out in quick succession, each wince-inducing, each drilling through the conference room window and slamming into the opposite wall. The British agent clutched his chest and collapsed, dead, on top of the prime minister.

The chopper's skids lifted off the heliport. Its nose dipped, its engine ground higher, and then it thumped away into the sky.

"Prime Minister," Cafferty shouted, "are you hit?"

"I'm okay," he said in a quivering voice. "I'm okay."

Ellen and Tom helped each other to their feet, then approached the prime minister, lifting the agent's dead body off him.

Shaken, Simpson took rapid shallow breaths. "Van Ness," he muttered.

Silence filled the meeting room for a moment, until the conference phone at the center of the table burst to life. Its crisp electronic rings reverberated around the room.

"Don't answer," Simpson blurted out. "We need a way out of here."

"He's isolated us," Cafferty said. "I doubt his plan was to simply steal your chopper. Why did you change locations at the last minute?"

"I didn't order the change. It came in from MI5 . . . No . . . surely the director isn't in on this! He can't be. Can he?"

"Yes, he can," Ellen said firmly. "I'm guessing Van Ness won't just let us walk out of here, so you need to get another helicopter here in minutes or we'll have to face whatever's coming. Trust me, with Van Ness, this won't be pretty."

The ringing stopped.

"We've got agents guarding all entrances," Simpson said. He fished his phone from inside his jacket, then selected a contact. After three faint rings, somebody answered. "Home Secretary. I want a chopper sent immediately to the roof of the De Jong building. I'm facing an assassination attempt. Send it now!"

BOWCUT SLIPPED HER GUN INTO HER CONCEALED HIP HOL-ster and grabbed a laser from the back of the van. Adrenaline coursed through her body. Whatever had battered the other van's doors off its hinges and darted into the basement wasn't human.

But exactly what, she had no idea. To her knowledge, the creatures weren't capable of surviving at ground level, where the oxygen rendered the air toxic to them. It mattered little. All she could do was deal with the facts, and she was pretty sure the laser was going to be of more use than her pistol right now.

"Good luck," Munoz said.

"Looks like the prime minister got off the roof safe. His chopper just lifted off."

"It's not him I'm worried about."

"Keep trying to get in touch with Tom and Ellen."

"Will do."

She hid the laser inside of her denim jacket and strode toward the De Jong Group's service entrance. It surprised her that no agents had guarded it, but from here she could see through the building's reception area. A few British agents milled around the front entrance.

It had all the hallmarks of a Foundation operation. Just like in New York, it had gotten people on the inside to clear a path for the coming assault. This time, she was ready to strike back with equal—

A brilliant flash of light erupted from the building.

A shock wave knocked her off her feet, instantly followed by a fireball. Dense black smoke gushed out of the service entrance. Shards of masonry and broken glass peppered her body and sprayed over the street.

Pain seared down her left side.

White noise filled her ears.

Car alarms wailed.

She groaned to her hands and knees and peered through the smoke, attempting to register what had just happened. Her father and brother had died during 9/11, and thoughts of that day spun through her mind as she scrambled to gain any kind of self-command.

A cry came from somewhere else in the street, desperate and weak.

Bowcut tried to stand but sunk back to one knee. Her injuries didn't feel severe. If anything, the blast had just stunned her. She checked the laser. A piece of shrapnel had split the casing. The weapon had saved her life, though it was now useless.

Munoz rushed through the haze and crouched by her side. "Are you okay?"

"I'll live." She coughed, grimaced, grabbed her ribs. "Help me up."

He wrapped an arm around her shoulders and she hobbled back to the van. Each painful step told her she wasn't fit for anything. She could barely hear from the blast. Her left side felt like she had been hit by a car. By all accounts, she should lie down and rest for a day or two in a hospital.

But she knew the fight was just beginning.

SIMPSON HAD GONE RIGID WHEN THE BUILDING SHOOK FROM the explosion. Cafferty felt the same, experiencing the internal dread he was sure the prime minister was going through. He struggled for breath, and his chest felt like it was about to explode. This had happened to him only once before—in the Visitors' Pavilion, after the torn-apart train rolled into the station, his wife and the passengers nowhere to be found.

He wondered if the plan was to simply kill the prime minister, Ellen, and him in an inferno, or something else more sinister. Van Ness had a sick flair for the dramatic. He had orchestrated a plane crash in Poland to kill half the country's administration on a flight back from Russia; there was no reason he'd resort to something as mundane as a bomb when the grandiose would sell the Foundation's agenda more readily.

"We need to get out of this building," Ellen said, and her voice helped him gain his composure. She was his rock in more ways than she knew.

"We've got a chopper coming in five minutes," Simpson murmured. "Can we hold out that long?"

"I don't know—"

The conference phone rang again.

"Goddamn it," she said. She reached across and hit the speaker button.

"I'm glad you answered before the building lost power

or disappeared entirely . . ." Van Ness' voice said in an official tone.

"He's gonna blow the building," Cafferty whispered.

"You disappoint me, Mr. Prime Minister," Van Ness said.

"What the hell do you want?" Simpson snapped back. "Do you think you'll get away with this?"

"Oh, I will. I always do. In an hour, a terrorist group will claim responsibility. That is, assuming you don't accept my final offer."

Simpson leaned toward the phone, scowling. "Which is?"

"Simple: the British government will continue to pay my fees in exchange for keeping your country safe. I watched your meeting with the Caffertys. Their theories are fascinating, I must say."

Cafferty edged closer to Ellen. He scanned the room but spotted no cameras or listening devices.

"Don't bother looking, Mr. Mayor. Surveillance is a bit above your salary as a public servant."

"And if I say no?" Simpson grunted, defiant.

"I can't allow a state to go rogue. The stakes have never been higher between humanity and the creatures. One misstep could be fatal. So, if you say no, I'll continue our deal . . . with your successor. I have one in mind."

The audacity of what Van Ness was threatening shook Cafferty. It was one thing to experience the attempts on your life, but another to hear a man discuss murder so casually, like this was simply a business negotiation.

"One thing more, Prime Minister. The deal comes with one condition. A caveat, if you will."

"Which is?" the prime minister asked.

"I'd like you to borrow your dead agent's gun. And I'd like to watch you kill the former mayor of New York and his lovely wife."

Ellen shot Tom a look, barely disguising her fear.

In the distant sky, a chopper appeared on the horizon.

Simpson shook his head. "You twisted son of a bitch. Go to hell, Van Ness."

"I'm afraid this is your final chance. There will not be another phone call—I'm going to the Palais Garnier this evening and simply cannot afford to be late."

"You're finished once we get out of here. The British government will hunt you down."

"Very well. Enjoy meeting the Foundation's newest weapon."

The call cut.

Moments later, the building's power went out.

"Newest weapon?" Simpson asked. "What in God's name does he mean?"

Before Cafferty could reply that he had no idea, multiple screams rang out from the lower floors. Cries of terror. And pain. He raced into the hallway, paused for a moment to figure out exactly where the chilling sounds were coming from, and pushed open the door to the fire escape steps. He then kicked himself for not picking up the dead guard's gun first.

People had evacuated to the lower levels to flee from the smoke that was now engulfing the building. Panic had taken a firm grip.

But the people at the bottom of the stairs were surging up the fire escape stairwell, directly against others trying to reach the road.

What are they doing—

Then he saw it.

Cafferty stared down in shock.

A creature—an actual, aboveground creature—whipped its razor-sharp tail into the throng of people, carving through three torsos, cutting a path upward. It reached forward and grabbed a man's head in its claws, then twisted it 180 degrees. A perfect, horrifying killing machine.

And it was coming up the stairs toward them.

Another member of the staff held his arm out to protect himself. The creature's tail sliced through his forearm, then whiplashed through the side of his neck, and blood coated the pristine white staircase walls.

Something appeared different about this monstrosity, something besides the fact that it was aboveground, seemingly impervious to both light and oxygen. Tom couldn't quite put a finger on it until he realized it was a little more human in form and slightly lighter in color than the ones that had attacked in New York. It also had only two arms, not four like the creatures underground. And it moved with a mission, a systematic kind of purpose that he hadn't witnessed before.

Was it being controlled? Could *a creature be controlled?*

The idea made him think of Van Ness . . . and made him shudder at the possibilities.

The carnage continued unabated. Only ten people remained alive on the stairs.

Nine.

The creature grabbed a woman in a white blouse

and raked its claws across her throat. Her carotid artery exploded outward.

Eight.

The smoke was becoming thicker by the second. The crackle of flames grew louder.

Snapping out of the mesmerizing massacre playing out below him, Cafferty sprinted back into the conference room. Ellen and Simpson, who were both peering toward the approaching chopper, turned to face him.

"We have to get out of here now," Cafferty shouted. He stifled a cough. His eyes stung and his throat burned. "Van Ness' new weapon is coming to tear us apart. It's a fucking creature!"

Ellen's jaw dropped. "What? How?"

Seconds later, one of the prime minister's staff—a man in a dark suit—lunged into the conference room, panicked. Another rasping scream came from the staircase, maybe only one level away.

Cafferty grabbed the dead agent's gun, and he and Ellen ushered the prime minister to the heliport, the three staff members closely behind. Even with the poor visibility due to smoke, he saw in their faces the same looks of hopelessness the people in the Pavilion in New York had displayed. A look of having encountered something beyond their wildest nightmares: a living monster that was actively hunting them down. Each fanned out to a different area of the helipad, probably thinking that the creature would go after one of the others.

As if those extra few seconds would matter.

Sirens blared in the distance.

A chair crashed through the conference room

window and skidded across the ground. Smoke billowed out of the hole. Cafferty raised the pistol and took aim. His chest heaved as he drew in a deep breath. He knew the bullets would have little impact unless he got lucky. A head shot in the right place. Maybe.

But it was one of the things his team had been practicing. The lasers were always key, but Bowcut had insisted they all have firearm training, just in case.

It was one thing grouping a clip in a paper target, though. Quite another when that target was darkness incarnate charging toward you. Cafferty steadied his arms.

The creature emerged through the dense smoke. Seven feet of solid muscle and razored edges. It stepped across the tarmac, eyeing the six people in turn. Blood dripped from its three rows of daggerlike teeth, and its tail swung from side to side. And it looked like there was some kind of small electronic box with a blinking red light attached to its head.

Cafferty gasped in disbelief. Had Van Ness truly found a way to control the creatures? This took things to a whole new level, and his mind went wild with the implications of the Foundation being able to weaponize the monsters themselves.

But immediate survival came first.

The female staff member, Stef, screamed. The creature leaped toward her, grabbed her by the shoulders, and clamped its teeth around her neck. Her eyes rolled up, then her limbs relaxed. It thrashed her body from side to side until her head tore free.

Cafferty's eyes streamed. He attempted to aim through the smoke but couldn't keep his now trembling hand steady. He fired twice in the general direction. Surprisingly, two rounds smacked into the creature's back. Frighteningly, it didn't even flinch.

The creature turned toward the two male staff members, who had both run to the far edge of the heliport. It bounded after them. One efficient swing of the tail tore through both their legs at calf level. A skull-crunching stomp of the heel to one of the men's head finished him off. The second man used his arms to drag himself up onto the edge of the roof, and he flipped off the side of the building. He screamed while falling all six floors, until his body hit the road.

Simpson sprinted back toward the conference room, likely thinking that with the creature at the farthest point away, he could make a run for the fire escape. But Cafferty knew it was pointless. Outrunning it wasn't possible.

If anything, this creature, like the others Cafferty had encountered, seemed to enjoy it when people ran. Whether it was their hunting instinct or some kind of sport to them, it hurtled straight past Cafferty and Ellen, grunting out sharp breaths as it went, and it caught Simpson by the meeting room entrance.

Smoke obscured most of the brutality. But they could hear, and it was ghastly.

Then one of Simpson's arms cartwheeled out of the smoke and slapped down against the heliport. Shortly after an extended scream, a pool of blood spilled across the roof.

Cafferty glanced skyward. The chopper was less than thirty seconds away.

"I love you, Tom," Ellen said.

Their fingers interlocked even as Tom took aim with his free hand.

The creature emerged from the smoke once more and stalked toward them.

"I love you, too."

The chopper was just about over the top of the building, but they had run out of time. Cafferty said a silent prayer. Sorrow welled inside him that it had to end like this. Butchered on the roof of a burning building, courtesy of Albert Van Ness.

He curled his finger around the trigger, knowing he probably had seconds to live. Scenes from his life raced through his mind.

His wedding day.

Ellen's face when he lifted her veil.

Their honeymoon in the Bahamas, a private dinner on the beach watching the sunset.

The beautiful Visitors' Pavilion before disaster struck.

The creature hunched to pounce.

Ellen squeezed his hand tighter.

This was it.

Suddenly, a brilliant red laser beam punched through the smoke and sliced the edge of the creature's neck. It let out a gurgling howl as it staggered to the side.

Someone limped out of the conference room wearing a gas mask. They fired again and cut the beam across the creature's head, sending a spray of bright yellow blood and brain matter across the concrete. The creature collapsed in a heap, and the electronic box attached to its head blinked red for the last time.

Cafferty puffed his cheeks. He had never felt closer to death.

Bowcut ripped off her mask. "What the hell is that thing?"

"Van Ness' new weapon," he spluttered. "I thought we were toast."

"Sorry. Had certain issues of my own to deal with."

Ellen rushed over to give Bowcut a hug. "Thank you!"

Sarah seemed uncomfortable with the show of affection but didn't let go of her friend.

Tom absorbed the sight, a strange moment of happiness—or at least relief—after such an ordeal. But his mind wouldn't let him enjoy it. "You know what this means?"

"Our timeline has changed. We can't wait for help—we need to stop Van Ness now." Sarah disengaged from Ellen and moved closer to the creature's corpse. She leaned down to inspect its body and the small electronic box attached to its brain.

The chopper thumped directly over the heliport and slowed to a hover. The side door opened, revealing a man in a dark green uniform crouched inside. He scanned the roof.

"Mr. and Mrs. Cafferty—where's the prime minister?" the flight sergeant asked.

"He's dead," Ellen replied as she quickly climbed into the cabin.

The sergeant eyed the corpse of the prime minister, torn apart on the roof.

"And the building is about to explode," Cafferty added as he and Bowcut leaped into the chopper.

"Are there any more survivors?" the sergeant asked.

Cafferty shook his head. "Anyone who didn't get out of the building earlier is dead already. I'm sorry, but we have to fly—now!"

The sergeant scrambled back into the cockpit as the chopper rose into the sky and powered away from the burning building.

Cafferty peered back at the carnage and considered the implications of what they had just seen. This new terrifying weapon at Van Ness' disposal. An evolved creature aboveground, able to breathe oxygen, able to withstand light. And under that madman's control.

A plume of fire belched up from the building's roof before he could finish his thought. An explosion boomed over the sound of the engine. The shock wave hit the chopper, rocking its body. Cafferty gripped his seat to avoid being thrown across the cabin. He watched out the window as the pilot regained control, speeding away from the De Jong building. Or, rather, what was left of it.

The building collapsed downward into a heap of rubble and fire.

"Diego!" Ellen said, looking at Sarah.

"He moved to a more secure location once I entered the building. He's fine."

"Thank God," Ellen said, relieved. She leaned her head against Tom's shoulder, their arms entwined.

It gave him little comfort.

Because he now believed Van Ness' words about the stakes never being higher between humanity and the creatures. The appearance of one in broad daylight had already told him that.

But it was Van Ness who was raising the stakes with this latest creation. Cafferty could only speculate how the Foundation had managed it. Not that it mattered how. What mattered was that it *had*. Which meant that the battle was coming aboveground, a prospect that momentarily sapped Tom of any hope. The mayhem and bloodshed of creatures storming through the packed streets of London—it was almost incomprehensible.

His team had lived to fight another day. The problem was he wasn't sure how many days they had left.

CHAPTER EIGHT

resident Amanda Brogan rested her elbows on the Oval Office's Resolute Desk. It had been commissioned by Queen Victoria from the oak of an exploration ship bearing the same name, then gifted to Rutherford B. Hayes in 1880. Right now, Britain was in the forefront of her mind. And the Foundation.

Six of her close team members sat on the two couches to her front. All stared at the TV screen displaying the shocking images from London. Thick black smoke billowed from an office block and flames burned brightly from the remains of the building. A headline scrolled below:

"PRIME MINISTER SIMPSON REPORTED DEAD. MILITANT GROUP LINKED TO ISIS CLAIMING RESPONSIBILITY."

She had met the prime minister eleven months ago after being sworn in following John Reynolds' disappearance. Brogan never imagined she would become America's first female president this way. She knew Reynolds chose her to round out his ticket—being a popular two-term governor from Ohio certainly helped him win the critically important state. But as vice president, she actually grew fond of Reynolds and trusted his word. Now, thrust into the presidency under such duress, Brogan felt like she had aged eleven years in the past eleven months. Every day the United States did not locate the missing former president, the stress on Brogan grew.

"It's a damned shame," Clive Webster, her silver-haired VP, said. "I liked the prime minister, even though he always had a stick up his butt."

Brogan gave him a reproachful look. "We should be thinking about protocols. I want everyone out for a minute, apart from Vice President Webster. Please review our threat level and see if there's anything we can do for the UK. There's going to be a lot of angry people over there; the least we can do is let them know that we stand firmly by their side."

The rest of the team filed out, leaving the two of them on their own.

Webster rose from the couch and moved in front of her desk. "How did they let this happen? They're lucky it wasn't the Queen or royal family."

"I want every resource offered to help their investigation. Do you think it was extremists?"

"Who else could it be? The CIA has verified increased chatter from ISIS in the past seventy-two hours. We knew something was coming."

He stared into her eyes for a moment. Brogan seemed unconvinced.

"What are you thinking, Amanda?"

"On first impression, this attack seems too sophisticated for ISIS, don't you think? A full-on attack against a secure location? How'd they get past British security? This building was on lockdown."

"How was it sophisticated? It looks like they let off a bomb and the building caught fire. It's probably luck more than anything. Or bad luck, I suppose."

"That bomb was set off *inside* the building, not in front of it. And there were multiple gunshots reported. It makes no sense."

Brogan stared out the Oval Office window at the south lawn and, in the distance, the Washington Monument. "Reynolds was convinced that the disaster in New York was in part an assassination attempt on his life by Albert Van Ness. He told me that in the past, Van Ness eliminated national leaders who hadn't toed his line. Now here we are, eleven months after Reynolds goes missing, and the British prime minister is dead."

Webster dragged a chair to the side of the desk and sat close enough that she could detect the scent of Old Spice. He peered toward the concealed cameras and mics around the room, then leaned toward her and said in a low voice, "You don't believe all that nonsense about subterranean monsters, do you?"

"No," she said forcefully, though she hadn't completely discounted it due to Reynolds' unbreakable belief about their existence. "But consider this. I've seen a long paper trail of the U.S. government paying Van Ness' Foundation for Human Advancement huge sums of money. The payments are hidden well, but they exist. What makes a private organization with almost no showings of public goodwill eligible for eye-watering amounts of foreign aid? Clearly, previous presidents believed enough to pay."

"But both the FBI and Homeland Security cleared the Foundation in their investigation of Reynolds' assassination."

President Brogan shot her vice president a stern look.

"Sorry—Reynolds' *disappearance*. Besides, have you heard from this Albert Van Ness character since you took office?"

"No," she admitted.

"I think it's a stretch to think he's somehow responsible for all this, or in bed with jihadists. I usually find the simplest solution is the right one."

Webster leaned in closer to the president.

"We don't need to delve into conspiracy theories just yet," he continued. "We've . . . you've . . . got a lot more important things to worry about, starting with preparing for a press conference about this attack. We need to say something soon, or the markets are going to tank even further."

Brogan drummed her fingers on the desk while she considered the possibilities.

Maybe I am taking this whole Van Ness thing too seriously.

Creatures. Kidnapping President Reynolds. Assassinating the prime minister . . .

It's bordering on insane.

But a nagging doubt remained in the back of her mind. Early reports had claimed Simpson's chopper had been spotted *leaving* the top of the building a few minutes before the explosion. The rest of the stories from the ground only added to her skepticism. Witnesses claimed they had seen people in the stairwell running back toward the upper floors. Why would they run up? A man had thrown himself off the top of the building. Why? An RAF chopper had arrived shortly after, but none of the reports followed up on that.

It all felt too convoluted for a simple explanation.

Somebody was hiding something.

"You're still thinking about it," Webster said. "Listen, it's times like this that you'll be judged by the international community. You can't let them see doubt in your mind. You need to be strong, resolute—assure Americans and the world that we will help the UK hunt down those responsible and bring them to justice. Stick with what we know, not conjecture."

She let out a deep sigh. "You're right."

"Now, let's discuss the—"

Somebody knocked firmly on the Oval Office door but did not enter. The president's secretary, Elizabeth Lopez, usually knocked and walked straight in.

Three sharp, authoritarian knocks rapped on the door again.

"Come in," Brogan shouted.

The door opened. One of the Secret Service Uniformed Division officers entered the office, stocky and bald, wearing his typical uniform of black trousers and a white shirt.

"Madam President," he said with a southern drawl, "I've got a letter for you."

The officer stepped forward and placed an ivory-colored sheet of folded paper on her desk. It had been secured by a red wax seal. He took two paces back and stood in front of her, motionless, staring over the top of her head.

Brogan leaned forward and studied the paper without touching it. Webster moved closer to her side and gazed down.

The seal looked like the eagle on Germany's national coat of arms, the differences being the talons were on the wing tips, making them look like arms. The tail was thin and serrated, and the head had three rows of jagged teeth instead of a beak.

Almost exactly how Reynolds had described a creature.

No, it can't be . . .

Brogan grabbed the paper and went to open it.

"I wouldn't," Webster said. "It might have a toxin inside."

"It went through our screening process," the officer said. "All White House mail is checked for toxins and x-ray scanned. It's clean."

The impulse to open the letter beat back any of her doubts. Brogan was 100 percent sure this letter was from Van Ness, and the timing appeared far from a coincidence. She snapped open the seal and unfolded the paper.

Dearest Amanda,

I'll keep this brief to avoid wasting your valuable time. We stand on the edge of extinction. The brink, if you will. Just as Sherlock Holmes had an epic struggle with Professor Moriarty on the lip of the Reichenbach Falls, humans and creatures are now locked in a similar fight to the death. There can be only one winner when neither party is prepared to compromise. One of our species is destined to plummet into oblivion. One will survive as the dominant force on the planet. It's a fork in the road for humanity. Taking the wrong path will consign us to history.

To that end, the Foundation for Human Advancement requires 2 percent of your GDP over the next twelve months. This funding will ensure the correct amount of resources is channeled into our global operation and to your own country's safety.

Please don't assume to know better like the previous president. John Reynolds is currently at my disposal and will be contacting you shortly with the finer details. Kindly heed my words, Madam President. I'm a man of action, which Prime Minister Simpson found out earlier today.

As a show of good faith, Amanda, I will currently spare your life. But the seriousness of my humble request does *need to be illustrated.*

Have a lovely afternoon.

Yours sincerely,
A.V.N.

Brogan's heart raced.

Suddenly, a solid red beam punched through the paper in her hands and hit the far end of the Oval Office. The wallpaper sizzled and turned black. The paper in her hand burst into flames and she threw it to the side and ducked. Webster dropped to all fours behind the desk.

The laser beam had come from somewhere in the Rose Garden.

The officer reached inside his pocket for his

weapon and raised his wrist to sound the alarm to the Secret Service. He opened his mouth to speak.

Before any sound came out, the beam cut to the left and carved through the officer's head at nose level. The top half of his skull slid off like a coconut getting topped. It bounced off his shoulder, then thudded to the ground by his boots. His whole body twitched.

Brogan watched in horror as his eyes rolled in their sockets and his lungs emptied.

A heartbeat later, he collapsed forward, his white shirt now a gruesome shade of crimson. The burst of blood from the officer's wound speckled the president's face.

The laser beam steadily moved to the left. It sliced through the portrait of George Washington and continued to burn a thin black line in the wallpaper toward the painting of Abraham Lincoln.

The president's secretary, Elizabeth, entered the Oval Office carrying a stack of documents.

"Elizabeth, get down!"

But the laser beam sliced through the woman's stomach before she could react. Her body crumpled to the floor, and blood sprayed the walls of the heart of democracy.

Brogan slammed her hand down on the panic button.

A siren split the air, repeatedly blaring a deafening tone. Suited members of the Secret Service charged in from either direction, grabbed the president and vice president, and rushed them out of the Oval Office, leaving the bodies of the officer and secretary behind.

"How the hell did this happen?" Webster shouted as he ran, hunched over in case another laser beam sliced through the White House walls.

Three Secret Service officers surrounded the president, three surrounded Webster. The rest covered their front and rear as they made their way to the Presidential Emergency Operations Center—an underground-bunker-like structure built to withstand any attack, last used on September 11, 2001.

The agents hustled Brogan into the dimly lit, long rectangular room. She took a chance to catch her breath and process the last few minutes.

Everything had happened so fast. And Reynolds was still alive?

Brogan still wasn't convinced of the creatures' existence. However, she was under no illusion that Albert Van Ness was a real danger to her and the country. It was time to take him seriously.

It was time to take him out.

"Get the new deputy prime minister on the phone.

"And Tom Cafferty, too."

CHAPTER NINE

We're about ten minutes out from Brize Norton Royal Air Force base, Mr. and Mrs. Cafferty," the flight sergeant said through his mic to their headsets. *"You'll be debriefed there."*

"Copy that," Cafferty replied.

He shot Ellen and Bowcut a weary look. They would undoubtedly be interrogated for hours about what happened in the meeting and on that rooftop. The prime minister was dead. Smoke still filled the air in the distance from the building's collapse. There would be so many questions, only some of which Cafferty had answers to. And he knew those answers would be hard to believe.

Bowcut was attending to her injuries in the back of the helicopter with the medical pack, T-shirt off, dabbing small cuts on her arm. The bruise forming down her left side made Cafferty wince, though the fact that she had fought through the pain to make it to the rooftop and save them didn't surprise him. The team members all possessed fight in different ways, and she was the best in physical terms. Tactically aware. A great shot. Good at thinking on her feet. Clinical. Reliable. Her history with the NYPD SWAT team and her courage on that day underneath New York City made her irreplaceable.

"What are you staring at?" Bowcut said to Cafferty. "You do know Ellen's sitting right next to you."

"I'm watching him," Ellen said in fake seriousness.

Cafferty laughed at being mocked in surround sound. It was probably the release of nervous tension on all of their parts, but he ran with it. "Just thinking how the team would be screwed without you. That's all."

"You pick the strangest times to give compliments."

"Maybe I do."

Bowcut wrestled on her T-shirt with a grimace and put on her jacket. There was a sadness about her that he couldn't quite put his finger on. Both her father and brother had been on the force, and both lost their lives on September 11. And then she had watched her boyfriend—and Cafferty's right-hand man, David North—give up his life to save their lives in those subway tunnels. Cafferty couldn't imagine the pain she was feeling. But there was more to her sadness than the grief of those losses. She seemed . . . unfulfilled. Perhaps killing Van Ness would fill that particular void.

If Cafferty didn't get to him first . . .

"Roger, go ahead," the flight sergeant said into his mic. "Sorry, say that *again*?"

The change in tone of the officer's voice caught Cafferty's attention. He wondered whether there had been another attack, and the chopper crew was just learning about it.

The flight sergeant turned toward Cafferty with a surprised look on his face. "Mr. Cafferty, we're patching a call through to your headset."

"A call? From who?"

"The deputy prime minister . . . and the president of the United States."

Cafferty's eyes widened, and he nodded affirmatively at the flight sergeant. Word had clearly spread. The headset crackled for a moment.

"Tom?"

"Madam President, it's good to hear your voice," Cafferty replied.

"Deputy Prime Minister Smith is listening in as well."

"Hello, sir. I am sorry for your country's loss today."

"Tell us what happened, Tom. Time is of the essence."

"Understood, Madam President. We were meeting with the prime minister to discuss launching a mission here in London to uncover Albert Van Ness' plans. Unbeknownst to us, Van Ness was listening and didn't like what he heard. He is responsible for the prime minister's death and the building explosion, despite what intelligence you may be hearing to the contrary."

"You don't have to convince me, Tom. Not after what Van Ness just did to the Oval Office."

Cafferty's eyebrows raised, but he held his tongue—he'd have to ask about that another time. "Madam President, we still believe Van Ness is planning something bigger here in London. A New York–scale event."

There was silence on the line as those words resonated.

Finally, *"Are you still prepared to launch your operation?"*

"We are," Cafferty replied.

"Then get to it, under the radar. Right now. And report back to us as soon as you know more. Tom, we need to stop him."

He thought of how long he'd been trying to convince everyone of that. But at least now he was going to have the help he needed. "We will. I won't fail you, Madam President."

The connection cut, and Cafferty replayed the conversation in his mind.

After what Van Ness just did to the Oval Office . . .

"So, Tom?" Ellen asked.

Cafferty leaned forward in the chopper to get the flight sergeant's attention, and the officer turned to face him. "So . . . we're going to have to turn the chopper around and head back to London," Cafferty said.

Bowcut and Ellen looked at him, confused. He smiled back at them with a newfound determination.

"Turn the chopper around . . . right now."

CHAPTER TEN

Darkness had fallen over central London and the streets were empty, possibly because this afternoon's attack had spooked people. A dead prime minister in an inferno would do that to most countries.

Diego had met up with the helicopter, and the full team was back together, dressed all in black, prepping in the van. Their intel led them to believe the Foundation was mounting some kind of operation in a long-abandoned stretch of the London Underground, and the time was now to see what it was up to.

Munoz glanced across from the driver's seat. "You sure you don't want me to go down there with Bowcut instead?" he asked Cafferty.

"I got this one," Cafferty replied. "It's only a reconnaissance mission. You're best off by the equipment, keeping a watch on us. Our eyes and ears on the street. You and Ellen stay here, Sarah and I will go take a look. Any problems, we'll need you both to save our asses."

"Copy," he replied, smiling.

"Look, our timeline has been sped up dramatically by today's events," Cafferty said, eyeing the look of concern on his wife's face. "I can't stress enough the importance of uncovering Van Ness' plan before he attacks again."

He realized his words did little to ease the pressure. He guessed Ellen was thinking about that horrible day underneath New York City. Or their son. Or the fact that they were going into action sooner than she'd like. But like Cafferty, she knew it had to be done. Sure, Cafferty had moments of self-doubt as well, but he had always tried to conceal them, especially around his wife.

Munoz pulled to the side of the road on Eversholt Street, right next to the 1960s-style Euston train station.

Bowcut leaned between the two front seats. "That unassuming door on the side of the train station building gets us in. Other than maintenance workers, I haven't seen anyone else come and go. So it's likely the Foundation doesn't have this entrance covered. It leads indirectly down to the old abandoned subway tracks."

"How indirectly?" Cafferty asked.

"Very."

Bowcut handed Cafferty a hi-viz jacket with NETWORK RAIL written on the back, making them look like official workers. "I digitally scanned the lock last week and had a master key cut—it should get us down there."

"And a map?"

She tapped the side of her head. "Got the map

right here. There are only so many places they could be down there. I've got two pretty good ideas, both deep abandoned stretches of track and an abandoned train station—perfect spots to be up to no good."

"Is there anything you haven't thought of?" Munoz asked.

She looked him directly in the eyes. "Failure."

The team smiled at her never-ending confidence and drive.

Cafferty slipped on the jacket. It had plenty of room to conceal a laser and pistol. For all he knew, Van Ness might have ordered a small army down there, with sentries covering every approach. That'd be the wise thing to do if they continued to take equipment underground. He reached back and grabbed a pair of infrared goggles.

Ellen handed him eight strobe grenades and he stuffed them in his pockets.

"Just remember," Munoz said, "if you guys go as far as the Thames, the chances are we'll lose you."

Sarah and Cafferty nodded, and then sat with Munoz and Ellen, observing the door for the next half hour. Nobody entered or exited. The pedestrians and commuters thinned enough for them to go in undetected. Eventually, the moment came when nobody was in view.

"Go now," Ellen said. "I love you."

"I love you, too," Bowcut replied.

Cafferty smiled, gave Ellen a quick kiss on the lips, and he and Bowcut jumped out of the van and headed toward the side door of the station.

Bowcut slipped the key in the lock, and they

entered a filthy stairwell that looked like it hadn't been used in about a century. Certainly not a place well trodden by the staff of Network Rail. A stench of brake pads, dust, and oil hung in the air, not dissimilar to the New York subway system. They climbed down several stories, the roar of trains getting louder and louder. At the bottom of the staircase, they unlocked a door, then another door, and another.

"Bingo," Cafferty said. They had reached the old abandoned London Underground tracks.

Cafferty activated his flashlight. His beam stabbed through the frigid blackness, illuminating the unused rails and years of dust and dirt.

"To your right," Bowcut said as she moved ahead of him, gun in hand. "Kill your light and flip on night vision."

He switched the flashlight off, and darkness enveloped them. The night-vision goggles kicked on and illuminated the tunnels with an eerie green glow.

They entered an area that looked as if it had been untouched since the 1960s. An old wooden customer service counter took up most of the left wall. To the right, four public telephones hung in a row, each with mold-speckled directories on a shelf beneath. Bowcut encouraged him toward a twin set of escalators.

Cafferty took the right, Bowcut the left. He gently placed his boots down on each step through fear of hitting a patch of grease and tumbling over a hundred feet to the bottom. Faded posters of plays and movies lined the walls. He could make out a few.

The Pawnbroker. Mary Poppins. Goldfinger. The temperature in the Underground noticeably increased when he neared the platform.

"Listen," Bowcut whispered.

Cafferty drew his pistol and crouched on the platform.

The outline of an old track led toward a tunnel. Old cables sagged along the wall at regular intervals. The filament lighting looked retro. Then a gentle breeze blew through the tunnel.

His heart rate spiked.

Bowcut's posture stiffened, too.

Back in New York, this had been a portent for the arrival of creatures. This time, thankfully, the breeze continued and didn't carry the same acrid stench. Cafferty strained to listen for any suspicious sounds. Rats squeaked and scuttled. The murmur of trains racing through distant tunnels rose and fell.

"Let's head down the tunnel," Bowcut said.

She eased herself down to the track and advanced toward the abandoned tunnel entrance, Cafferty following. Anticipation rose inside him. He had always considered himself a politician, a paper pusher and a bullshitter. But since surviving his initial encounter with the creatures, this felt like a fresh start, and he welcomed the exhilaration it brought. He felt alive. Focused. Worth something more than a speechmaker to a cynical press pack.

It was amazing how putting yourself in danger made you feel like your life had meaning.

"Diego, you hear me?" Bowcut whispered.

"*Loud and clear,*" he replied through the earpiece.

"We're heading east."

"Roger that."

Cafferty and Bowcut continued along the path at the side of the track. Each step took them farther into the pitch black until he could only see a few inches in front of his face. Drips of water into a pool echoed through the tunnel. Eventually, after five minutes of creeping, they reached a split in the track.

Bowcut paused. "First option is left."

They carried on for another five minutes and reached another disused platform. The route beyond had been bricked up.

"That way leads to the live system. We need to head back."

After retracing their steps to the split, they took the right tunnel.

Two minutes later, the glow of artificial light appeared at the end of a sweeping section of track.

Bowcut stopped. "Get down," she whispered.

"I take it that's not supposed to be there?" Cafferty asked.

"The far end of this tunnel leads to where I've seen the Foundation heading in and out of the Underground. I just didn't know how far they'd come down the line." She raised her cuff mic. "Diego, we've found something in the right tunnel, close to below University College London."

"Copy, be careful."

Cafferty dropped to a crawl position and eased himself forward using his knees and elbows. Bowcut moved by his side, pistol extended. Sweat trickled down his back as they advanced. When they rounded the shallow bend, they both stopped, raised their goggles, and squinted toward the bright light.

"What are they doing?" Cafferty whispered.

Up ahead, two men dressed in all black hovered over assorted metal crates and a ten-foot hole dug right through the old subway tracks. Power tools and boxes of supplies were stacked against the right wall. Above the hole was a metal frame and pulley, and above all that was a brilliant white globe hung from the ceiling, blazing down onto the circular breach. It bathed the entire area with light so bright it was near impossible to look at, as if the sun itself had somehow risen underground in London.

"That ball of light tells me one thing," Bowcut said.

"Creatures." Cafferty thought for a moment and took in the entire scene: the pulley, the equipment. "My God, they've dug down to a nest."

"Exactly. We need to call this in—"

Gunshots split the air, ricocheting off the walls all around them. Instinctively, Cafferty and Bowcut flattened themselves on the ground. Before they knew it, the two men were nearly upon them, pistols in hand. They raised their guns to fire again.

Bowcut kicked Cafferty out of the way a split second before a spray of bullets dug into the ground where he had just been lying. She rolled left, planted her elbows on the old railroad ties to steady her aim, and unloaded six bullets in rapid succession at the men. All six hit. Two bullets in each of their chests, and a fatal bullet for each right between the eyes. Their bodies crashed to the ground, only a few feet away.

Silence returned to the subway tunnel. Bowcut kept her gun aimed firmly at the construction site, expecting that at any moment more of Van Ness' men would come rushing at them, or a creature would burst out of the hole and rip them to shreds. If there were more bad guys here, there's no way they didn't hear the gunfire.

Silence.

She nodded at Cafferty, and he helped her to her feet.

"Nice shot. And . . . thanks."

"Any time," she replied.

They carefully and quietly approached the construction site. A mound of dirt was piled against the wall.

"There must be a creatures' nest right under our feet. Why would they want to breach it, though?" Cafferty asked.

"Maybe Van Ness wants revenge and plans to unleash these monsters in the London Underground, like he did in New York," Bowcut replied.

Anything was possible with Van Ness, but something about what he was seeing didn't seem right to Cafferty.

"Van Ness exposed the nest in New York as punishment against the United States, true—but his ultimate intention was always to *destroy* the creatures . . . and kill the president in the process. Kind of a two-for-one deal. But this—I feel like there's more going on here."

The beaming light from the globe above their heads became almost unbearable the closer they got to the breach. Certainly bright enough to keep any creatures at bay, for which they were grateful. But it made it hard to see and was making the already warm underground chamber hotter. They shielded their eyes as best they could. When they reached the breach, they both glanced downward.

A long shaft descended from the subway tracks maybe a hundred feet and opened up into a huge cavern below. The light didn't quite penetrate the deep, but the familiar screeches of angry creatures below their feet filled Cafferty's ears, and he was certain it was a nest.

"Jesus Christ," Cafferty said. "They're right below us."

But Bowcut wasn't looking down; she was more interested in the crane and pulleys built over the hole the Foundation dug, studying them carefully. "Tom, what do you think they used this for?" she asked.

"I imagine to dig out the hole or to pull something up?" Cafferty replied.

"I don't think so. Look at the way the crane is designed, the way they have it bolted down, and the way the pulleys are set up. They were lowering something *downward*, something very heavy."

It baffled Cafferty while he studied it. "What would they be lowering down into a nest?"

Bowcut studied the surrounding equipment and boxes. "Um . . . Tom."

Cafferty followed her gaze to an enormous empty crate in the corner. On the side of the crate was the radioactive symbol and assorted warnings. An unused Geiger counter lay in front of it.

"Holy shit, Tom. This could be very, very bad."

Her understatement made this almost laughable. But there was nothing funny about the situation or whatever was contained in these boxes. What had Van Ness done? "We have to go down there and see what it is."

"I knew you were gonna say that," she muttered. Louder, she said, "Okay, but we're gonna need Diego down here. He's best suited to examine whatever it is they put down there."

"Agreed." Cafferty activated his comm. "Diego, we're gonna need you down here, stat."

"Roger that," Diego replied through the earpiece. *"Find anything yet?"*

"I have a feeling we're about to," Cafferty replied. "Bring down some extra rope and come fully armed. Ellen, hold down the van and tell us if you spot anything unusual or anyone suspicious entering or exiting the station. We already took out two of Van Ness' men. Anything happens down here, it's up to you to alert the president and deputy prime minister."

"I don't like the sound of this," Ellen replied. *"Please be careful."*

"I don't like it, either. But this was always the plan. And so was being as careful as we can."

Which probably didn't mean all that much when you were standing above a nest with millions of creatures in it.

Bowcut headed back through the tunnel to guide Diego to the breach, leaving Tom alone with his thoughts and the screeches below. He kept thinking about how his obsession had almost destroyed him. Was he equally obsessed now with taking down Albert Van Ness? Blind to the damage it was causing others? Cafferty couldn't deny he was singularly focused on the Foundation. But he also couldn't deny that Van Ness had to pay for what he did. Also, if Van Ness had developed the technology to control the creatures and use them as a weapon *aboveground*, then he definitely was a bigger threat than Tom ever imagined.

The sound of movement in the tunnel snapped him out of his thoughts. He raised his gun.

"Don't shoot," Diego's familiar voice said as he and Bowcut came around the bend. "I'm just a lowly MTA worker from Brooklyn who took the Tube and got lost down here somehow."

Cafferty smiled and lowered the weapon.

He knew Munoz liked being part of a capable team, despite having the odds stacked against them. It had been the case ever since their first official meeting in the Beekman Pub. He liked having the pragmatic engineer on his side, too.

"All right, whadda we got?" Diego asked, scanning the construction site and the hole dug down to the nest. He peered into the breach. "Damn."

Assorted handheld electronic devices were stacked next to the crane, and charts lay on the ground around the hole. Diego picked one up curiously.

"Mmm, this says the cavern below us is three thousand feet deep. Holy hell."

Diego continued to scan the site and quickly eyed the empty crate.

"Uh-oh."

"That didn't take long for you to spot," Cafferty said. "What do you think it could be?"

"High-tech X-ray equipment? Maybe they are creating a detailed map of the nest."

"Care to take a look down there with us?" Cafferty asked.

"Do we have a choice?" Diego replied rhetorically.

"All right then. Let's climb down to hell."

CHAPTER ELEVEN

S o, how're we doing this?" Diego asked.

Bowcut moved by his side. She unfastened his backpack and grabbed a rope. "We throw strobes into the breach to push back any nearby creatures, and we all keep one lit on our belts at all times. This should keep the creatures at bay. I'll rappel down first, you both follow behind."

"That nest has gotta be full of methane like New York, don't you think?" Cafferty asked.

"I'm sure," she agreed. "We've got twenty minutes down there max, before we lose consciousness. So let's move fast."

"You don't gotta tell me twice," Diego said. He took deep breaths to keep calm. He had no problem getting involved in the action, even as the thrill battled internally against the fear of death. He reminded himself he was capable. He was the man who single-handedly saved President Reynolds, the man who took out the Foundation's top agent, who had infiltrated the Secret Service.

The gangster turned good . . . turned gangster. Sort of.

The disaster in New York had changed him. It was as if invisible chains had snapped off his previous vow to follow the straight and narrow. Back to being street Diego with a legit cause.

"Ready?" Cafferty asked.

"Let's do it."

Munoz squeezed the sides of a strobe and threw it into the hole. Intense flashes blasted from the sphere as it plummeted. He had nicknamed them "disco balls" but it had never caught on with the team—*their loss*, he thought. When the strobe hit solid ground somewhere below, hundreds of shrieks exploded out of the breach, though they quickly grew fainter as the creatures fled from the blinding light.

Munoz started humming "I Will Survive" as he watched the dangerous dance playing out below them until a sharp look from Sarah cut him off.

"Would you prefer I sing 'I Need a Hero'?" he asked. Bowcut finally smiled.

Meanwhile, Cafferty threw in another strobe for good measure. Bowcut had already secured the rope. She slung her lasers over her shoulder, then rappelled down, leaning back, boots planted against the wall. She lowered herself through the man-made tunnel for maybe a hundred feet.

Toward the bottom, the tunnel opened up into a massive, cathedral-sized cavern thousands of feet deep, with small caves peppering the walls—very much like the one below the Hudson River. It was like hanging over the Grand Canyon—if the Grand Canyon was filled with lightning-fast monsters bent on wiping every human off the face of the earth.

She could hear the screeches of the creatures in the shadows, shielding themselves from the powerful strobe lights. It was a cacophony louder than the Giants games her father and brother used to take her to. Bowcut could also feel the air was different. Without gas masks, as they hadn't expected to enter a breach, they had only minutes to uncover Van Ness' plans with this nest.

Below her was a rocky overhang with some kind of large man-made device on it—probably whatever Van Ness' men had lowered down. She tossed a strobe grenade onto the ledge, and unseen creatures bolted to safety. Bowcut's boots hit the ledge and she quickly whipped out her laser for any creature bold enough to strike.

"I found something," she called up to Cafferty and Munoz, who were in the process of descending.

"On our way," Diego shouted back, halfway down the breach with Cafferty. As they neared the cavern below, the sound of the creatures grew louder.

Munoz attempted to copy Bowcut's rappelling technique. After sixty feet of descending, though, his feet slipped, and he dangled over the abyss, clutching the rope in a white-knuckled grip. He told himself to stay calm and drew in a deep breath. He hadn't done anything like this since a disorganized team-building exercise a few years ago, and even back then he didn't pay much attention because the instructors had done all the hard work for them. He gradually lowered himself, inch by inch, gaining confidence as he neared the ledge, and eventually his boots hit the ground. Cafferty landed next to him moments later. They stood on the rocky ledge and looked out on the expanse, in awe of what the creatures had carved out of the earth.

"It's oddly beautiful," Diego said.

"Too bad everything in here wants to rip us to shreds," Cafferty replied. He scanned the walls of the cavern for any signs of an impending attack, but the strobe lights were doing their job.

"All right, let's see what we've got," Diego said, approaching a large glass case perched on the over-hang. Inside the thick glass sat a three-foot-long dense metallic cylinder. A black wireless antenna protruded from the small hole on the left side. It led to a module inside with a tiny blinking green light. Wires from the device connected to a timer. The timer counted down methodically.

25:07:23
25:07:22
25:07:21

With each blinking flash, the clarity of the situation increased. All he could do was stare in disbelief.

"Holy shit . . . is it a bomb?" Cafferty asked, but Diego ignored him, still studying the device and the markings on the case itself. "Diego?"

Cafferty stared at Munoz, a sickly green cast to his face.

"Diego," he asked again. "Is it a bomb?"

"This . . . this isn't just a . . . *bomb*," Diego said, his voice trembling. "It's a thermonuclear bomb.

Big enough to wipe out these creatures . . . and all of London. And probably much of southern England."

Cafferty's eyes widened and he shot a look at Bowcut.

"And it goes off tomorrow at . . ."

Diego glanced at his watch.

". . . midnight."

CHAPTER TWELVE

Albert Van Ness relaxed back in his chair. He loved his south Parisian château's library as a place to unwind after a busy day. Logs crackled in an open fireplace. Thousands of books packed the antique mahogany bookcases that hugged the three other walls. Some of the tomes had been in his family for several generations. Tragedies by Daniel Caspar von Lohenstein and Andreas Gryphius. A seminal work on philosophy by Immanuel Kant.

He belonged here among other great minds.

It was his quiet time in his personal space. He raised his glass of brandy and breathed in through his nose, and he savored the rich aroma. Van Ness went to take a sip—

The phone on his writing desk rang. He powered his chair over and picked up the receiver with annoyance. "Speak."

"*Our London team is no longer reporting back,*" Edwards said through the phone. "*Something is wrong.*"

Annoyance shifted to anger. He squeezed his brandy glass in his hand nearly to the breaking point.

"Have the British discovered our plans?"

"I don't believe so, sir. We would have spotted their military or police force moving into the Underground."

"Which means a small team must have moved in, undetected."

"It is possible that—"

"Silence."

Van Ness gazed across the library at his father's vast collection of books about political ideology and war strategy. *The Art of War* by Sun Tzu. *On War* by Carl von Clausewitz. *Guerrilla Warfare* by Che Guevara. And, of course, *Mein Kampf,* with an inscription by Hitler himself.

A military genius wasn't coming after the Foundation, though. In fact, he didn't think any existed in modern times. No, it was that politician he had already broken once.

"It's that damned American. It's Cafferty and his team," Van Ness said icily. "How long ago did our team stop responding?"

"About twenty minutes."

"They are still in those tunnels."

"How do you know that, sir?"

"Because I know that man. He won't be able to resist what he sees. To put it more directly, the man cannot stop himself. And neither can I."

"What would you like me to do?" Edwards asked.

"Have a team sweep the nearest unguarded Underground entrance in the vicinity and I suspect we'll discover what I want." Van Ness hung up the phone and sipped his brandy.

Cafferty was a growing irritant, one that needed to be dealt with more directly.

A few minutes later, the phone rang again and Van Ness answered.

"Sir, our UK Four team just carried out a sweep around the nearest unguarded station and spotted Ellen Cafferty in a van."

"But no one else?" Van Ness asked.

"No, sir."

He smiled. "Perfect. Bring her to me, would you?"

"I'm sorry, bring her to you?"

"That's right. Capture her and bring her here to Paris. Cafferty will follow, I assure you."

"Wouldn't it be easier to just trigger the weapon, sir? This is a deviation from our plans . . ."

"Easier. Yes, yes, I suppose it would be," Van Ness confessed. "However, you know what I would like most?"

"What's that, sir?"

"I'd very much like to see the former mayor on his knees, begging me, before I show him what it's like to lose someone you love. To see all his short-sighted plans come to nothing. To know he has no power and, worse, no clue about the powers that he is trying to oppose. Then, when he has witnessed his stupidity, when his spirit is broken, I'd like him to watch what I do to those who defy the Foundation. Ours is a great undertaking, and no politician from a dirty little city is going to upset that when presidents and prime ministers accede to our demands."

Van Ness sipped his brandy.

"You will bring his wife to me, and he will learn

there are things in this world besides the creatures worth fearing."

"*I'll see it's done*," Edwards said.

Van Ness smiled to himself, knowing he would rest well this evening. "Good night, dear friend."

CHAPTER THIRTEEN

Munoz had known insane before, but never at this level. He listened to Cafferty quickly relay to Ellen up top what they had found in the cavern. Finished, Tom turned toward him and Bowcut.

"Can either of you disarm it?" Cafferty asked.

"Are you kidding me?" Munoz shook his head while snapping photos of the weapon with his phone. "For all we know, even opening the glass case could set it off. I wouldn't know where to start."

Cafferty peered at the bathtub-sized device in its strange glass casket and imagined an enormous mushroom cloud blooming above the London skyline, then a scorching blast wave flattening the city in the blink of an eye.

"Neither would I," Bowcut added. "They didn't train us how to disarm nuclear weapons on the SWAT team. My question is this: Why tomorrow at midnight? Are they timing it for some reason?"

"The bastards did the same for the inaugural run

of the Z Train," Munoz spat. "So . . . what's happening here in twenty-five hours?"

None of the three had an answer.

"We have to alert the deputy prime minister and the president," Cafferty said. "Evacuate as many people as possible."

Munoz shrugged. "I dunno. I wouldn't act so fast, Tom. See that antenna sticking out the side? I think that's a remote detonator."

"So . . ."

"So Van Ness can probably detonate the bomb whenever he'd like."

"Jesus . . ." Cafferty whispered to himself.

"I betcha if Van Ness sees people evacuating the city, it's game over, man."

The three continued to stare at the weapon of mass destruction sitting right in front of them. The power to destroy millions of creatures—and millions more people—in an instant. A truly nuclear option, with no chance for discussion or nuance. This was Van Ness playing judge and executioner, having no time to even bother with a jury.

"Either way," Cafferty said finally, "we need to tell Brogan and the British authorities what's going on right away."

"Agreed."

Bowcut wrapped her hands around the rope to begin the ascent. "All right, let's get out of—"

Suddenly, all the brilliant strobe lights that had been protecting them on the ledge flew off the ground and off their belts into the vast cavern below, pulled by some unseen force. They were plunged into total and utter darkness, and the silence in the cavern—a silence they hadn't even noticed—was now deafening.

"They're using their telekinetic powers!" Cafferty shouted, rapidly pulling out his laser. "Fire!"

In that instant, a creature's tail whipped from behind a rock formation right at the team. Cafferty fired his laser and tore the creature's tail off only inches away from severing his and Diego's legs in half.

Bowcut and Diego pulled out their lasers and fired in all directions, slicing through dozens of creatures scaling the walls, rapidly bounding toward them, moving in to kill their prey. Two creatures crashed onto the small ledge, lunging forward with their powerful legs right at Cafferty. He fired rapidly while stumbling backward. The dazzling red beam zipped through the darkness and sliced right through the creatures' abdomens. Their guts spilled out, steaming messes that filled his nostrils with a burnt, putrid smell. Both corpses collapsed to the ground in heaps at Cafferty's feet.

He looked down at the dying creatures, illuminated only by the red glow of Bowcut's and Diego's rapid laser fire. Those soulless black eyes brought everything back from the New York nest. The snarls. The teeth. The spine-tingling shrieks. The thrashing tails.

He froze, mesmerized by the depth of black in those now sightless orbs.

Bowcut fired continuously. She switched her aim to a creature on the right wall and sliced off its legs. It slid down with a roar.

"Watch out!" Munoz bellowed.

A creature leaped off the wall right at the distracted Cafferty. He looked up in terror with no time to react, and the creature's leg battered his shoulder. Claws raked his arm, tearing through his flesh. He crashed to his knees and swayed over the front of the ledge. Blood dripped from his fingers and pattered against the rock. He was finished, and he breathed a good-bye to Ellen—

Diego's laser beam burned right through the monster, carving it into pieces as it towered over Tom. Streams of hot blood spattered Cafferty's face, and he frantically wiped his eyes. The carcass crashed into him, forcing his body to fall backward over the edge. He somehow was able to grab the lip of the overhang, but with the wound in his arm, he wasn't going to be able to hang on.

In just a matter of seconds, he was saved from death only to be facing it once more. He was going to plummet thousands of feet down and could do nothing to stop it.

As his hold weakened—the blood loss draining his energy, the blood on his hands causing his grip to slip—a strong hand grabbed his shoulder, pulling Cafferty firmly back onto the ledge.

"I gotcha!" Bowcut said, still firing her laser with her free hand.

Not that it was doing much good.

Creature after creature crashed onto the tiny ledge, shaking the very rock they were standing on. Cracks began to spider their way across the carboniferous limestone rock under their feet.

"There's too many of them!" Diego shouted, firing at all angles, searching for where the creatures had gathered in the overwhelming darkness. "We're sitting ducks on this ledge!"

Cafferty nodded a quick acknowledgment. And even though he knew they had to climb back up the rope, he was also sure they'd be torn to pieces if they attempted it. He fired his laser and sliced through three creatures in rapid succession, for all the good it was doing.

Munoz continued to fire as well, until a tiny reflection of light caught the corner of his eye when he fired into the darkness. He glanced down quickly and traced its origin to an unused strobe grenade that had gotten wedged under the thermonuclear bomb. The single strobe had not been yanked off the ledge when the creatures focused their telekinetic powers.

"Cover me!" Munoz shouted, and even before his team could react, he dove for the grenade.

Their working so closely together the last year paid off, though, as Bowcut and Cafferty spun, blasting away at the dozens of creatures closing in from all sides. Brilliant red beams speared directly over Munoz's head, making the place appear like a demented underground disco. As he dove, all he could hear was Donna Summer playing in his head.

Last dance. Last chance for love . . .

The adrenaline coursing through his body was making him crazy.

Creatures smashed into the ledge all around them. The team was surrounded on all sides with no way out.

Munoz crashed to the ground, driving the air out of his lungs. He could hear his impending death scuttling and screeching its way toward him, and he reached under the bomb. His fingers grasped the strobe and pulled . . .

But it was stuck.

This is it . . .

"*No!*"

Munoz got a better grip and pulled with all his strength. The ball popped out from under the bomb, and he used the momentum to let himself be turned onto his back, squeezing the sides of the silver sphere.

It came to life.

It came to *light*.

A brilliant flash of white burst out of the strobe grenade in all directions at the speed of light, painfully blinding the creatures instantly. The screeching turned from that of a triumphant predator to an animal in pain, and the creatures leaped off the ledge at breakneck speed, disappearing into every dark crevice and cave they could find. In seconds, Bowcut, Munoz, and Cafferty were once again alone on the ledge. Creature blood soaked every inch of the overhang, and still-sizzling appendages were piled all around them.

"Holy fuck . . ." Diego said, desperately trying to catch his breath.

Cafferty took the flashing strobe grenade from Munoz, clutching the life-saving device as if it were the most precious thing he'd ever held. Bowcut helped Munoz to his feet.

"Thank you for saving my life again," he said to her.

"Thanks for saving ours," she replied, looking at the strobe grenade.

"Am I the only one singing Donna Summer?" Munoz asked. Bowcut cracked a smile.

Cafferty winced at the pain from his wounded arm and the gashes on his legs, but he smiled as well. They were alive, and that was due to acting like an actual team.

We can fight them if we stick together.

Suddenly, a loud cracking sound came from underneath their feet. They looked down, only now realizing the splintering in the limestone ledge had reached critical levels.

"The ledge is gonna snap!" Bowcut shouted, noticing it as well. "Climb the rope! Climb!"

"But what about the bomb?" Cafferty yelled, firmly affixing the flashing strobe grenade to his belt.

The splintering sound grew louder. Large chunks of the overhang cracked off and plunged downward into the depths of the cavern.

"There's no time!" she snapped. "*Jump!*"

The three leaped for the rope just as the entire ledge—and the bomb—plummeted into the abyss below.

"*No!*" Cafferty screamed, as they hung dangling over the darkness, shock waves of pain running through his arm.

"Is the bomb gonna blow when it hits bottom?" Bowcut asked.

"I don't know. Maybe . . ." Diego answered, clinging to the rope.

"How long?"

Diego did the math quickly in his head, based on the data he had seen in the chart up top. "Three thousand feet deep . . . if we're still here in twenty seconds, we're good."

Twenty seconds.

The three of them hung over the depths of hell, silently counting down in their heads. Twenty seconds. Not enough time to climb up. Not enough time to warn anyone. Not enough time for Cafferty to tell Ellen he loved her. Not enough time for him to apologize for failing his team, for failing New York, for failing himself.

Cafferty hung his head down, counting the seconds, waiting to learn his fate.

He had dreamed about taking out Van Ness for so long that he never really accepted the possibility of failing his mission. His hubris in New York cost the lives of more than a hundred people. His hubris here was about to cost the lives of millions.

Ten seconds.

It was too much for Cafferty to bear, the thought of it ending this way, incinerated at a temperature of 150 million degrees Fahrenheit. The thought of getting beat by Albert Van Ness. The thought of *losing*.

Five seconds.

Bowcut, Munoz, and Cafferty held their breath.

Four.

Three.

Two.

One.

Silence.

No detonation. No nuclear holocaust.

"Goddamn it, we're still alive!" Diego shouted.

Bowcut let out a primal, exuberant scream.

Cafferty held on to the rope silently. Slowly, determination spread throughout his bruised body.

This war may kill me—Van Ness may kill me—but not here, not in this place, and not like this.

"The bomb must have split apart on impact," Munoz added.

"Okay, let's climb," Bowcut said, lifting herself hand over hand back toward the breach and subway tunnel above. Diego and Cafferty followed closely behind, the flash grenade keeping the creatures hiding in the shadows. Cafferty's eyes stung, pain seared from the gouge on his arm, and blood trickled down his leg, but he'd be damned if they didn't make it to the abandoned Underground.

Bowcut reached the top first and helped Munoz and Cafferty up. For a moment, the three sat on the tracks in silence, catching their breath, taking fresh oxygen deep into their lungs.

"I'm going to bring Ellen up to speed," Cafferty said, lifting his comm to talk.

"One sec," Diego said, staring at the assorted handheld electronic equipment next to the crane. One of the tablets was blinking. He lifted the iPad-sized device and looked at the screen, which read:

    24:52:18
    24:52:17
    24:52:16

"My God," Diego said. "It's still counting down. The bomb is still intact. At the bottom of that nest. Three thousand feet down."

The team's spirit faded with the realization.

"There's no way the British can recover that in time and stop it," Bowcut said.

"We're fucked," Diego replied morosely.

Cafferty's head pounded and anger coursed through his body. He tried to quiet the rage and focus. *There must be a way . . .*

"The remote detonator!" Cafferty shouted. "Van Ness has the ability to trigger the bomb at any time."

"Yes," Diego replied.

"So it stands to reason that he can remotely turn off the timer as well."

"Yes . . . yes, I follow."

Determined, Cafferty locked eyes with his team. "We're going to Paris. We've got to stop that bomb from wiping out London."

Cafferty didn't need a vote—he could see Bowcut and Munoz agreed. He activated the comm to relay the plan to Ellen.

"Ellen, we're heading back topside, lots to fill you in on," Cafferty said.

Nobody responded.

"Ellen," he repeated. "Are you there?"

Still nothing.

"Could just be the reception," Diego said, but his words had little conviction. The reception had been fine before.

All three exchanged looks of concern, then broke into a sprint through the tunnels. Their boots pounded up the dilapidated escalator stairs, and they raced through the old ticket hall, along the corridor, and up the flights of stairs. Cafferty shoved the door open and hurtled into the street.

"Oh my God," he gasped.

Munoz and Bowcut flanked him as he approached the dark, powerless van. Its front window had completely frosted over and so had the lights. A creeping sense of foreboding turned into a sinking feeling in the pit of his stomach when he drew closer. The driver's- and passenger-side windows had been smashed in. He moved around to the back and opened the now unlocked doors.

Ellen was gone.

The interior of the van showed signs of a struggle. *Ellen was gone.*

A small white rectangle caught his eye, lying on the center of the floor. Cafferty reached inside and plucked it between his fingers.

It had the Foundation's name printed across in bold letters and the address for its Paris headquarters below.

Ellen was gone, and Van Ness had her.

And it was his fault.

"What is it?" Munoz asked.

Cafferty didn't reply. He couldn't. Instead, he attempted to control the rage erupting inside him like a supervolcano.

"Tom," Bowcut said. "Is it the Foundation?"

He slowly nodded. "He's got her."

Enraged, Cafferty crumpled the card in his hand and balled it into a fist. The thought of Ellen being accosted by Foundation thugs raced through his mind. *If they touch her . . .*

But this was bigger than Ellen. She was everything to him, but he wasn't the only one on this team. And he definitely wasn't the only one in this city. He stood there, his mind flipping back and forth, rapid-fire, between Ellen and the lives of the millions of innocent people all around him.

Cafferty was on the brink. He could feel it.

Ellen's kidnapping now confirmed that there was only one way to stop Van Ness, the man who was blackmailing the world and threatening humanity's existence with nuclear war and a terrifying new type of creature that could live aboveground.

"We're going to Paris. We're going to stop this bomb. And then . . ."

"Tom?" Munoz asked.

"And then I'm going to kill him."

CHAPTER FOURTEEN

Ellen had lost track of her kidnappers' car route since they had left the major roads surrounding London. All she knew was that they had initially headed west and were now winding their way through the dark countryside. The female driver, who appeared to be the leader of her captors, glanced over her shoulder toward the back seat. A stone-faced man sat by her side with a firm grip on her shoulder.

The multiple zip ties bit into Ellen's wrists as she tried to force them looser, straining against the rigid black plastic, but they held firm. The same happened with her ankle restraints. Escape appeared unlikely at present, though she hadn't resigned herself to whatever fate the Foundation had planned. Her experience in the caverns below New York had taught her that, and the knowledge that she needed to get back to little David reinforced her already cast-iron will to survive.

Perhaps I can reach out to this woman on a personal level. If even a scrap of humanity exists inside of her . . .

"You're British, right?" Ellen asked.

"Very perceptive," she replied sarcastically. "And you're from New York."

"You can't be comfortable with London being reduced to ashes."

The woman eyed Ellen through the rearview mirror. "If you knew what I've done and had seen what I've seen, you'd know it's an acceptable loss."

"Acceptable loss? You have to be kidding me."

"If it's any consolation, my brother lives in the city."

"How is that a consolation? You're prepared to let him die?"

"For the Foundation's mission, I'd let *anyone* die."

Ellen could hear it. Her captor had drunk the Kool-Aid. She was a true believer. Converting her to the good side was unlikely. But what other choice did she have? She pressed on.

"How does killing millions of people, including your brother, help defeat the creatures? Where's the logic in that, if the Foundation wants to protect humanity?"

"I'm sure Mr. Edwards can enlighten you on the plane," the woman replied.

The mention of Edwards being on the jet sent her mind racing. She knew he was Van Ness' number two, and if he had come along for the ride, this appeared more than a simple assassination.

It was probably another one of Van Ness' games. A power play. The twisted German thrived on manipulating people for his own amusement while putting them into the exact position he wanted them.

And knowing Tom and his impulsive nature, he

would oblige. She just hoped he didn't do anything rash and walk directly into a trap.

The driver flipped open the glove box and grabbed a pack of Marlboro Lights. "Mind if I smoke, Mrs. Cafferty?"

"I'd prefer you didn't."

The woman lit the cigarette anyway and took a deep drag. She lowered her window a couple of inches and groaned with satisfaction as she puffed out a stream of light gray smoke. The man holding Ellen didn't move an inch.

The stench invaded the back of the car. It reminded her of being trapped in one of New York's surviving cigar lounges, though the bad attitudes that lingered alongside the smoke in those places was thousands of miles away from here.

"Oh, and one request," the woman said, eyeing Ellen through the rearview mirror.

"And that is . . . ?"

"Shut the fuck up until we arrive. To be perfectly blunt, your accent disgusts me."

For the next few minutes, the car continued to snake around country roads until the woman flipped on the turn signal and navigated through an open chain-link gate.

"We're here," the man said casually, speaking for the first time. "Get ready to move."

Ellen forced herself up and peered out the window.

Spotlights blazed down from the roof of an aircraft hangar. To the right of it, a single runway stretched into the darkness. A Learjet sat at the near end. Its back door was open, and a set of steps led down to the tarmac. Ellen wondered how many people knew this place existed. Woodland surrounded the entire private airstrip. She couldn't see any commercial signage or anything else to betray the location.

The woman steered the car onto the runway. She grabbed her phone from the center cup holder. Before she had a chance to dial, two stocky men, dressed head-to-toe in black, descended the Learjet's steps.

"A word of warning," the woman said. "If you want to keep your pretty smile, don't struggle with the guards. If I didn't know better, I'd say they get off at punching people's teeth out. And probably have no problem with smacking a woman around."

"Thanks for being so considerate," Ellen said.

"I'm just doing my job," she replied.

"That's what concentration camp guards claimed, too. I suppose you're not that different if you're willing to let millions die for your boss' twisted ideology."

The woman turned in her seat. "A second word of warning. Say anything like that in front of Van Ness and it'll be the last thing that comes out of your mouth." And then she flicked the still-glowing cigarette butt at Ellen's face.

Ellen screamed, but she barely got burned.

The woman began to laugh.

Ellen defiantly spit right at her face, bringing the woman's laughter to a quick end.

"You bitch—"

Both back doors flew open, letting in the cold night air, and one of the men pushed the driver away before she could attack Ellen.

"You know better than to play with Mr. Van Ness' toys," he said.

The man slipped a knife from his belt and sawed through Ellen's ankle restraints with the serrated edge of the blade. Ellen used all of her inner strength to not smash her knee into his face. He was shaven headed with a nose that looked like it'd been broken several times. He grabbed her by the shoulders and heaved her into a standing position on the runway.

The stench of airplane fuel hung in the air.

The Learjet's two engines whined.

A thin, bald man stared down from one of the plane's windows.

The Foundation lackey took a firm grip of Ellen's shoulders and marched her to the plane. She didn't see the point of resisting. Spitting was one thing, but she knew there was no way she could take one of these guys, let alone two. Besides, she had her hands tied behind her back. She had no clue as to her location, so had no idea where she would escape to. And she valued her teeth. The way ahead was to remain subservient until a better opportunity arose.

"Up the steps," the guard ordered. He shoved her in the back. "Right now."

Ellen climbed into the brightly lit cabin. Two sets of oversized cream leather seats faced each other. On the far left one, a balding, skinny old man in a beige suit gave her a wry smile. Closer up, she recognized him from Bowcut's reconnaissance photos in Paris and Munoz's portfolios of the known Foundation staff. Just like the woman in the car had said, Van Ness' number two had been waiting for her.

He didn't appear particularly threatening or intimidating, but then again, neither did a faucet riddled with Legionnaires' disease.

"It's nice to finally meet you, Mrs. Cafferty," Edwards said in a raspy voice.

"Are you pretending this has any scrap of civility?" she barked back at him.

Edwards peered beyond Ellen at the guard and motioned his head toward the seat opposite him. Once again, a shove propelled her forward. The guard stayed close behind; his breath warmed the nape of her neck. He removed her wrist ties and twisted her shoulders, forcing her down into the seat. Then he moved around the back of her and secured her to the seat with a thick black strap.

Ellen glanced across to Edwards, who returned a neutral expression. If the man had any emotions, she couldn't tell. He stared back at her silently, studying the woman.

"What do you want from me? What is this all about?" she asked.

"What this is about . . ." he replied in a monotone voice.

Slowly, he reached inside his jacket pocket and pulled out a jet-black razor-sharp creature claw. He grabbed her arm quickly, holding it down on the armrest.

"What the hell are you doing?"

". . . is *this*, Mrs. Cafferty."

He scratched the sharp tip down her arm, causing her to wince and leaving a long visible mark on her skin. Visions of her first encounter with the creatures made her swallow hard and close her eyes. That claw circling her pregnant belly, gouging her flesh, and corkscrewing down toward her unborn baby.

The jet jerked forward and picked up speed along the runway. Edwards leaned back in his seat and slipped the claw back in his jacket pocket. He didn't make a sound. He just stared at her with the same expressionless face. On the psychopath scale, she guessed he was off the charts.

The Learjet's wheels lifted off the runway and they powered into the night. Ellen looked out the window to avoid Edwards' creepy stare. She felt his eyes on her the whole time it took to break through the clouds and reach a cruising altitude underneath the star-studded sky.

"But first, there's some business to attend to," Edwards said, picking up where he left off despite the minutes of silence. "Mr. Van Ness would like your husband in Paris."

"Why not kidnap him, then?"

"Oh, I'm sure you'd agree that the emotional turmoil this will put him through is much more fun." A smug smile spread across his face, the first emotion he had displayed, but it quickly dissipated. "But you already know how to put your husband through emotional turmoil."

"Excuse me?" Ellen asked.

"You know, inserting Lucien Flament into your life was my idea. I can only imagine how seeing that French 'reporter' on his big day tore your husband apart inside. Still, you should thank me for providing you with a child. How is little David?"

Fire burned in Ellen's eyes. She ignored the question and looked away.

Edwards' spindly hand gripped the back of her head and twisted her face toward him. His expression had transformed from stoic to intense. He glared into her eyes, unflinching. "I asked you about little David."

"Leave him out of this."

"I'm sorry, but you and your husband brought him into this when you started your deluded pursuit of the Foundation. What did you expect would happen?"

"No," Ellen whispered to herself as it appeared her worst fear was about to materialize. "Not David . . ."

Edwards slipped a phone out of his pants pocket. He scrolled through the camera roll to a video, hit play, and held the screen toward her face.

On-screen, Ellen's parents pushed David's stroller through a public park close to their home in West Virginia. He sat facing out, wearing his red fleece coverall decorated with penguins. This was part of the retired couple's daily routine since agreeing to look after her son. Ellen had done the same walk several times.

The video continued tracking her parents. A normal-looking woman dressed in yoga pants and a vest walked by her parents, greeting them warmly as she passed. She was clearly a familiar face to them, perhaps a neighbor. As the elderly couple passed, though, the young woman abruptly turned around, no longer smiling, and silently followed them, matching their stride. The woman glanced toward the secret camera for a brief moment, then drew a pistol fixed with a long silencer and switched her aim between the backs of Ellen's parents.

Ellen's hands balled into fists. Little David . . . her parents . . . they had no way of knowing they were trapped in the Foundation's web. And any reaction from her now could put them in further danger.

She held back her anger. She held back her shouts and insults.

She held back her tears.

"It does amaze me how easy it is to ingratiate yourself into people's lives, to become their trusted confidant, their best friend, and, on rare occasion, their lover. Tell me—did you consider putting Flament's name on David's birth certificate?"

Once again, Ellen refused to rise to his barbed comments. But if she ever had the chance, she'd drill a bullet through this monster's brain.

"Nothing to say?" Edwards asked.

It took all Ellen's willpower not to tell him to go fuck himself. But she could still see the video of her parents with David. Could still see the gun pointed at them. Instead, she calmly said, "You've already captured me. I'm sure Tom will follow to France. So why stalk my child and parents?"

"If your husband does anything not according to our plan—and I mean anything—my team will kill your child and your family. Their deaths won't be fast."

Ellen bowed her head and drew in a deep breath. She had little chance to escape and even less of a chance to warn her parents about the grave danger they were in.

"Oh, there's no need to be so upset," Edwards said.

"You just threatened to kill my family!"

He leaned closer. "Yes, but you shouldn't let that worry you. You see . . . you won't be alive to see it happen."

CHAPTER FIFTEEN

S hafts of moonlight shone through the barred window into the small, filthy cell. Reynolds sat in the corner, clutching his knees and slowly rocking back and forth. His ribs ached from the kicking the guards had given him for throwing his tray of food. His jaw did, too—that was for mouthing off. The Foundation had also turned the heat up and down at regular intervals, and the temperature was dropping again.

Others had clearly been kept here against their will before him. Someone had attempted to scrawl what looked like a phone number on the wall, but it was incomplete. Dried smears and spatters of blood betrayed the previous violence. He was kept in almost total silence, apart from the sporadic echo of distant voices. Worse was the feeling of death that hung in the air.

The image of Van Ness and the idea of his insane demands kept swirling in his mind. The deranged lunatic thought he could blackmail the United States. Reynolds figured Van Ness was smart enough to realize America would not capitulate, even with the former president's pleading. Which made his life worthless to the Foundation.

So why am I being kept alive?

Reynolds shivered and hugged himself tighter. Ice crystals started to form on the window beyond the steel bars. His only hope lay with the CIA tracing his location and attempting a rescue. But those chances were slim, if the Foundation had indeed kept him hostage for almost a year. He didn't doubt Van Ness' words, though, because of his thin arms and legs, the visible ribs, and a shrunken gut where he once sported a paunch the ex-marine in him had always hated the sight of.

The silence was interrupted by the sound of multiple footsteps approaching the cell.

His refusal of food had been hours ago, and the guards had informed him that his next meal was breakfast at sunrise. His mind spun at the thought of who was approaching and why.

Reynolds groaned to a standing position and winced at the stabbing pain in his ribs. He vigorously rubbed his arms and body so he could stand tall and firm to meet whoever was coming for him.

Outside, a bolt screeched along its rail.

The door creaked open.

Two guards stood there, emotionless. One had a large canvas bag slung over his shoulder. The other pointed a pistol at Reynolds' face.

"Outside," the one with the gun commanded. "Mr. Van Ness is waiting. If you make us late, I'll knock your teeth out."

"Maybe you'll get yours knocked out if I stall," Reynolds replied defiantly. "I'll accept that trade."

Another guard walked in front of the cell, armed with a cattle prod. This was the stocky South African man who had threatened the beatings earlier, then consequently delivered on his promises.

"You sure you want to test me?" the guard said ominously.

This time Reynolds decided against resisting. He headed between them, along a dark corridor. A strip-light flickered overhead, momentarily brightening more cell doors on either side. Moans and wails came from several of them. Considering the Foundation had the balls to take the president of the United States, he reckoned that it had a few more blackmail prizes here. Perhaps even other foreign leaders who refused Van Ness' demands.

The guard with the pistol walked by his side, shoving him in his back every few steps. He resisted the temptation to attack.

Whatever the consequences, so be it.

Two more guards waited by a large steel door at the end of the corridor. That made five, the most he had seen, though he had little doubt this was a much larger operation.

They heaved open the door to reveal the same vast warehouse with the chair and TV in the middle of the black flooring. And the creature still behind the transparent section, with a few more shatter marks on the glass. The corpse it had been tossing around was now just a pile of guts and limbs.

A video camera on a tripod had been positioned

in front of the glass facing the creature. Reynolds guessed Van Ness would enjoy watching him suffer the same fate, then the video would be shared with the world. It would make watching even the vilest hostage video seem like a picnic in comparison. It would also prove the Foundation could take out anyone. He swallowed hard at the thought of his family and friends witnessing him being ripped to shreds.

"The boss is already on-screen," one of the guards called out with a Dutch inflection as they entered the warehouse. The various guards Reynolds had encountered so far had spoken in an array of accents, mostly European, he guessed, which could point to his likely location. He searched his memory again for the slightest recollection to back up his assumption.

Nothing.

"Back in the chair," one of the guards ordered.

Reynolds slumped down and rested his back against the chilly metal support. He kept a straight face despite the burning pain in his chest and arms. Van Ness faced him on the screen. He sat behind an antique dining table with portraits on the surrounding wood-paneled walls and peered at Reynolds through the screen.

A guard snapped the manacles around Reynolds' wrists and ankles.

A shuddering boom echoed around the warehouse. Reynolds looked over his shoulder. The creature had smashed against the glass again, then hunched down, staring at him with intent. It met his eyes with a stifled shriek.

Everyone left the warehouse, oblivious to the threat, apart from a single armed guard. He kept his aim on Reynolds' head.

"Good morning," Van Ness said. "I've sent a message to President Brogan to expect your call. I'm sure she'll listen to what you have to say. Don't disappoint me, John."

Reynolds shook his head. "It's John now, is it?"

"I'm a civil man, John. As long as you do what I ask."

"And how exactly will you force me to do what you ask? You can beat me further, threaten me with that monster. It won't matter. The United States does not negotiate with terrorists, no matter what I say. If you're going to kill me, get it the hell over with."

"Let's not travel down that road just yet, John. The destination doesn't end well for you."

"Does it piss you off that all of your efforts to capture me has come to nothing?" Reynolds smiled in defiance, even though he realized the consequences. "Do your worst. I'll die thinking about your death when we finally come for you."

"We?" Van Ness let out a deep sigh. "There is no 'we' right now. There's humanity versus the creatures. If you want us to remain the dominant species, then you'll do as I ask. Please, John. I'm not a cruel man—don't force me to be."

"Call the president yourself," Reynolds replied. "I won't help you. You've captured me for absolutely nothing."

"Oh, I must politely disagree," Van Ness said. "You see, capturing you shows the United States—

and the world—that nobody is unreachable, no government can protect you. I have unlimited resources, unlimited power. You give me maximum leverage when negotiating, don't you see? Former Mr. President, you are effectively my toy."

It infuriated Reynolds how Van Ness was treating this like a business meeting rather than pure terrorism. This wasn't about him talking. The Foundation didn't need him for that. It was a power game, pure and simple. A show of force. The ultimate humiliation and there was nothing he could do about it.

"Fuck you," Reynolds replied.

On the video screen, Van Ness took a sip from a glass of water.

"Very well, John, you leave me with no option." Van Ness lifted a phone to his ear. "Bring them in and make it fast. I'd like to get on with my day."

Three people staggered through the warehouse entrance, hands bound behind their backs, each with a guard shoving them forward. All wore orange coveralls. All had sacks over their heads. One man, two women, judging by their figures.

"What game are you playing?" Reynolds snapped.

"This isn't a game. You've tested my patience long enough, and it's in your hands to end this."

The three hostages were positioned between Reynolds and the TV.

A guard ripped the sack off one of the women's heads.

Reynolds bolted in his seat. "You son of a bitch."

"Meet your former secretary," Van Ness said coldly. "I believe you two shared some good times in the Oval Office, am I right?"

The president's former secretary, Adele Ringwood, stared at him. She attempted to scream something through the dirty gag tied around her mouth, but the cloth muffled her words. Tears streamed down her cheeks. Her blond hair was unkempt and greasy. She appeared nothing like the confident woman who had stolen his heart and almost caused his impeachment.

The guard with the canvas bag dropped it on the floor. He pulled open the zipper and produced a weapon similar to a medieval mace, only shiny and fashioned from steel. He moved behind Ringwood and raised it over his head, preparing to strike.

Reynolds hadn't seen this coming. He hated himself for not actively pursuing Van Ness while he had the chance. Now others suffered because of him. He briefly wondered about the identities of the other two hostages before returning his focus back to the screen. "Is capturing and killing innocent people your way of saving humanity, you twisted fuck?" he bellowed.

Van Ness replied, "Do it."

The guard drove the mace down. It connected to the top of Ringwood's head with a dull crunch. She dropped to her knees, wavering as blood dribbled down her face and pattered onto the floor. He swung at her again and battered the weapon against her temple.

Ringwood slumped to the ground, facedown. Her legs twitched several times. The guard leaned over and wedged his boot into the small of her back to rip out the mace. He slammed it down twice more against the back of her head, each blow making the weapon's retrieval easier as her skull gradually collapsed. Reynolds winced at the blood spilling across the ground.

Anger burned inside him. Pure hatred. Van Ness needed to pay for this. Everyone in the Foundation did. Tears began to stream down his face.

One of the guards dragged Ringwood away by her feet back toward the cells. Her body left a glistening trail of blood on the warehouse flooring.

"I imagine you must feel helpless," Van Ness said. "I imagine many people around the world have felt that way in the face of your country's aggression."

Reynolds fought back his tears and the urge to vomit. "Go to hell."

Van Ness glared at him. "Unmask the next one."

A guard whipped off the sack covering the male hostage.

Billy Reynolds, his nephew, stared at him with fear in his bloodshot eyes. Nineteen years old. A college student majoring in political science at the University of Virginia, same as Reynolds had done decades earlier.

"You seem quiet," Van Ness said. "Will you speak to President Brogan on my behalf now, John?"

The implication was clear: concede to Van Ness' demands or watch another murder. He felt like his insides were being ripped apart.

"Don't you value your nephew's life?" Van Ness asked. "My business is saving humanity; I'm uncompromising about that and you'll come to appreciate it one day, if you comply. Now, will you talk?"

"You're a monster."

"No, my friend, I'm fighting the real monsters."

Reynolds bucked hard against his restraints. For the first time in his life he felt useless, unable to even remotely dictate proceedings. And he had hardly any time to think.

Before he could respond, Van Ness said, "Do it."

"*No!*" Reynolds cried out.

The guard stepped behind Billy and pulled an ice pick from behind his back. He clenched his teeth and slammed it into the top of the nineteen-year-old's head.

The tip of the pick exploded out of Billy's left eye. Blood sprayed over Reynolds' legs.

Billy crumpled to the ground like a puppet with its strings cut. The guard smashed a boot against his jaw, but he didn't move a muscle. The first blow had already done the job.

Tears streamed down Reynolds' face and he shook his head no, head slumped downward.

It was no consolation that his nephew's death had been swifter. Reynolds needed a way to stop this. He couldn't hold out any longer. But he knew that even if he did what Van Ness asked, he wouldn't get him the results he wanted.

More would die—*he* might die—and it was because Van Ness wouldn't listen to reason.

How does someone convince a madman?

Another guard dragged Billy away, leaving a second bloody trail.

Reynolds closed his eyes for a moment. He couldn't imagine how it could get any worse. He blamed himself for the deaths of Ringwood and Billy. His stupidity had led to this. He should have known the true severity of the situation following the Z Train disaster instead of focusing on weeding out the traitors.

"Next," Van Ness commanded.

The head sack was ripped off the final person left alive.

His *mother*, Jacquelyn.

Eighty-seven, widow, she wouldn't hurt a fly. Her thin gray hair was pasted against her head, partially through blood caked on her scalp. She gave her son a look of confusion. Her hands quivered from Parkinson's disease, and a guard had to prop her up to stop her from falling.

"Do you want to know what it feels like to lose your mother and there's *nothing* you can do to stop it, Mr. Reynolds?"

"Don't do this . . ." he muttered, broken.

"My mother was crushed to death by thousands of kilograms of crumbling concrete when American and British bombs destroyed my town of Dresden in 1945. Your government murdered half a million civilians in that mission. Did they forget to teach you that at university?"

"Please, stop . . ." Reynolds whispered.

"Will you call the president?" Van Ness shouted. "Or shall I toss your mother into that cage?"

His mother shivered, realizing the peril of her situation after seeing the blood trails from the other hostages.

The first two deaths had already pushed Reynolds beyond his limits. Seeing his frail, innocent mother being torn to shreds by a creature was too much to handle.

"I won't ask again," Van Ness shouted.

Reynolds raised his eyes to the screen. "I'll do it."

"I knew you'd come around, John. You agree to relay my demands to the new president?"

"Yes."

A guard approached Reynolds, hit the speed dial on a phone, and planted it to his ear. The ringtone chirped four times before someone answered.

"White House switchboard."

"This is John Reynolds. I need to speak to President Brogan."

"President John Reynolds?"

"Yes, goddamn it."

"Sorry . . . Give me a moment, sir."

Reynolds waited. The longer he stayed on the line, the better chance they'd have of tracing his call. Van Ness glared at him.

"President Brogan" sounded through the speaker.

"Amanda, it's John Reynolds. I'm being held hostage by the Foundation."

"Do you know where?"

"No. And I'm sure you understand the Foundation is listening."

"Of course."

Brogan sounded firm. Reynolds liked that, though it probably meant the end of him.

"They want me to relay certain information," Reynolds said. "A ransom."

A reply didn't come straightaway. Eventually President Brogan said, *"I'm sorry, John. We refuse to talk terms with Albert Van Ness. But I have a message for* him. *Tell him we're coming for him."*

Reynolds grinned. "I think we're in Europe. Do what you can—"

The guard ripped the phone from his ear.

Van Ness shook his head. "You don't realize what you've just done."

One of the guards spoke into a walkie-talkie. A moment later, he grabbed Reynolds' mother by the collar and led her away.

Reynolds had expected the screen to cut—an uncompromising sign of arrogance from Van Ness that he was above the events. But instead, Van Ness stayed on-screen, gazing at him with a neutral expression as if this were all business.

A guard pushed the old woman along a gangway above the creature's enclosed space, on top of what appeared to be a trapdoor.

"Do it," Van Ness said.

"Put me back on with Brogan!" Reynolds shouted desperately.

"We'll discuss that in a moment," Van Ness replied, ignoring his pleas. He sipped from his water glass and placed it back down on the antique table. "Do it."

A guard pulled a lever next to the old woman. The trapdoor swung open.

"NO!" Reynolds cried out.

The frail woman dropped into the transparent lair of the creature and hit the ground hard.

Reynolds couldn't bear to watch, but he couldn't take his eyes off the spectacle. The creature leaped over to Jacquelyn's crumpled body and slashed at her coveralls with its claws. Within seconds, it had shredded through the material and gouged her stomach.

He squeezed his eyes tight as screams echoed around the room. The creature wrapped its hands around the old woman's face, then repeatedly slammed her limp body against the glass.

"So who shall be next, John?" Van Ness asked. "We've got three better guests lined up for you. Or maybe I'll choose you next. Will you speak to the administration again, or shall we continue with this?"

Reynolds sunk in his chair and shook his head no.

He knew he'd be next in terms of punishment. But dying seemed preferable to dealing with this sick asshole and his crazy demands.

"Make him see the error of his ways," Van Ness commanded. "But make sure he can still talk."

A guard wrapped him in a tight headlock. Another released him from his seat, and they dragged him back toward the cells.

One way or another, Reynolds knew his death was coming.

CHAPTER SIXTEEN

The clock ticked closer to midnight. Brogan stared at the conference phone in the center of the table, in shock. She had expected Van Ness would call with his demands—which she would refuse—but she never expected this: John Reynolds was alive, and the Foundation had taken him. Now it was a case of waiting to see if the NSA could trace the exact location.

Near silence filled the White House Presidential Emergency Operations Center, broken only by the hum of the air conditioner. That's the way it had been since Reynolds' desperate voice had erupted through the speaker. Webster and four members of the Secret Service sat on the opposite side of the table. Other members of her team had been listening in from the Situation Room.

The split in resources had been purposely coordinated by her, at least for today. The assassination of Prime Minister Simpson and the attempt on her life had planted enough distrustfulness for her to keep a degree of separation from the wider team.

Van Ness could no longer be allowed to keep removing national leaders at his leisure. To her, the Foundation appeared nothing more than a high-powered racket, like the Bilderberg Group with a lethal edge.

"The CIA has analyzed the voice pattern, Madam President," a Secret Service member said. "Confirmed—that was President Reynolds."

"I always had a feeling the crafty old dog was still alive," Webster said. "Let's bring him home before we turn our attention to the Foundation."

"We'll do both," Brogan replied. "If Van Ness thinks he can get away with this, he's sorely mistaken. We need immediate intel and an overwhelming military response."

"You don't need to tell me. That said, our next moves require delicate sequencing if we're to succeed."

"I don't disagree," Brogan said, although her voice sounded unconvinced.

"But you don't fully agree?" Webster's brow furrowed. The hard-nosed New Yorker never liked his opinion being questioned, though his steadfast nature was part of the reason she had selected him as her VP. "All I'm saying is we don't want to scare the horses."

Brogan returned his frown. "Meaning what?"

"Most Americans think John Reynolds is already dead, so if we bring him home, we're heroes. Perhaps it's not a bad idea to negotiate with Van Ness. We can use that time to get a fix on Reynolds and work on getting him out. We'll deal with the Foundation afterward. If Van Ness finds out we're launching a military attack on him, he'll kill Reynolds and disappear underground. Let's take it one step at a time. Remember—the public won't forgive us if we blow this."

She resisted the temptation to roll her eyes. Yes, Webster was an election-winning machine and his rhetoric had the power to inspire people, but this was about more than public perception. It was about democratic principles. The life of a president. The scourge of Van Ness.

One thing she intended to find out was why the Foundation acted like it did and why it had gotten away with its behavior for so long. After all, it was one crazy old man heading up a bunch of fanatics. History dictated that these kinds of small groups never successfully imposed themselves on the world for any protracted period of time. That's what made it all so baffling. How had the Foundation slipped under the global radar for so long without, to her knowledge, being seriously challenged?

A tone pinged by the Emergency Operations Center entrance.

On the entry pad screen, Tony Roscoe, the head of the NSA, and General Burns from Joint Special Operations Command stood waiting outside—the first in a suit, the second in uniform. Both serious-faced, with folders tucked under their arms. Both the type of middle-aged men Brogan had to battle on a daily basis as the first female president. But both were beyond suspicion as far as she was concerned.

"Let them in," she ordered.

One of the Secret Service briskly walked over to the pad and punched in a code. The door's thick steel bolts clanked open. He waved Roscoe and Burns inside the room, and they headed over to Webster's side of the desk.

"We've got a location for Reynolds," Roscoe said. "The call came from a small warehouse in the Swiss town of Schaffhausen."

Burns slipped a satellite photo out of his folder and slid it across the table. "The warehouse is on the edge of town. We've traced the ownership several layers back to the Foundation for Human Advancement."

"You're absolutely sure?" Brogan studied the picture. "He's there?"

"All I can say for certain is that the phone call originated from that warehouse," Roscoe replied.

Excitement rose inside of her. She had feared they would tell her that Reynolds was being kept in Paris, which would've brought several unwanted complications, but a warehouse on the outskirts of a small Swiss town . . .

"Do we have anyone in the area?" she asked.

The general nodded. "Close, and it's a good team. If you want, we can hit the place at first light."

"We shouldn't rush," Webster said. "The Swiss need to know what we're doing first. And I still think we should reengage the conversation with—"

"No," Brogan said, cutting her vice president off. "We act first. I'll deal with the Swiss government once we get John Reynolds safely home. General, I want an extraction plan ASAP. Let's go save the president."

Burns gave her a firm nod. "Yes, Madam President."

Burns and Roscoe left the room.

She finally felt like the administration had gotten onto its front foot. First, they save the president. And then they destroy Albert Van Ness.

CHAPTER SEVENTEEN

The first signs of dawn brightened the snow-capped peaks of the Upper Rhine Valley. Master Sergeant Suarez peered through his binoculars across the murky valley toward the picture-perfect town of Schaffhausen. Lights twinkled from the hundreds of houses clustered on the banks of the mighty River Rhine. The sixteenth-century Munot Fortress, a circular fortification with a single white tower, dominated the land above.

Nothing stirred.

Nothing hinted at why he and his team were here.

It was hard to imagine such beauty shielded such evil. It looked more like the front of a Christmas card than a town that had held the president of the United States prisoner for almost a year. Suarez had never expected to carry out a live operation in these surroundings, especially in the civilian clothing of jeans and a winter jacket. This place was near paradise compared to his previous operations in Iraq and Afghanistan, and he thought it was a quiet assignment, which he had looked forward to. Not that he wasn't prepared. He was a soldier through and through, and he took that seriously.

But nothing exciting was supposed to be happening in Switzerland.

Four unmarked vans, all different makes and models, sat in the turnout behind him, each with its engine idly humming. Smoke belched from their exhaust pipes and drifted away in the chilly breeze.

Suarez zipped his jacket up to protect his neck from the cold.

His group of soldiers had been given the responsibility for the rescue early this morning. The twelve-person team had no intentions of screwing this up. They had been training a German commando team when the call had come in. Since then, the unit had spent the time poring over blueprints of the industrial warehouse beyond the town. Readying their gear. Moving into position.

Their plan was approved. Now it was just a case of waiting for the final confirmation to execute.

Suarez wanted this more than any previous mission.

This was bigger than Bin Laden.

His helmet cam would broadcast directly to the White House Situation Room. Two teams of six would simultaneously hit both ways into the warehouse. They were trained for this. A pair would stay outside of each entrance to stop anyone from entering and to provide covering fire for the choppers if required. Then a rapid building clearance. Grab John Reynolds. A flight back across the border to their base in Germany.

Of course, this was neutral Switzerland, and

they were mounting a secret military action on its soil without permission. He couldn't even begin to imagine what kind of political shit-storm this would create. But that, to him, was irrelevant. Politics were for politicians. He had his orders, and he was going to execute.

Two figures trudged up the side of the road toward the turnout. A woman and a man. Both dressed like typical hikers in boots, walking trousers, Gore-Tex jackets, and wool hats. Their boots crunched on the icy grass as they approached. Suarez instantly recognized them as the forward reconnaissance team, Staff Sergeants Ross and Suzuki. They had already radioed in with their ETA, and as usual, they were right on time.

Staff Sergeant Ross stood by Suarez's side as he continued to watch the slumbering town for signs of movement. She stamped her boots to clear the ice.

"Well?" he asked.

"We've only got a single heat signature," she said.

"Seriously?"

Ross nodded. "Looks like a man tied to a chair in the large central area. There's a table with an electrical appliance next to him."

"He isn't guarded?"

"Maybe they abandoned him, knowing we traced the call. He's likely chained down . . ."

"Possible, I guess. Is he alive?"

"We've picked up some movement from his body. He's alive."

"What if it's not him?" Suarez questioned, almost rhetorically.

"The cell signal *originated* from that warehouse,

now confirmed by both the CIA and Homeland Security, sir. Who else could it be?"

He pursed his lips. "Could've switched him out."

"And left one of their own tied up all night? I don't know, seems like a stretch."

"True. But it's still so damn strange. Relay this intel back to the White House, and let's get confirmation they still want to proceed."

"Copy."

The two staff sergeants moved to the rear of the nearest van and climbed into the back. Suarez considered the unusual scenario. He had expected the two teams would have to fight their way in. Now, if their entry triggered alarms, they would most likely have to fight their way *out* when the Foundation reacted.

The only thing his team had been briefed on about the Foundation for Human Advancement was that it was a civilian group that had tried to blackmail the United States. That much he had already guessed, considering it had killed the former president's detail in the hills around Camp David and then taken him hostage. How nobody knew anything about this group being a threat until now seemed odd. Its supposed charitable status, then this . . . It wasn't like it was linked to any fundamentalists or other known players.

That said, with the kind of planning it took to snatch a president on U.S. soil, Suarez didn't expect this to be easy. But who these people really were and their ultimate aim remained a mystery.

He let out a deep sigh.

The facts by themselves bordered on the realms of fantasy.

Staff Sergeant Ross approached again. "We have confirmation from the White House, Master Sergeant. We are a go."

"Very well."

The orders from the White House were clear. They had to go in right now to recover John Reynolds. No turning back. No hesitation. The eyes of the administration were on his team and expected immediate action. No, demanded it.

If the Foundation had men guarding the president, Suarez expected they'd be trained mercenaries. If that was the case, so be it.

Let them try.

They would be met with a welcoming committee of lead-filled justice.

"Captain," Suarez said through his comm. "Our team is a go."

"Copy. Let's move in," the captain said through the earpiece.

The rear doors of the van slammed shut.

A wave of excitement ran through him. He had feared the administration would pull back his team at the last minute and leave this job to the Swiss Special Forces Command. They were good, but his team was better.

The faint buzz of choppers echoed in the distant sky.

He jogged to the passenger door of the van and climbed inside. A soldier named Darryl Scott sat in the driver's seat.

"The boss says he's in there alone," Scott said.

"So it appears," Suarez replied.

"Appears?"

"You know better than to expect the expected."

Suarez slipped his Glock into his holster, grabbed his short-barreled M4 from the footwell and rested it against his thighs. He already had the stun grenades in his pockets. He left his helmet by his side to avoid any obvious signs of suspicion when they rolled through town, in case the Foundation had sentries watching the roads.

"It can't be this easy," Scott said. "What are you thinking?"

"Same as you. If they had the muscle to grab Reynolds, they won't just let us waltz in and ride off into the sunset without a fight."

"So what? They're hiding underground?"

"Doubtful, based on the schematics. The place is built on solid rock. I'm guessing they'll be close."

"I don't think they'll enjoy their first date with us."

Suarez smiled at the soldier.

Scott shifted the van into gear. He pulled onto the road and descended toward the bridge that would lead them through Schaffhausen. The other three vans followed, keeping their distance sporadic. As they drove lower into the valley, the natural light decreased, and the vans' headlights stabbed through the gloom.

"*We're sticking to the original plan,*" the captain said over the earpiece. "*There's a chance they're in rooms that avoid heat detection. If they descend on the location, two in each team fall back. Radio silence until we reach the warehouse.*"

Suarez kept his eyes glued to their surroundings. They crossed the bridge that spanned the Rhine and headed through the old town at a speed of thirty miles per hour. He had read that Schaffhausen was one of the best-preserved places from the Middle Ages, but taking in the cultural scenery was the last thing on his mind. Instead, he focused on potential threats. A few people ambled along the sidewalks, all wrapped up to face the cold. Nobody gave the van a second glance.

Scott navigated through a series of tight streets until the buildings thinned. The satnav indicated that they were two minutes away, and like the aerial images had shown, they hit open countryside.

The sun had risen farther into the morning sky, and shafts of light brightened the snow-covered vineyards that lined the hills.

Suarez ran the details of the mission through his mind again and again. He was to lead one of the teams through the south entrance. Head up a corridor with plenty of small rooms leading off—possibly cells or ambush points. Then through a doorway to the large central area. That was where Reynolds was, or at least the heat signature of a man tied to a chair.

"Just imagine," Scott said. "Us bringing him home."

"Focus up, soldier," Suarez replied.

Nowadays, Suarez felt calm during the moments before a mission. He put it down to having a wife and two daughters. In his younger days, adrenaline and bravado had fueled him into constant chatter. The army was his entire life. Scott was his partner in close-quarter combat, and they had fought together during the Battle of Fallujah. Unlike him, though, the Connecticut man had never changed. It wasn't a good or bad thing, just different. That said, he trusted Scott more than anyone to have his back.

They reached the crest of a hill and the warehouse appeared a few hundred yards to their front. The size of a football field. Made from corrugated steel. A glass-fronted entrance at the south end, which appeared to be an easy obstacle. No cars parked outside. No visible lights on the inside.

The distant group of houses appeared dormant. Lights out. Sleepy. But he expected they would. However, the Foundation *had* to be watching. Anything else seemed far-fetched considering the prize it held.

Scott slowed the van when they neared the side road leading to the building.

In the rearview mirror, the other vans closed into a tight formation.

Suarez put a round in the chamber.

This is all too easy.

The second and third van roared past them and headed for the north entrance; the fourth pulled up close behind as they sped to the southern end. The tires screeched on the gravel and threw up frost and dirt as they came to a crunching halt in front of the double glass doors.

The van's back doors flew open.

Suarez and Scott immediately jumped out into the freezing morning air and took up covering positions, rifles shouldered. Another two team members covered the hills at either side, eyeing the ridgelines through their scopes.

One member of the team rushed to the entrance holding the battering ram—or the "enforcer," as they liked to call it—a long piece of steel with two hand grips and a blunt front end, designed for breaking open locks. More of the team covered him as he smashed the tool against the warehouse doors. They buckled inward and the windows shattered. The second swing hammered them open, revealing a dark reception area.

Suarez sprang to his feet and crept inside, searching for trip wires or alarm systems. He scanned the dusty desk, clearly not used in years judging by its state and the faded calendar on the wall behind. Chairs in the waiting area lay on their side; cobwebs stretched between them. The place appeared derelict, which came as no surprise. He hardly expected a receptionist waiting to book them in for an appointment to see John Reynolds.

Scott and two others immediately followed him into the building.

Two waited outside, as instructed, to guard the entrance.

"We're in," the captain said through Suarez's earpiece from the northern entrance. *"No signs of the enemy. Move to the main area."*

The long corridor with the multiple rooms on either side lay beyond the door, which was ajar, so didn't present any access problems. Scott led the way. He slowly pushed the door fully open, and the light mounted on his rifle punched through the darkness to the far end, roughly eighty yards away. It highlighted a steel door that was also ajar. He swept his beam along the left and right walls.

Every solid door to the side rooms had been closed. None had windows for the enemy to fire on the team as it advanced.

Suarez slipped past Scott and moved forward, hugging the left wall, ready to fire. Two others moved along the right side using a leapfrog technique, covering each other at all times.

Dried footprints covered the stone floor, and a trail, perhaps of blood, ran underneath one of the doors. Suarez had visited a black site before and this wasn't too different. Discreet on the outside. Benign. But the walls concealed a multitude of things that would spoil the public's breakfast if shown on the morning news.

Suarez neared the steel doors and dropped to one knee.

His team followed suit.

A gentle breeze whistled through a crack in the roof.

His earpiece let out a quiet static hiss.

A bead of sweat trickled down his back.

Suarez hit his transmit button. "No hostiles. We're heading into the main area."

"*Same*," the captain replied.

He remained conscious that every move he made was being watched by staff in the White House. This fact repeatedly spun in the back of his mind, and now they were all encountering the moment of truth. Suarez rose to his feet, keeping his rifle aimed forward, and he stepped through the gap at the side of the steel door.

The other three in his team followed and fanned around him.

Two small ceiling lights blazed down on the center of the cavernous area, highlighting a man in a suit with greasy, shaggy hair. He had the same build as Reynolds, and the dirty charcoal suit looked like the type the former president used to wear for his addresses.

The rest of the space remained in pitch-black darkness.

"Cover me," Suarez ordered. He broke into a fast jog.

The echo of the other team's footsteps approached from the opposite side of the warehouse. Two of their flashlights cut to different parts of the vast space.

The place appeared empty apart from a few cardboard boxes. The black rubber floor had been cut into sections, for whatever reason. The odd design was the least of his concerns.

Reynolds' arms and legs had been secured with manacles and padlocked to the chair. His head slumped to one side, as if sleeping. Or dead . . . maybe. Until his right arm twitched. A wire ran from his finger to a device on the table next to him—perhaps a polygraph.

As Suarez closed in, the distinctive stench of human decomposition hit him. He knew it well enough from Iraq, where it had emanated from the piles of rubble in Mosul. That was after a couple of days, though. Reynolds had apparently been on the phone yesterday night to the administration. There was no way his body would have time to degrade enough to create this odor.

Suarez approached the man in the chair carefully. He had the pallor of a waxwork. White mottled skin. Purple lips. Eyes half open. He was dead.

And it wasn't John Reynolds.

Electrodes and heat packs had been attached to the corpse's arms, legs, and shoulders and led to a bank of batteries on the table next to him, continually electrocuting the man while keeping him warm. That explained the heat signature and the body twitches, now gruesome and robotic to the eye. Inspecting the body with his flashlight confirmed this person had been dead for a while.

The captain came to a halt next to Suarez in front of the twitching body. "That's not the president."

"No shit."

Suarez grabbed the corpse's hair and lifted the head back.

"Jesus Christ," the captain blurted out. "That looks like Blake Mansfield."

The secretary of defense who had gone missing after the Z Train disaster. Some had called him a traitor for reasons that were never made public. The accepted story was that Mansfield was on the run after screwing up the rescue operation under New York City. The FBI and Homeland Security believed he didn't want to face the inquiry and a public trial and fled. Cowardly, perhaps, and extreme, but there had been no intelligence that he'd been taken by the Foundation. Clearly they were wrong.

Even if this was Mansfield, it didn't explain what

the hell was going on. All the fears of this mission going sideways washed over Suarez, and his eyes darted left and right, trying to penetrate the now suffocating darkness of this massive room. The signal from Reynolds' call originated from here. The intel insisted it couldn't have been from anywhere else.

But what did that really mean? Because this guy wasn't Reynolds, and that meant something was seriously wrong.

Suarez scanned the table. Beyond the bank of batteries, two phones sat in holders facing each other. A simple, untraceable relay using burner phones. But it wasn't just that. They connected to an encrypted relay device. The signal could've hopped all over the world before linking back to here. Whoever had placed this knew exactly what they were doing and had experience in clandestine operations, enough to fool the CIA and Homeland Security.

Reynolds could be anywhere.

Suarez's heart hammered against his chest while he considered what this meant.

The captain reached inside Mansfield's blazer and pulled out a crisp piece of paper. He unfolded it, and a look of confusion grew on his face as he read the words.

"What does it say?" a voice said in their ears from the White House Situation Room.

"It says: 'President Brogan, if luring your men here and killing them doesn't convince you to negotiate, my next avoidable action will cost the lives of millions on U.S. soil. The choice is yours. Sincerely, Albert Van Ness.'"

The captain turned the paper toward Suarez. He focused his light on the sheet and ensured his helmet cam was angled at it, allowing everyone in the White House Situation Room a chance to read the neatly penned words.

His team had heard the contents of the letter and immediately spun back to face the way they had entered, scanning for any sign of the trap the note threatened.

Suarez hit transmit. "Status outside?"

"All clear on the south side," one of his team replied.

"All clear on the north," one of the captains said.

There was nothing. No attack. No sound in the warehouse. Everything was still.

Suddenly, an odd, mechanical grinding noise broke the silence, coming from both ends of the main area of the warehouse.

"Move out, NOW!" the captain yelled.

Flashlights focused on the steel doors at either end as the teams turned to retreat. But both slammed shut within seconds before anyone could reach them, trapping the soldiers inside the room.

The mechanical grind stopped. Moments later, a hiss filled the air.

Scott swept his beam along the side of the wall. Others followed suit to trace the source of the sound. Eight large white tubes had extended out of it, pumping out what was so far an odorless gas.

"Could be toxic!" the captain shouted.

"We need a way out," Suarez bellowed.

"We'll search the north end," the captain replied. "You take the south."

"Only fire if absolutely necessary. Whatever that gas is could be flammable."

"Agreed. Let's move."

Suarez, Scott, and the other two members of his team raced back toward the steel door in a tight formation. The footsteps of the other group pounded against the ground as they made their way back into the darkness at the opposite end of the area.

They searched the walls for doors, ventilation shafts, any way to escape, until they made it back to the steel door. Suarez cut his beam across the ceiling and came across a security camera, carefully concealed in the rafters.

The Foundation had been watching them. It had known exactly when to remotely lock both strike teams in the main space, and now they were likely being poisoned, if the note had spoken the truth.

"Dammit," he shouted as he inspected the steel door. He had yet to feel any effects from the gas, but that didn't mean it wasn't happening soon.

A low hum, coming from the center of the warehouse, broke his thoughts.

From the opposite end, mounted lights from the other soldiers' M4s speared through the darkness and focused on the area to the right of the corpse.

A section of the ground had started to rise into the air, roughly the size of a bus, and it slowly extended toward the roof. It was a hatch of some kind. Covering what, Suarez didn't know.

"*What the hell?*" someone said through his earpiece.

Piercing shrieks split the air, emanating from the

hatch. They were like nothing Suarez had ever heard before. The soldiers had nowhere to take cover. They spread, dropped to one knee, and took up firing positions.

The hatch was now fully elevated. From both ends of the warehouse, four beams focused on the gaping black chasm in the ground.

The shrieks grew louder and reverberated around the walls.

"Fire at anything that rises from that hole," the captain commanded.

"What about the gas?" someone replied.

"Fuck the gas," Suarez said. "Shoot on sight."

And he meant every word. The shrieks had triggered memories for him. The claims of the survivors after the Z Train disaster, in which Mansfield and Reynolds had both played their part. Stories of uncompromising creatures that had torn people limb from limb. Their chilling howls. Most had laughed at the stories and had put them down to stress, or to some of the survivors getting together and coming up with a huckster plan to make a fast buck.

It didn't seem funny or cheap right now.

Suarez's pulse pounded in his ears. He curled his finger around the trigger. He drew in a deep breath as he peered through his sights.

Dark figures exploded out of the ground. At least ten. Twenty. Thirty. All raced toward the far end of the warehouse at unbelievable speed before he even had chance to aim and fire.

The other team's muzzles flashed, all four rifles firing rapid shots.

"*Holy shit*," the captain yelled.

Several tracer rounds streaked through the warehouse. Other rounds battered into the wall to Suarez's right. "Get down!" he shouted.

His squad hit the ground flat and quickly took prone firing positions.

Suddenly, the two ceiling lights cut out, and the team was plunged into near darkness, save for the lights on their weapons. The four beams swept across the huge space. For a split second, one would focus on a massive black creature making its way back across the floor before it darted into the shadows.

Suarez's light focused on the body of Blake Mansfield, still being slowly electrocuted. A tail whipped into the light, gleaming and serrated. It lashed against the body's lifeless head and ripped off the jawbone entirely.

A single blood-curdling scream crossed the warehouse before quickly dying out.

Shots fired, illuminating the far end of the warehouse, before they, too, were abruptly snuffed.

Then silence.

The warehouse grew quiet, but Suarez could still feel the presence of the coiled violence surrounding them on all sides. The only sound he could hear was the gas pouring into the warehouse, filling every inch with God knows what.

His body shook with fear, adrenaline, and anger at the desperateness of their situation. He pictured his wife and daughters. Thought about how he should have done more to stop this mission.

He grunted in frustration.

"Let's fuck 'em up!" Suarez shouted.

Shrieks punctuated the guttural breaths that were closing in on the team's position. The soldiers fired, but they couldn't seem to get in any effective shots before the dark figures darted to the left and right.

Then multiple footsteps charged, heavy and growing louder by the second.

Out of the darkness, a tide of creatures raced at them. Claws extended, a keening wail echoing off the walls. Everyone opened fire, spraying the approaching wave of black armor with bullets.

A few of the creatures screeched in agony and went down. Most of the bullets, however, appeared to have little effect. They had seconds before their position was overrun.

Suarez briefly flashed his light over to Scott. Sweat poured down his friend's face, and terror filled his eyes. Yet he didn't waver from his duty, quickly and efficiently changing his magazine and aiming. Before he could fire, though, two clawed hands grabbed him by the shoulders, lifted him in the air, spun him, and piledrove his head into the ground. Even above the firing and the shrieking, Suarez heard the sickening crunch of his buddy's vertebrae disintegrating. Another one of his team let out a gurgled scream.

All three M4s fell silent around him after another scream.

He sprayed the contents of his magazine to his front until it ran dry.

He didn't have time to reload.

Creatures crowded around him within a heartbeat. Loads of them, all with rows of spiky teeth, thrashing tails, and a glossy musculature that was at once alien and alluring. They stared at him through soulless eyes, as if deciding which one would kill him. He flipped onto his back and reached for his holster.

He knew it wouldn't be enough, but he'd fight until he drew his final breath.

For a brief second, he imagined the chaos in the Situation Room as they watched all this unfold, then his focus returned to his wife and daughters.

Suarez raised his pistol toward the closest creature's face.

He whispered into his headset, hoping the White House would hear, knowing there was no way out. One last magazine. Then, torn to shreds.

"Tell my family I love them."

He fired the gun.

Suddenly, a massive fireball consumed the entire warehouse as the gas ignited.

The last thing the White House heard was Suarez screaming as flames scorched his body to an unrecognizable crisp.

CHAPTER EIGHTEEN

I n the White House Situation Room, the on-screen transmission from the helmet cam cut to fuzzy gray. Shortly after, it was replaced by a view from a chopper, closing in on Schaffhausen. President Amanda Brogan hardly had time to blink before the feed showed a huge ball of fire roaring into the clear blue sky.

"My God," somebody uttered behind her.

She stared in disbelief as an explosion ripped open the warehouse's external structure. It blasted away the walls and flattened the vans outside.

All communications from the ground fell silent.

Orders barked out of the desk speaker, telling the teams by the warehouse entrances to stand by. Nobody replied. Repeated attempts to contact those inside failed, too. The footage had already made it a foregone conclusion as to their fate.

Brogan spun her chair to face her staff. Everyone had crowded around her end of the table to witness this hastily arranged operation. All had watched in horror when the creatures had emerged and butchered the special forces team. The ones guarding the entrances had also stood little chance of surviving the subsequent explosion.

Twelve good people gone.

She knew their deaths were always a possibility, but not like this. Her stomach sank at the utter futility of their deaths. Van Ness set up a trap, for no other reason than to deliver another message to the president.

And the creatures . . .

Any doubts Brogan had had about their existence were long gone. They were beyond anything she'd ever seen. Brutal. Overwhelming. She was terrified.

Vice President Webster sat directly to Brogan's front. The silver-haired motormouth from New York usually had something to say. Instead, he just stared at the feed showing a plume of black smoke belching from the snowy hills of the Upper Rhine. The other seven staff members looked at the president in expectation, waiting for her first words after witnessing the surreal carnage. Their facial expressions matched her internal emotions. Confusion. Shock. Fury. A sense that they could no longer contain the threat of Albert Van Ness.

No words came. All she could think was that everything Reynolds and Cafferty had previously told her about Van Ness had been true. Before this moment, she had struggled to believe the full extent of their claims. Before this moment, she couldn't justify the funding to investigate the Foundation for Human Advancement.

Why didn't I listen?

"Madam President," Webster eventually said.

"Wait."

It had all seemed so outrageous, like the stories of Area 51. When President Reynolds purged half his administration after the events in New York, rumors abounded in Washington and the press as to the reason. The Van Ness rumor seemed the least credible, despite Reynolds' apparent cast-iron belief in the conspiracy. Brogan had thought President Reynolds made the Foundation the scapegoat for some reason, but she never really considered this. *What if everything Reynolds believed was actually true?*

Then John Reynolds was abducted.

Eleven months of fruitless searching had followed.

Reynolds' call late last night had confirmed it was the Foundation.

And now, there was no denying the creatures' existence.

A sense of paranoia rose inside Brogan. She studied the faces of her staff, searching for a hint of betrayal. Reynolds had told her about Mansfield's links to the Foundation, and he had paid the ultimate price, despite being a traitor.

Surely not one of these people.

"Madam President," her chief of staff, Karen Weatherford, pressed. "Those creatures—"

Brogan held up a finger, cutting her off. Despite her diminutive frame, Weatherford was a formidable force—highly strategic and often underestimated. But Brogan didn't want to lose her train of thought with so many things currently battling for her attention. She focused back on the people around her.

If Van Ness can get to my Secret Service, if he could get to Blake Mansfield, can anyone in this room be trusted?

But there was no time to begin her own purge. For now, she needed to lead.

"As hard as this sounds, we need to forget the creatures for a minute," Brogan finally said. "What's the word from France?"

Webster met her glare. "President Tessier isn't playing ball. He'll only allow a raid in Paris by his own military. But he will only do that if they have sufficient proof of illegal activity in their country. The French would consider any covert action by the United States to be—"

"Goddamn it." She slammed her fist against the desk, cutting him off. "I want our teams there right now. I'll deal with President Tessier."

"We need to deal with the Swiss, too—" Webster added.

"They can fucking wait! I want everyone focused on Paris."

"But Reynolds could be anywhere."

"President Reynolds is no longer our mission. We need to take down Van Ness. If we can save Reynolds in the process, great. But we need to stop Van Ness, NOW."

The JSOC general nodded in acknowledgment and left the room.

"I want to know what they're planning on U.S. soil," Brogan said to the remaining members of her staff. "Get the CIA all over this damned Foundation until we're clear to move on Van Ness."

"He might be hedging his bets," Jim Swain replied.

The director of national intelligence and former senator from Indiana had a reputation for being cautious. Still, he had a long and distinguished career and was the last person Brogan expected to flip against his own country.

"What do you mean?" she asked.

"We've been keeping an eye on the Foundation since Reynolds told us about the potential threat. From what I gather, most of their activities are in Europe or Asia. Nothing here as far as we know, apart from that shit-show in New York. The threat could be just that—a negotiating tactic to get the money he wants."

She shook her head. "We cannot afford to take that risk with further American lives. He said *millions*."

"Madam President, before launching another attack on another sovereign country's soil, let's study the man. Let my team analyze his movements and speech patterns. Then you take a video call with him to negotiate, and we analyze the video to see if he's bluffing."

"That works? Explain."

Swain leaned over the table.

"There is publicly available video of Van Ness at various charitable events over the years. Events where the man didn't feel threatened. These videos can give us a baseline analysis of when he's telling the truth. Like most people, his micro-expressions are the big giveaway. There are muscles in the human face that people cannot control when they're lying. Even the best poker faces in the world. It's there for a fraction of a second, but we'll see it. So when you video conference with him, we'll be able to tell if he's bluffing."

"It's as simple as that?" Webster asked.

Swain smiled. "It's a bit more complex. We'll need you to baseline him again during the call, using information we know to be true about his history. We'll prepare questions for you, like asking him the same thing in different ways. By the time we ask about his threat, his micro-expressions will betray him."

"It might be worth a shot," Webster chimed in.

"You're not suggesting we deal with him directly!" Brogan spat. "The man ordered the deaths of more than a dozen of our people. The United States does not negotiate—"

"Madam President," Webster replied, "you launched an illegal operation on foreign soil. Do not underestimate the fallout from this botched operation. Re-engaging with Van Ness might be the best course of action."

"Don't forget Van Ness set up this butchery specifically for our eyes," a new voice chimed in. Brogan looked across to McCann, her grizzled director of counterterrorism. He had what the French president Tessier and Vice President Webster appeared to lack: nerve. "As Madam President just said, the Swiss can fucking wait. And frankly, so can the French."

She smiled at his bluntness. "Are there any measures we can take outside of official channels? Anything to get things moving faster?"

McCann answered authoritatively. "There's plenty we can do off the books, but it'll take a day for our teams to infiltrate Paris under the radar from surrounding countries. We do have another, faster option, though."

McCann appeared uneasy as he uttered the final sentence. Then again, Brogan guessed everyone was feeling this way after seeing the creatures in action for the first time.

"What's the *other* option?" she asked.

"Tom Cafferty and his team—"

"You're not serious?"

"Plausible deniability, Madam President. His team acts independently—it's not an official government operation. That would temper French political anger, if they are discovered."

She eased back in her chair. "Do you know where they are?"

"We lost Tom's signal after he went into the subway tunnels in London. I'm sure we'll hear from him shortly, when he has updates."

"You think we send him after Van Ness under the radar? Would he do it?"

"If you think Van Ness has a hard-on for us, just wait till you see Cafferty's drive to take down the Foundation. Trust me, he'll do it. He could get there in under three hours."

Swain moved to McCann's shoulder. "It isn't the worst idea in the world. We keep Van Ness distracted while Cafferty's team gathers intel on the ground. All the while our teams secretly move into place by tomorrow night."

"Van Ness won't be expecting it," McCann added.

"He was expecting us today," Webster said.

"He's not wrong," Brogan replied. "And because of Cafferty's open hostility against the Foundation, we have to assume they're watching him, right? From what we've seen from the Foundation so far, do we really believe they would let someone come after them without taking precautions?"

"Anything that gives us a jump on the Foundation is worth pursuing," Swain insisted. McCann nodded.

Brogan considered the proposal. International diplomacy with the French would be slow and difficult. It was a matter of pride; they didn't like being told what to do. The possibility also existed that President Tessier was in Van Ness' pocket. In fact, the more she thought about it, the more it made sense. His stubborn refusals to act against the Foundation despite its headquarters being situated in the heart of Paris were testament to this.

The visceral images of the creatures attacking the special forces, the blackmail, and the attempt on her life were more than enough motivation to act decisively. The uniqueness of the situation meant it wasn't time for conventional thinking, though. National governments in the past had likely already made the same mistake a hundred times over with the Foundation.

"Call Cafferty as soon as you pick up his signal," she said. "Once we've spoken to him, arrange a call with Albert Van Ness. And prepare those baseline questions you want me to ask him."

"Madam President, we're setting up another mission for failure—" Webster added.

"This decision rests on my head," Brogan snapped at him. "McCann, Swain—let's get this done. I want regular updates on the progress."

The two men looked visibly relieved, for whatever reason. Perhaps like her, they had also come to a similar conclusion. To take down Van Ness, they needed to do something different.

That much was obvious.

He had directly threatened the United States.

He had kidnapped a president.

He had killed twelve good men and women.

He seemingly had creatures under his control.

Enough was enough.

"I want Van Ness, dead or alive," Brogan said determinedly. "Preferably dead."

CHAPTER NINETEEN

Van Ness powered his wheelchair along a sub-terranean corridor that had only recently been carved out of the solid rock. At the end of this fresh section of the complex, he had a new weapon to test. A white-coated weapons technician flanked his left side, half jogging to keep up.

The man was out of shape, which wasn't a crime in modern society. It was his neatly manicured mustache that irritated Van Ness, the time involved to wax the ends into points. Effort was one thing within everyone's control, but a person applying it pretentiously rather than intelligently had always vexed him. Visual eccentricity was the domain of the weak, a conformist's vainglorious way of attempting to stand out.

The guard to his right had no such egotism. Clean-shaven. Stocky. Dressed from head to toe in black, clutching a rifle. Fit for the job; striding with purpose. Just like a creature or anything else in the animal kingdom, his focus was on the task at hand. In the wild, it was all about a relentless drive for survival by whatever means. Van Ness had the same primal focus for humanity in the epic struggle against the creatures.

No wasted effort on vanity.

Never giving an inch.

Fighting for the right to stay at the top of the food chain was the only path forward. Soon, everyone would come to realize this, whether by force or an understanding that he was the only person with the vision to ensure an ultimate victory that would echo through the ages.

For all he knew—for all anyone knew—the final escalation in the ultimate death match might begin tomorrow, right after Van Ness struck with overwhelming force. He wondered how the creatures would react when faced with annihilation.

His eyes narrowed as the wheelchair continued to hum forward.

It made the insolence of the U.S. administration and John Reynolds a major irritation. Again and again, he had spelled out the cost of success and the price of failure plainly, only to be met with cynicism and disregard. And to be branded a terrorist was insulting. They had no clue what danger humanity was truly facing. He'd make them understand.

Van Ness slowed his speed as he approached the end of the corridor and stopped in front of a metal door. The guard halted by his side, stoic and expressionless. Just the way he liked his employees unless prompted.

The technician paused for a moment to catch his breath. He eyed Van Ness, likely spotting an external sign of his impatience, and keyed in a code on the entry pad. The door punched to the left with a pneumatic hiss.

Everything beyond the entrance looked perfect, exactly how Van Ness had instructed during the design phase. A large spherical turret, made from graphene glass, extended from the rock face, roughly a hundred feet above the operations center's dome. It housed the biggest pair of twin lasers ever constructed, controlled by twin joysticks that extended from the console on the wall. The lasers were the size of medieval lances with supercharged packs as their base. The turret and lasers were capable of independently rotating to all parts of the cavern via the powerful mechanical arms. There was nothing in the world like this—a flawless lightning-fast defense system that responded to any motion and could fire hundreds of lethal beams each minute. Pride swelled inside Van Ness.

"Just like the *Millennium Falcon*'s gun well," the technician said, cracking a smile.

Van Ness stared the man down, and the smile quickly faded. He made a mental note of the technician's face for future reference. Right now wasn't the time for pettiness, especially when he had a new weapon to test. Two months ago, Van Ness' underground lair had suffered a power outage during the final phases of construction. The massive globes of light that bathed the entire facility with brilliant light went out, and creatures swarmed the outside of the complex. The four automated turrets on the operations center's roof had sucked all power from the backup generators after having to blast thousands of creatures. Hundreds more smashed themselves against the thick, impenetrable glass for a frightening hour until power was restored.

The unpredicted experience, which like everything seemed obvious with the benefit of hindsight, had worried Van Ness enough that he created an extra layer of protection with a secondary power source, one that would run the entire complex for weeks at a time. It included more lasers in strategic positions and massive oxygen tanks on the cavern floor, ready to beat back the methane in seconds.

"It's r-ready for you to try," the technician nervously stuttered. "Of course, the lasers automatically track movement and protect the facility at all times. But if you'd like to operate it manually for some reason . . ."

The technician gleaned the answer from the look on Van Ness' face.

"So, once you approach the console, a monitor descends in front of your face to give you an enhanced picture of the cavern with calibrated crosshairs for the lasers. The left controller moves the turret. The right one aims the laser. Hit the button on top of it to fire. The controllers only respond to your palm prints, sir."

Van Ness tutted. "I'm aware of the design."

He powered his wheelchair to the console. Directly below the turret, one of the huge globes blazed brilliant white light on the caves and crevices in the immediate vicinity. Faint shrieks, muffled by the glass, came from outside. Creatures were never far away, lurking outside the light, waiting for the chance to attack. That's why Van Ness built his fortress inside the creatures' nest—to show them humanity's dominance.

Van Ness gripped the joysticks. The weapon system detected his palm prints and thrummed to life. As it booted up, the mild vibrations sent a shiver through his body. A screen flipped down from the ceiling and stopped in front of his face. It blinked to life, displaying a dark cave directly opposite the turret within the red crosshairs.

Van Ness angled the left controller down and to the side.

The turret spun diagonally down fluidly.

Van Ness moved the right controller in the same direction.

The twin lasers rotated down. He watched the screen as the crosshairs swept past boulders and caverns until it came to rest on another small, dark cave. This was one of the favorite hiding places for the creatures to launch their repeated, pointless attacks against his strength.

He tapped both controllers, slightly adjusting the angle of the turret and laser to test their sensitivity. Both moved smoothly and seamlessly according to the pressure he applied. His team had managed close to perfection.

Van Ness allowed himself a smile.

Then he hit the button on the top right controller.

Two thick beams sizzled from the tips of the lasers. They zipped toward the cave in a flash and blasted the ground just inside the entrance.

A collective shriek rang out, the red-hot lasers eviscerating anything inside that cave in an instant.

They're always there. Always waiting.

"Impressed?" the technician asked.

"Send my congratulations to the team."

Van Ness spun the turret to face the right side of the cavern and indiscriminately fired at dark areas. The weapon acted like an extension of his body. Beams speared through the stale air and blasted away shards from the rockface. He had not felt physical power like this for almost thirty years. Not since that damned creature had broken his back down in the depths of a Florida sinkhole.

A pedal by his left shoe caught his attention. "What's that?" he asked.

The technician glanced down at Van Ness' painfully thin legs, immobile and incapable of pressing it down. He swallowed hard.

"Well?" Van Ness pressed.

"A prototype, sir. A *superweapon*, if you will."

"Explain."

"It's a next-generation strobe grenade launcher with a bit of a twist. These new strobe grenades shed their outer skin before lighting up. Hundreds of highly reflective foil particles disperse in the air before the strobe activates. When it does, the light reflects off the foil particles in millions more angles than before. There's literally nowhere for a creature to hide. If we ever lose primary power again, these babies will clear the cavern fast."

"I don't remember that as part of the design." However, he liked the idea, though it had an obvious problem. "And how am I supposed to use it?"

"I don't . . ."

"You don't what?"

"I mean, we haven't . . ." The technician dabbed a handkerchief on his forehead to wipe away beads of sweat. "We'll create a new firing mechanism immediately."

"You better. A demonstration, if you please."

The technician edged around Van Ness' wheelchair. He punched his loafer against the pedal. A strobe grenade rocketed out from above the turret toward the center of the cavern. A moment before it began its descent, a glittering silver cloud exploded from its surface.

The grenade's light activated when it began falling at terminal velocity. Its strobes reflected in all directions off the tiny silver particles. All parts of the cavern lit up as if under a giant searchlight.

Thousands of shrieks split the air instantly. Van Ness could feel the creatures' pain below.

"Excellent," he murmured. "Truly terrific."

"We'll install a button on the command desk for you."

"See that you do. Today."

Van Ness returned the turret back to its original position and released the controllers.

A green notification icon had appeared on his communications pad. He pressed his index finger against the screen to reveal the message.

Ellen Cafferty had arrived. He smiled.

It was time he greeted his first guest.

VAN NESS ACCELERATED HIS WHEELCHAIR ALONG A BRIGHTLY lit, polished corridor toward the underground complex's conference room. Four guards marched to his left, four to his right, all aware of their duties once they met the new arrival. Their boots hammered the stone in perfect step over the sound of his chair's electric motor, like they were in a small military parade. He wondered if his father, Otto, had ever been in a similar situation with the SS marching through the streets of Berlin in 1942. That was history, though. He was currently in the business of making it.

The conference room doors automatically parted and he wheeled inside. Cafferty's wife stood facing him at the far end of an oval-shaped mahogany table.

Ellen Cafferty glared at Van Ness with hatred in her eyes. Her creased sweater and pants and smudged makeup gave her a disheveled look. "You bastard," she growled.

"Please don't swear. That kind of language is reserved for the uneducated or the uncouth. You are neither."

"You're twisted, deranged," she replied.

"Am I?" Van Ness whispered to himself introspectively. "No. No, I don't feel that way at all."

She studied him as if lost in thought, then said, "The governments of the world will stop your—"

"They'll stop *nothing*! The world will bend to my will, or they'll face a far worse fate than dying at the hands of these creatures!"

She visibly shook at his words. He took no pleasure in that.

What he had in mind for her was a hundred times worse.

"You mean nuclear annihilation?" Her shoulders

dipped as she struggled with whatever had been used to bind her hands behind her back.

"*Yes!*" Van Ness forcefully replied. His gaze felt like it could burn a hole right through Ellen. She looked away, trying to control her fear.

He slowly regained his composure and lowered his voice again. "I'm sorry I raised my voice, Mrs. Cafferty. But don't you see? I'm the only sane leader on the planet. Who else is taking our long-term existence seriously?"

Ellen's face twisted into a grimace. "Sane people don't build underground fortresses and attempt to blow up major world cities."

"To paraphrase Martin Luther King Jr., 'Human progress is neither automatic nor inevitable . . . Every step toward the goal of justice requires sacrifice, suffering, and struggle; the tireless exertions and passionate concern of dedicated individuals.' Is this not the same?"

"You actually believe your own bullshit, don't you?" she snapped back.

"Again with the swearing." Van Ness rubbed his temples. "I see there's no convincing you, Mrs. Cafferty. So I'll get to the point."

"Enlighten me," she replied defiantly.

"Your husband is on his way to Paris as I speak. I'm going to make him watch you get torn limb from limb. While it doesn't advance the world, it'll teach him a lesson he won't forget for the rest of his short life."

CHAPTER TWENTY

Munoz drove the van at high speed along the A20 motorway on the way to the Calais ferry to get to France. Cafferty sat by his side, trying the White House yet again. He needed to alert the president and deputy prime minister of the thermonuclear bomb under London.

Thunder rumbled in the angry morning sky, and rain battered the windshield. The screeching sound of the wiper blades went straight through him, though it was only a mild discomfort in the grand scheme of things. He stared straight ahead at raindrops dancing off the saturated road surface.

In a matter of hours, Cafferty potentially faced his long-awaited first and likely final dance with Albert Van Ness. As dramatic as the idea appeared in his mind—the two of them opposite each other, with only one of them surviving—the lives of millions depended on his success, including his wife.

The Foundation kidnapping Ellen had left his reasoning scrambled and his pulse rate at the speed of a drum roll, but he told himself she wasn't his number one priority—stopping that bomb was.

Or am I kidding myself?

Van Ness has made this personal.

"What's going through that head of yours?" Munoz asked.

"Nothing good."

"Ellen?" Munoz replied softly. "I get it, Tom, but remember we're also facing a big mushroom cloud over London."

Cafferty nodded in acknowledgment. Both scenarios to him spelled a nightmare. He appreciated Munoz's empathy, though he understood deep down that millions took precedence over one. It was a hard pill to swallow, and he hoped it would not come to that.

The countdown timer on the nuclear bomb beneath Euston Station flashed through Cafferty's mind. He glanced at the digital clock on the dashboard—they had a little under thirteen hours until midnight.

They had to get today right, against near impossible odds. If they didn't . . . the crushing thought nearly consumed him.

It didn't help that they had no clear plan on how to get to Van Ness. Bowcut had done reconnaissance on the Foundation's building in Paris, but the place was essentially a fortress. But perhaps it would be as easy as walking in the front door. The business card left in the van was clearly an invitation for Cafferty to pay Van Ness a visit. He knew he was being baited, but what choice did he have?

This entire operation was a gamble, pure and

simple. In fact, this whole endeavor had always been one. They were just four (*three*) people with limited resources against a shadowy, multinational entity that had the upper hand in nearly every category: numbers, technology, money, and intelligence about the creatures. It was more than just a gamble, then—it was a long shot. One in which almost every outcome for Cafferty and his team meant their deaths . . . and the deaths of millions of others in London tonight, and perhaps millions more across the globe in subsequent days.

Even knowing all that, though—or, perhaps, *because* they knew that—no one in this van would have considered any other course of action. Their lives compared with several million didn't need much time for deliberation. They had placed their chips on the table, and the wheel was going to spin however it spun.

But that didn't mean they were going to just let the house take their money.

"Are the lasers charging?" Cafferty asked Bowcut in the back.

"We'll be ready, Tom."

"Get me in the room and I'll waterboard a Foundation bitch if I got to," Munoz insisted, half kidding.

Cafferty couldn't help but smile, knowing that despite Diego's words and violent past, he'd never stoop to the level of torture. The Brownsville man had more class and integrity than anyone Tom had ever met. More, the engineer's penchant for optimism made him an invaluable member of the team. Even now, as they sped toward an impossible—and potentially deadly—situation, the fact that Munoz could crack jokes meant that hope wasn't completely lost.

I only wish that Ellen could hear them and draw the same hope from Munoz's quips that I am.

Cafferty's phone rang in his hand, pulling him from the dark path those thoughts were about to lead him down.

"It's the White House," he said, surprised.

"Wasn't it just *you* trying to call *them*?" Bowcut asked.

Cafferty threw her an uncertain look, even as he put the phone on speaker and answered. "This is Cafferty."

"Tom, this is President Brogan. I'm here with Jim Swain, the director of national intelligence."

"Hello, Madam President. My team is listening in as well. I've tried to reach you."

"Tom, we need you and your team to get to Paris immediately."

Cafferty shot a confused look at Bowcut and Munoz. "Madam President—we're on our way there now."

"You are?"

"Yes, Van Ness kidnapped my wife. I'm going after her."

"My God, I'm sorry."

"Madam President, there's . . . more," Cafferty said, stumbling with his words. "Van Ness has planted a thermonuclear bomb underneath London."

"What? Jesus . . ."

"It detonates at midnight tonight, Greenwich Mean Time. There's no way to stop the bomb unless we get to Van Ness' detonators, which we're hoping he has in Paris. We'll get there."

"We must tell the deputy prime minister immediately. There could be more bombs."

"More bombs?" Bowcut said.

"Van Ness has threatened to kill millions of Americans if we don't cooperate. We thought he might be bluffing, but now . . ."

"We told you to take him seriously. We *told* you the Foundation wasn't a group to mess with. God, we told—"

"I know, Tom," the president said in a resigned voice, cutting off Cafferty's tirade of mounting frustration, just as Bowcut was putting her hand on his arm to calm him down. He took a shuddering breath, listening as Brogan continued.

"You were right, and you can't believe how terrible it feels to sit in this seat, knowing we might have prevented this. But," she said, more resolute than before, *"that doesn't mean we're done fighting. While we have special forces moving into Paris, they'll arrive too late. I hate to put this on your shoulders, but you need to do whatever it takes to stop Albert Van Ness. We will support you however we can. If we don't hear from you before midnight, we'll be forced to take overwhelming action. Do you understand?"*

"Yes, Madam President."

"One other thing. President Reynolds is still alive. Van Ness is using him as a pawn to get what he wants. If you find out his location, you must let us know."

Cafferty was caught off guard by this new information. He looked at Bowcut, who he was certain mirrored what must have been his own look of surprise. What was Van Ness' end game? Was this all part of his plan?

"I understand, Madam President. That bomb under London can be detonated at any time. If the deputy prime minister evacuates London, there is a possibility that Van Ness might set the bomb off prematurely."

"Understood. That might be a risk we have to take."

"Madam President, is there any kind of intel or support you can give us? We're flying a bit blind at the moment, and Van Ness is expecting us. I'd like to gain the upper hand in some way."

"Tom, this is Jim Swain. We might have something that can help your team out."

Cafferty and Bowcut locked eyes with each other, inquisitive. "We're listening."

"Now, this is highly classified. A reminder that it is top secret."

Bowcut snorted.

"Did you say something?"

"With all due respect, sir," Bowcut said, "with all the shit going down, you can shove your top secret up your ass."

There was silence on the White House end for a moment. Then President Brogan said, *"Jim, just tell them what we know. We'll worry about national security after we're sure we still have a nation left to secure."*

"Yes, ma'am. Sorry. So, the thing is we've cracked the Foundation's firewall and encryption to gain access to their computers."

Incredulous, Diego chimed in. "How? I've been working on cracking that for over a year—their systems are literally impenetrable."

"I'm sure you're very good at what you do, Mr. Munoz, but we have access to some toys you wouldn't believe. In this case, we used a quantum computer to crack the encryption."

Swain was right—Diego couldn't believe what he was hearing. "But quantum computers are barely in their infancy—they're more a myth than an actuality. Even if they did exist, there's no way they could crack into anything in their current form," Diego replied.

Munoz knew a lot about the subject. In theory, quantum computers could crunch numbers a hundred million times faster than a traditional computer, easily cracking the most advanced encryption available. The technology would literally change the world . . . in about a decade, which was how long it would take to build a working quantum computer.

To everyone's surprise in the van, Swain chuckled.

"I'm glad some things are still classified. I assure you, though, that our quantum computer is not an infant. We will transmit to your team the details of how to gain access to the Foundation's computers. Once inside, you'll find details and schematics of their Paris headquarters that should help in your mission."

"Thank you," Cafferty said.

Bowcut looked up suddenly. "With your fancy computer, can you access their remote detonator? Turn it off?"

"Honestly? I doubt we'll have the time. If there is such a device, it's been kept separate, probably for this exact reason."

"Damn." She looked at Tom, shrugging. "Worth a shot."

He nodded.

"One last thing, Tom."

"Yes, Madam President."

"Go save your wife. And make that asshole pay."

He was processing all the new information when she said that, but in the back of his mind, those exact thoughts were ever present. He was going to save Ellen.

And Van Ness was going to pay.

With his life.

CHAPTER TWENTY-ONE

By the time the team had arrived in Paris, Munoz had secretly combed through massive amounts of data from the Foundation's network. He prayed this quantum computer was as smart as the director of national intelligence implied. Because if the Foundation knew he was rooting around inside its servers, the mission was over. It would slam down a new firewall, and the three of them would once again be flying blind. It wasn't certain Munoz would find anything here that would help, anyway, but without this information—without something that gave Cafferty an edge—Tom's unquestioning drive ensured he was as good as dead.

And so was Ellen, and probably Sarah and certainly the people of London.

So . . . no pressure, Diego, he thought.

The ferry ride and the drive to Paris had been relatively uneventful (although Sarah had to shout at Munoz to drive on the right side of the road a dozen times once he had taken the wheel). They had wended their way through the capital, and now the van was parked near the Parc du Champ de Mars. The Eiffel Tower's wrought-iron lattice structure lay at the end of the long, thin area of parkland, reaching majestically into the cloudy sky. Commercial offices and stores lined the roads at either side. Bowcut studied the tallest building in the area—the only thing close to a skyscraper. It was the official headquarters for the Foundation for Human Advancement, conspicuously out in the open, considering its secret and sinister mission—further evidence that the French government had capitulated to Van Ness' demands ("Not the first time France has given in to German pressure," Munoz joked).

Twenty floors of black glass and steel, the Foundation was at odds with the nineteenth-century buildings that took up the rest of the boulevard. On the next block, a vintage Parisian café sat between two fashionable clothing outlets. But the trio's eyes were drawn to this monstrosity, particularly its top floor and its grayed-out windows, which— according to the schematics—were designed that way to conceal the office of Albert Van Ness. The fact that he had gained planning permission to construct such an eyesore said a lot about his reach. The building was a monument of darkness in the City of Light.

During Bowcut's surveillance over the past few months, the building appeared to be a normal office building—men and women in smart clothing working routine hours every day like any other job. But that's where normality ended. No one entered or exited the building without passing through the most advanced full-body scanners and facial recognition Bowcut had ever seen. The building emanated a magnetic field from all sides, too, blocking any attempt to listen in on what was happening inside. Most peculiar, it was cut off from Paris' electric grid entirely, it had its own water supply, and it was not connected to any external phone lines; rather, it utilized internal satellites. Basically, the building was spy-proof. One thing had been clear to Bowcut at the time—there was no way to sneak into that building undetected.

"Tell me you found something, Diego," Sarah said, hoping the info Swain had given them provided an in for Tom.

"I found something," he replied.

"What do you have?" Cafferty asked. "We've got less than eight hours before that bomb explodes. Can you get us into that building?"

"We're not interested in getting into that building," Diego replied.

"We're not?" Bowcut asked.

"Nope. We need to get in *there*."

Munoz pulled up schematics from Van Ness' servers showing a massive underground operations center built hundreds of feet below the Foundation's official headquarters.

"And, Tom," Munoz continued, "you won't believe this, but . . ."

Cafferty studied the schematics. "Jesus Christ," he said.

"What?" Sarah asked.

"That deranged son of a bitch built a secret command center *inside* a massive creatures' nest, underneath the heart of Paris. Look at this."

The three studied the various schematics and details of the underground lair.

"Trust me—Van Ness isn't in that office building. He's down there," Munoz said.

"Agreed. So how do we get in?"

"There's no way we get in through the office building—security is too tight. And to get down to the command center, there's a heavily guarded elevator shaft. We won't even be able to get close."

"I sense a *but* coming up," Bowcut said.

"But . . ." Munoz continued smiling. "Half a mile away, there is an access port that secretly connects to the old catacombs deep below the city. It looks like an emergency hatch hidden right among the tombs."

"Where?"

"Just east of the Crypt of the Sepulchral Lamp, down a passage on the right marked as private. There's a single titanium door at the end with a combination wheel. Open that hatch, and the tunnel descends to the underground command center and to a loading bay. That's how we can enter the facility."

"How do we open the hatch?" Cafferty asked.

"You didn't bring me along on this mission for my looks, did you?" Munoz said.

"Actually, we did," Bowcut said. "We thought you being so ugly would distract the bad guys while we went about our business."

Munoz laughed. "Fine—be that way. Now I'm not going to tell you what I found."

"Diego . . ." Tom growled.

"Right. Anyway, it's amazing what you can find

if you dig deep enough," Munoz said. He pulled up detailed tech specs for the hatch from the Foundation's servers. He highlighted what seemed to be a random line of numbers:

043046

"Four, thirty, forty-five." Diego seemed particularly pleased when he said it.

"Do those numbers have any kind of significance?"

Diego, ever the conspiracy theorist, smiled. "Of course. It's the day Hitler committed suicide in the Führerbunker: April 30, 1945."

"Of course you would know that," Bowcut muttered.

He seemed surprised. "Yes—it's pretty common knowledge. You see, Hitler—"

"Focus, Diego," Cafferty said, knowing how much Munoz liked discussing random trivia. "You said Hitler died in forty-five, though—this number is forty-six."

"Right. A little more digging, and it turns out 1946 is when Otto Van Ness founded the Foundation for Human Advancement—exactly one year after Hitler's suicide."

An interesting coincidence, Cafferty thought. "And you think that's the passcode?"

"Yes. It doesn't make much sense to have included it in the plans, but what else could the numbers mean? And considering how Van Ness operates, it's in line with the arrogant hubris he tends to display. Look at his building: it doesn't blend in. Then look at the command center: it's in the *middle* of a nest. Couple all that with the firewall, there's no doubt he thinks he's at the height of power . . . and cleverness."

"Guess he didn't count on you being cleverer," Sarah said with a clap on Munoz's shoulder. He smiled at the rare compliment from the normally taciturn ex-cop.

"Good work, Diego," Cafferty said. "Let's gear up and take out this cocky bastard."

"One more thing," Munoz interjected. "Um. There's a reason no guards cover the hatch in the catacombs."

Cafferty and Bowcut—who had been assembling their weapons in the back—stopped what they were doing and turned to listen to Diego.

"The hatch is considered secure because of what's inside it."

Cafferty had a sinking feeling in his stomach. He knew what Munoz was about to say.

"It seems that the tunnel connecting the hatch to the underground lair is . . ."

"Full of creatures," Cafferty said, finishing Diego's sentence for him.

Maybe Van Ness had the right to be so cocky.

CHAPTER TWENTY-TWO

Albert Van Ness relaxed in his wheelchair, gazing up at the screens in the operations center. One displayed BBC news footage of London being evacuated. He watched with cold indifference. At least they had a chance to flee the city, unlike the citizens of Dresden.

Let them flee. It won't save the city, and the creatures will be destroyed along with it.

His conscience was clear—the Foundation wiping out yet another deadly nest, ultimately protecting humanity in the long run. The logic was undeniable.

The elevator's mechanism cranked to life, and the transparent car plunged from ground level down its long glass shaft. He never grew tired of marveling at the Foundation's feats of engineering.

Twenty staff members buzzed around their work-stations, all ready to switch the video feeds and detonate the bombs of his choosing. Beyond the re-inforced glass of the command center, the brightly lit nest with millions of creatures hiding in the shadows served as a constant reminder of the stakes.

Edwards exited the elevator, walked over, and sat next to him in the middle of the huge dome. Van Ness' loyal number two stared at several overhead screens that had maps of America on them. One map had a blinking red light over Nebraska, the other South Dakota. Video feeds from the ground showed both states calm and tranquil, bathed in morning sunshine.

"You think President Brogan will take our offer?" Edwards asked.

"Doubtful. As my father always said, only the democratic nations' hypocrisy outweighs their sense of self-worth. The next few minutes will dictate how much damage their egos will inflict on their own populations."

Edwards glanced down at the desk's digital clock. "Almost time, Albert."

"This is the real start, my friend. The day we've talked about for years."

"Yes, sir. Although . . ."

"Yes?"

"I want to urge caution when dealing with Brogan."

Van Ness slowly turned his wheelchair toward him. "I beg your pardon?"

"There is the possibility that no matter what we do, Brogan still decides to strike back, and hard. Our actions could harden her stance and backfire on us."

"Harden her stance? She *will* fold. What other choice does she have? She can no longer underestimate what I'm capable of, not after Reynolds and the Oval Office and Switzerland. And once she capitulates, the rest of the nations will fall in line or be destroyed trying to fight us. Don't *ever* question my strategy. There is nothing I won't do, no one I won't sacrifice, to defeat these creatures. You understand? Do not doubt the Foundation's vision."

Edwards tried painfully to look resolute. "I don't, Albert. We've built the Foundation together, we'll see it through."

"My *father* built the Foundation," Van Ness snapped back. "Not *we*. We are simply standing on the shoulders of greatness. We're the inheritors of humanity's greatest savior, and we will succeed in my father's mission. Even if I have to kill nearly every single man, woman, and child on this planet to do it. As long as even a small pocket of humanity survives—the chosen, the pure—then we've succeeded."

Edwards maintained eye contact but appeared visually uncomfortable. Van Ness could tell his number two was trying hard not to blink, swallow, or otherwise appear in any way not fully committed.

Van Ness continued staring at him for a full minute, studying the man carefully. Edwards had loyally worked by his side for more than two decades. Van Ness anticipated some employees might not have an appetite for what he was about to do, but Edwards could not be one of those doubters.

Eventually, the left screen burst to life, showing an incoming call, and he turned his attention away from Edwards. An image formed of a conference room with the crest of the president of the United States behind three bulky leather chairs. Van Ness straightened his shoulders. He felt fully in control.

In his element, actively overseeing every step of the plan now that it had reached the end game for the United States and the UK. And while there were still others to convince (not including the Russians, though he considered them untrustworthy bedfellows), he knew that these two were the key for the rest of the dominoes to fall into place.

On-screen, President Brogan sat in the central chair, seemingly all business. He instantly liked her more than President Reynolds, who had a penchant for showmanship. Two off-the-shelf American politicians sat on either side of Brogan. Dull jackets and solid-colored ties. The kind of men who were best suited to sell used cars but had somehow failed up the government ranks. Their irrelevance already worked to erase them from his focus.

Edwards assumed his position next to Van Ness.

The operations center fell silent as all eyes turned to the video call.

The Americans glared at Van Ness. The pure hatred oozing through the screen was palpable, and he delighted in it. Savoring the moment, he refused to open the conversation.

They had his demands. And they had called this meeting.

"Mr. Van Ness," President Brogan eventually said. "I take it the other gentleman is Allen Edwards?"

"That is correct, Madam President. And who may I ask are the underlings by your side?"

The president ignored the slight dig. "This is Jim Swain and Bob McCann, my directors of national intelligence and counterterrorism."

Both men silently nodded.

"Ah, I see. Interesting," Van Ness said, though his tone made it clear that he didn't think it was interesting at all. "It is too bad I am not a terrorist. It might have made more sense for your Treasury secretary to be here instead, no?"

"You're holding us hostage for money. You've kidnapped and killed and threatened. If that's not a terrorist, I don't know what is. But let's not argue semantics—it's already highly irregular for us to call a meeting like this. But you've proven to be a difficult and dangerous individual, Mr. Van Ness, and *that* I take very seriously."

Van Ness waved his hand dismissively. "Amanda, I am not your opponent. It's the creatures who are *our* opponents. I thought you would've realized that after what they did in New York and Switzerland."

"You mean what *you* did in New York and Switzerland. Those death tolls are on you."

"Oh, tsk tsk. Wars have casualties, Madam President. And I assure you, the next great world war *is* coming. Now, shall we discuss my offer?"

"Your *offer* is a nonstarter. I'm here to order you to disarm the bomb underneath London, return President Reynolds, and share any intel and technology that can be used by the legitimate governments of this world to fight the threat you are so concerned about—or face the consequences."

"You . . . are ordering . . . *me*?" A slight smile crept up Van Ness' face.

"That is correct. You have *our* demands."

"I have them, but I am not certain I can comply. Why would I disarm that bomb, Amanda?" he said, deliberately ignoring her title. "You do realize there is a nest of creatures right underneath London—millions of them. They are killing machines. They hunt us for sport. They study us to learn how to eradicate us and have already made forays onto the surface—surely the deputy prime minister told you about the incidents happening all across the city. They are rising, first through the cracks in our subway tunnels, then through the basements of our deepest buildings, and will soon be overrunning our streets. They are stronger than us. They outnumber us. They evolve faster than us, and it appears—based on what we saw in New York—that they are trying to crossbreed to produce even more lethal killers. Ones that will be able to operate on the surface without the fear of oxygen or light. London *will* be destroyed one way or another, Madam President, either by my hands or their claws. So the answer to your demand is . . . no. I will not disarm that bomb. And no. I'm not done with Reynolds."

Van Ness stared at Brogan, boring a hole through her with his intensity.

"As for sharing my inventions, how un-capitalistic of you," he said with a mean smile. "Perhaps instead, you pay me what I ask, and I simply take care of the creatures for you. Yes, yes . . . I believe that's the best possible solution . . . seeing how it's the precise one I offered you before."

Van Ness turned to Edwards with a smile across his face.

"This is great fun, my friend."

The comment unnerved the president.

"One other thing, Amanda," Van Ness continued. "Kindly tell the CIA buffoons to your left and right that there's no need to profile me. I'm sure Langley will study this tape and report back to you that I'm deadly serious. But I can save you the time: I am, as ever, a man of my word."

Swain and McCann shifted uncomfortably in their chairs, looking away from Van Ness' silent, piercing gaze.

Brogan broke the silence. "This is your last chance to agree—"

"No, Madam President," Van Ness said, cutting her off. "This is *your* last chance. To *survive*. Do you accept my offer?"

President Brogan leaned forward as if to drive her response home. "No," she said. "We do not accept your offer."

"Very well." Van Ness turned to his number two. "Allen, would you kindly destroy the next nest?"

"Yes, sir."

GLORIOUS SUNSHINE BEAT DOWN ON THE LOW MOUNTAIN range that splintered Rapid City, South Dakota. Rob Scaffidi sheltered his eyes with his palm to take in the view from the summit. Beyond the bustling neighborhoods, the Black Hills National Forest stretched as far as the eye could see. His hiking partners, Sherrie Tennant and Angela Blaikie, trudged to his side.

A cool breeze whipped their bodies, bringing welcome relief after the lung-busting ascent up the trail. Rob thought everything looked picture perfect from this vantage point. The countryside. The sun reflecting off the windows in the town. The group's next stop was Mount Rushmore. Adrenaline flooded his body; he had wanted to see it up close his entire life. He turned in its direction, went to raise his binoculars . . . and froze.

A brilliant, blinding flash of light consumed the entire sky, coming right from that direction. The light was a thousand times brighter than the morning sun, immediately blinding Rob, who gave a strangled sob.

A fraction of a second later, an enormous mushroom cloud exploded into the South Dakota sky.

The ground shook below their boots.

"My God!" Sherrie screamed.

"Is it a . . ." Angela cried out.

Before any of them could move, a shock wave smashed their bodies against the rock face, and a deafening boom split the sky.

A rumbling roar built in volume.

Rob let out a sharp breath through his teeth. He raised himself to all fours, covering his eyes to no avail. If he could see, though, he would have realized the futility.

A wall of raging fire was racing over the mountains and hills, consuming everything in its path.

The firestorm tore through Rapid City, population seventy thousand. None of the hikers had time to even blink before the million-degree wave incinerated them instantly to ash.

VAN NESS RESTED HIS CHIN ON HIS KNUCKLE AND STARED AT the overhead screen. He had watched the South Dakota footage until the Foundation's camera had been destroyed by the bomb, so he knew the job had been done. The nest beneath Mount Rushmore was no more.

"It's done, sir," Edwards said.

Van Ness sat and waited, staring at the president the entire time.

In the White House, another minion in a suit rushed into view and whispered something frantically in President Brogan's ear. The color instantly drained from her face.

"What have you done?" Brogan shouted.

"Only what you made me do, Madam President. I am sorry for your country's loss." He sipped from a glass of brandy. "My favorite brandy. You should try it. Allen, let's send her a case—"

"You're insane! This is an act of war!" she shot back.

She had visibly lost her temper, and Van Ness sensed an opportunity. As much as he wanted to deal with them in a conventional manner, his father had always said that the only message those opposed to them truly understood was violence.

"We're already in a war," Van Ness replied, lacking any emotion in his voice. "The only war that matters. So I ask you again, Amanda. Does the United States accept my offer?"

"The only thing we'll accept is you burning in hell!" she shouted back.

Van Ness lowered his glass of brandy and massaged his temple. "Unfortunate," he replied. "Please don't take what happens next personally. It's just business, Madam President."

Van Ness turned to Edwards. "Allen, I'd like to send President Reynolds my final regards."

"Yes, sir."

The Foundation cut the video feed to the White House.

CHAPTER TWENTY-THREE

John Reynolds sat shivering in the center of the dark warehouse. The freezing cold manacles dug into his wrists and ankles. Nobody had been around for a few hours, not even for the customary bucket of water over his face or the mocking insults. He growled in frustration at the situation. The three futile deaths. His own mother. Potentially more deaths coming, solely as torture . . .

The television in front of him flickered to life, casting a pale glow over his withered body. He slowly raised his head, squinting against the light. When his eyes finally adjusted, he saw Van Ness on the television screen, sitting there in his wheelchair, staring at him as if he were a curious specimen in a petri dish. "Good afternoon, John," he said. "I'm sorry to say our time together must come to a fitting end."

"Go to hell."

"The creatures would certainly enjoy that, wouldn't they? Dragging us down to hell. Consider this a mercy, then—though I take no pleasure in what needs to happen now. So much life lost because of you and your country's intransigence. I am not a cruel man. I was not your enemy, until you made me into one."

"Not our enemy? You could have helped at any time. Instead, you used fear and blackmail and *murder* to advance your own agenda. So go fuck yourself," Reynolds spat back.

"Language, John. Please." Van Ness pressed a button on the console by his side. "Could you kindly look downward, former Mr. President?"

In the blink of an eye, the flooring below Reynolds turned from jet black to transparent. The circular section around him was on a set of large steel hinges. His chair sat above a vast chasm. Reynolds could see millions of bodies crawling throughout the dark rocky enclaves. Claws and tails thrust out from caves, and all he could think of were the tunnels under the Hudson River . . . and his mother's body being torn apart.

A single light on a ledge in the cavern caught his attention. He squinted to get a better look. Next to the light appeared to be a large, rectangular bomb, only a few dozen feet below the president.

Reynolds swallowed hard. "Where am I?"

"Exactly where I want you to be."

"Where, goddamn it?!"

"You're sitting on top of a nest."

"I know that," Reynolds shouted back. "Where?!"

"Why, I brought you home, John."

"Home?"

"You're in Lincoln, Nebraska."

A mechanical grinding noise filled the air. The

roof above him parted from the center, revealing the crisp Nebraska sky to his confused eyes.

"Why—"

"This part, I must confess, *is* personal, John," Van Ness said, interrupting Reynolds while refilling his brandy. "When the floor opens, you will sadly fall. I imagine the creatures will enjoy their momentary prize. But I set the thermonuclear bomb to detonate thirty seconds later. So don't fear—your wife and children, who moved back to this horrid little city, will not have to bear the same death as you. Theirs will be a bit more . . . instantaneous."

Reynolds turned away from the screen. He clenched his teeth. Wished that he had played things differently. But he refused to give Van Ness any pleasure. The bastard was tormenting him for his own sick game and didn't deserve a response.

"Look at me, John," Van Ness commanded.

He ignored the request.

"What was it you texted me from that New York subway tunnel?" Van Ness asked quietly.

The words came to him.

You failed. Now I'm coming after you.

"Truer words have never been spoken. You came, you saw . . ."

Van Ness hit a button on his control pad.

"You failed."

The four steel bolts that secured the chair legs to the ground snapped free. Reynolds rocked back and forth. He toppled backward and slammed hard against the ground.

A moment later, the circular hatch groaned downward.

His chair slid toward the chasm.

He struggled against the manacles with all of his might, but even if he were able to free himself, nothing was stopping his fall.

Reynolds plunged downward, free-falling into the abyss.

The piercing sound of creature shrieks filled the president's ears.

A tail lashed out of the darkness, carved through Reynolds' biceps, and his severed arm separated from his body, even as it still remained locked to the arm of the chair. He could see the fingers, now no longer attached to him, still wriggling of their own accord, until blood spurting from the stump caused him to turn away.

Reynolds screamed as his body descended faster and faster through the cavern.

A creature leaped out of the darkness and clamped itself around his falling body. He looked into its soulless eyes before it crunched its razor-sharp teeth into his face. Talons punctured his neck and squeezed hard. Blood sprayed from the president's body as the creature tore him apart in midair.

The unbearable pain and fear ended in an instant, when the thermonuclear bomb incinerated the entire nest and wiped the middle of the Great Plains off the map.

ANOTHER AIDE RUSHED INTO THE WHITE HOUSE SITUATION Room and said, "Madam President, we've received a report of another explosion, in Lincoln, Nebraska."

President Brogan froze.

A second nuclear attack on American soil in the space of twenty minutes.

John Reynolds' hometown.

The team around the table looked at each other, openmouthed. Chaos immediately spread in the Situation Room.

The news of the detonation in South Dakota was only just sinking in. Now, two nuclear strikes. Hundreds of thousands of Americans dead. Brogan fought back her nausea.

"General, take us to DEFCON 1 and begin evacuating every major city in America." She turned to Swain. "Is Van Ness in Paris?"

"Absolutely. Facial recognition software picked up Edwards outside the building an hour before our call."

"Send our fighter jets into France—I want that building wiped off the face of the earth, *now!*" she commanded.

"Madam President," Swain quickly interjected, "I don't think he's doing this from that building. We've been combing through the Foundation's servers. Van Ness has built a massive underground bunker, nearly a mile below Paris, inside a creatures' nest. A conventional military strike from the air will not stop him."

"Well, we can't nuke Paris—" McCann added.

"If it saves millions more lives, we damn well can!" Brogan said, cutting him off. She knew this was an overreaction, but the options were limited.

Except she knew that really wasn't an option, either. She took a moment to calm herself and considered the choices.

"Get me the French president," Brogan said. "No more negotiating, no more waiting, and no damned politics. If his military won't help ours, then they are our enemy, too, complicit in the first nuclear attacks in seventy years. Understood?"

The president's staff nodded in agreement.

"General, send our troops into Paris. Let's hit him with everything we've got. I want that building infiltrated and Van Ness' bunker destroyed. Karen," she said to her chief of staff, "inform the leadership of Congress of our impending attack, but make sure they know in no uncertain terms that this is happening with or without their support. The United States has declared war on the Foundation for Human Advancement."

"What about Cafferty's team?" Swain asked.

"Let's pray they're able to stop Van Ness before he attacks again. But we can't count on that."

She looked around the table.

"The Foundation for Human Advancement represents a clear and present danger to our nation, to the entire world, and we're ending its reign of terror . . .

"Today."

afferty's shoes pounded the stone as he led Bowcut and Munoz along the dimly lit corridors of the Paris catacombs. Thousands of stacked bones lined the walls, gruesomely topped with skulls. He had briefly read some of the literature on his way into the exhibit, attempting to appear like a typical tourist, and the bodies of more than six million people had been laid to rest here. It sounded like a lot, but nothing compared with the upcoming death toll if he didn't take down Van Ness.

Inside his heavy wool coat, a fully charged laser was strapped to his right side. A holstered pistol hugged his left ribs. Strobe grenades filled his pockets. He kept his arms tensed by his sides, ready to draw a weapon if the team came across a member of the Foundation.

But there was only one person's forehead he actually wanted to put a bullet through.

But first, they had to reach him.

At six in the evening, only a few visitors remained,

and none was going in the same direction as the team. No one looked particularly suspicious, but the team wasn't taking any chances and discreetly followed visitors' movements once they passed.

Bowcut and Munoz moved closer to his side when he got beyond the Crypt of the Sepulchral Lamp and near a roped-off passage. Everything appeared exactly how Munoz had described.

They approached the hatch, hidden there right in the middle of the skulls and bones.

"No going back now," Munoz uttered under his breath.

Cafferty keyed the code—043046—into a pad by the side of the hatch. He smiled grimly. He hoped today would be another moment in history that a dictator would meet his end.

Bowcut drew her pistol.

Munoz clutched a strobe grenade in one hand, a laser in the other.

The door opened with an electronic grind, revealing a smooth, carved tunnel in the bedrock. Bright lights blazed from the ceiling. Fifty yards ahead lay a single glass entrance with darkness beyond.

The team cautiously entered the corridor, and the hatch automatically closed behind them with a hollow thud.

Munoz spun to face it, studying the hatch from the inside. "Guys, I'm not sure we can get back out this way even if we wanted."

Cafferty shrugged. There was no going back anyway. The only direction they could go led to Van Ness, Ellen, and a potential way to stop a nuclear bomb from detonating. Nothing else was worth contemplating. He strode along the tunnel toward the far entrance, then abruptly stopped.

Bowcut also froze, then grabbed her laser.

The faint sound of shrieks emanated from beyond the glass.

Not one or two, but hundreds . . .

Cafferty studied the thick glass entrance. He had seen this type of glass only in the space shuttle on the deck of the USS *Intrepid*. It was nearly impenetrable.

Nearly.

The temperature had risen once the hatch had closed. A bead of sweat trickled down Cafferty's temple. He turned to Bowcut and Munoz. "You guys ready?"

Munoz shot him a nervous smile and raised a strobe grenade. "Not just ready. Excited, boss!"

Cafferty gave him a tight grin, once again reminded how crucial Munoz's infectious optimism was this last year.

Bowcut gave a firm nod.

Cafferty went to pull the glass door open, but he managed to heave it only a few inches because of the sheer weight. He wrapped both hands around the steel handle and dragged it open. An intense, acrid stench wafted out. A moment later, the deafening sound of piercing shrieks filled the air.

Munoz hurled his strobe grenade into the darkness. It bounced along the ground, then disappeared out of sight.

Brilliant flashes of light illuminated exactly what they were facing.

A set of steps led down to what appeared to be an underground storm drain, roughly fifty yards long and twenty feet wide. At the far end, light reflected off another glass entrance. But that wasn't the problem.

Hundreds of manic creatures thrashed around at the bottom of the drain. The strobe had given them nowhere to run. Some hurled themselves at the far entrance, ramming into the glass. Some scaled the walls. Most turned to the team and tore toward them, claws extended, mouths open, tails whipping.

Van Ness had lined the corridor with hundreds of creatures, trapped with no way out. Feeding troughs lined the walls. He had fed them like pigs. No wonder he didn't need guards stationed at either door.

"Oh shit," Munoz said.

That about sums it up, Cafferty thought as he ripped out his laser.

Before he even fired, a bright red beam from Bowcut's weapon sliced through the closest creatures, who had rocketed up the stairs and came within a few feet. One hit the ground and skidded to a dead halt inches from Cafferty. Its blood oozed around his shoes.

Munoz fired to the right, cutting down three creatures that had raced along the wall toward them. He pulled out two more strobes and hoisted them deeper into the corridor, but they only served to increase the creatures' fury.

Cafferty squeezed the laser's trigger and sent a red-hot beam along the center of the drain. He kept his finger depressed, sweeping across the central pack, carving through the black mass.

Bowcut and Munoz covered the left and right,

firing on anything that came at them along the smooth stone walls and ceiling.

Cafferty kept firing ahead as he slowly descended the twenty steps, picking his way around the sizzling corpses. His face twisted into a grimace. He used to fear these monstrosities, but right now he had nothing but contempt for them. Visions of David North's brave last stand raced through his mind. His best friend and head of security had ensured the survival of the people on the train in New York City. Between North's death, the kidnapping of Ellen, and Van Ness' impending nuclear attack, Cafferty seethed with anger and was propelled by determination . . .

Until a claw dug into his ankle, and he was pulled down the stairs. He crashed along the stone steps, covering his head to protect it, but banging up his elbows and back. At the same time, a sharp pain shot up his leg from where the claw had pierced his ankle.

He came to a halt against the ground, still curled in a ball. Any second, he expected a tail to lacerate him.

When that didn't happen, he forced himself to jump up, swinging his laser toward the decapitated corpse of the creature that was on the ground with him, and instantly sighed with relief. He must have sliced the monster into pieces farther up, and the claw had reflexively grabbed him as he made his way past. It still held on to his ankle. He winced and shook his leg free. He looked back up to where Munoz and Bowcut were cutting their way down toward him. Together, the team's three beams tore through the remaining black figures until nothing was running at them or away from the glare of the strobes.

After a minute, the place fell mostly silent, apart from a few pained murmurs. Cafferty had never felt more on top of a situation involving creatures. At long last, he was managing things on his terms and closing in on his prey. They finally had a way to Van Ness.

They finally had a chance to actually stop him.

Bowcut and Munoz moved between the smoldering bodies and gave a few surviving creatures the coup de grâce with laser shots to the brain. They caught up with him on the ground.

"You okay?" Munoz asked.

Cafferty wiped sweat from his brow. He ripped off his coat, tore off a few strips to wrap up his ankle, and dumped the rest on the ground.

"Let's go."

He moved to the opposite door and heaved it open. Bowcut slipped inside first, then Munoz, then Cafferty.

Toward Van Ness' underground lair.

SARAH DEPLOYED A STROBE AND CREPT THROUGH A NARROW tunnel, laser at the ready, switching her aim between the dark spaces that were sheltered from the light. The heat this far beneath the ground provided a sharp contrast to the chilly Parisian winter above. Like Cafferty, she dumped her jacket and moved forward in her form-fitting black T-shirt. From here, she guessed it didn't matter who saw her extra holstered weapons and bandolier of strobes.

Shrieks echoed all around, but somehow this felt different from New York and London. More . . . *managed*. As if Van Ness had orchestrated everything belowground.

Does Van Ness already know we're here?

She had purposely taken the lead. There was no doubting Cafferty's motivations; she wanted to kill Van Ness, too. But they would be facing a human enemy. It was one thing to kill a creature, but another to take a human life. She didn't enjoy the prospect, but her time with NYPD SWAT had at least given her the tools to deal with such a possibility, to do so with all feelings stripped away. Cool and calculated. There'd be no mistake of letting emotions overtake rational decisions. That's where she feared Tom was at, and with such a small team, they couldn't afford a single mistake.

But it wasn't a human they encountered first.

A tail lashed from a cave and slammed into the rock by her boots. She dropped to one knee and fired into the darkness. Her beam lanced through two creatures who had been waiting in anticipation.

Munoz and Cafferty edged to her side.

Ahead, beyond the mouth of the tunnel, artificial light brightened what looked like a vast natural cavern.

"Wait here, guys," she said. "Let me check this out."

Both men nodded.

She moved forward in a crouching run until she neared the end of the tunnel. Then she dropped to a leopard crawl and edged forward.

When she craned her head into the cavern, Bowcut took a sharp breath. Blinding globes hung at different levels, washing the vast space, maybe the size of a baseball field, in white light. Two hundred yards in front of her, a glass dome covered an area where twenty people sat at workstations. A glowing, transparent elevator shaft extended from it and went all the way up to the ceiling. Perhaps a thousand feet up.

It showed the Foundation's abilities in a way she had never witnessed before. Sure, she knew it was a powerful foe, but this . . .

It was breathtaking.

It was insane.

Finally able to shake herself from the sight, she took in the details of her surroundings and noticed, off to the side, a loading dock that had been carved out of the rock, just like Munoz had described. There was a series of five sturdy-looking metal doors connecting the dock to the glass dome and assorted fork lifts around the area.

She switched her focus back to the glass dome.

Four turrets jutted from the top with twin barrels on each. She wasn't certain what they were until one swung around and sent a powerful laser beam zipping into a dark cave.

Bowcut struggled to push a heavy rock off the tunnel's edge into the cavern below. The small boulder rolled and fell into the cavern.

Within seconds, one of the turrets swung toward it, the lasers leveled, and fired. It blasted the rock to pieces as it fell. The intense heat from the nearby blast added unwelcome warmth to Bowcut's already glistening face. The lasers were fast, accurate, and presented a massive problem if they wanted to cross the cavern to get to the glass dome. She scanned the immediate area to see if they could make it across by darting between cover, then she crept back to the team.

"What's the situation?" Cafferty asked.

"Good news and bad news."

"Good first," Munoz said.

"We've found their center of operations."

"And the bad?"

"We need to move fast between boulders if we want to make it to the complex in one piece."

Cafferty frowned.

"He's got big-ass versions of these," Bowcut said, motioning to her laser gun. "And they are motion activated."

The team gave each other a knowing look, then nodded and edged toward the mouth of the tunnel. They were all in. This road had led them here, to two possible outcomes:

Their death . . . or his.

CHAPTER TWENTY-FIVE

Van Ness sat behind the desk in his subterranean office. The false windows on three sides of the room displayed crystal-clear high-definition images of the rolling foothills of the Bavarian Alpine Foreland. His father had loved taking him hiking there when he was a child. The memory of it brought him solace. He had hated slogging up the steep trails as a kid, but it had taught him a valuable lesson: the things that hurt us the most in life are usually the best for us.

As father and son would look out from the top of that gorgeous Alpine vista, Otto would say, "Imagine those vile creatures running wild over the Fatherland, taking the lives of everyone you know, destroying all you love, all that we've created. One day, when I'm gone, the survival of our race, of all humanity, will be in your hands, son."

This was the day.

Not *a* defining moment, but *the* defining moment.

But the fulfillment of those dreams had to wait a few minutes. Van Ness' thoughts drifted back to the story about the sound his mother made, the tiniest beginning of a scream snuffed out instantly under the colossal weight of a building.

Those vile creatures . . . taking the lives of everyone you know . . . destroying all you love . . .

The world would pay for its crimes. And the dream would be born again.

Van Ness sliced a piece off his filet mignon and groaned with pleasure as he slowly took a bite from the perfectly prepared steak. His chef could never quite match the exquisite experience he had at Delmonico's in New York City so many years ago, but this was close.

Van Ness dabbed the corner of his mouth with a napkin and took a sip of his favorite Italian Pinot Grigio. Only pretentious fools selected their wine based on their meat. He had once thrown a glass of water in the Brazilian president's face after the idiot attempted to correct him on his order. That said, meals were an excellent time for reflection and strategizing, which was why he had always eaten alone.

Three wall-mounted screens directly ahead showed him feeds from the Foundation's operations. Edwards controlled the content, and they currently displayed footage of long traffic jams out of London and two distant shots of the detonation sites in the United States.

He went to spoon some glazed brussels sprouts onto his plate, watching the people flee from London with amusement.

The phone on his desk let out low electronic pulses.

Van Ness sighed and thumbed the speakerphone button. "What is it, Edwards?"

"We've got company."

"Which we expected. Why are you disturbing my dinner to state the obvious, my dear old friend?"

"It's more than that," Edwards replied, hastily trying to cover the panic in his voice. "The French defense minister just called to say he didn't have a choice but to join an American attack on our building after the bombings. They know about this bunker as well and plan to take it out."

Van Ness laughed mildly. "Let them try. They'll never get through the defenses up top. It's a shame we can no longer count on the French president for support, but we'll deal with that in time."

Those last words made him drop the spoon, though. His smile quickly dissipated, and his hand tightened into a shaking fist. He had put that cretin in office. He had let France off the hook for a decade in exchange for protecting his operation in Paris.

Well, those protections were clearly no longer needed, were they?

"And how about the hatch in the catacombs?" Edwards asked.

"Now that the resourceful Thomas Cafferty thinks his team hacked us and has made it through safely, blow the tunnel. Seal us in. Let's see the Americans and their allies try to blast their way through that."

"And what of this Cafferty? Is he not a distract—"

"NO," Van Ness snapped back. "No. Let him come."

"Yes, sir. Anything else?"

"Nothing has changed. If anything, our momentum—our timeline—only speeds up."

"Understood."

"We're standing on the great precipice of history, my dear friend. It's time to take the leap."

Van Ness cut the call and gazed forward.

The monitor on the right switched to a display of the main entrance of the Foundation's headquarters up top. At least a dozen dark vans screeched to a halt outside. The back and side doors flew open and heavily armed French assault teams jumped out. Some ran down the narrow passages at the sides of the building, though most stormed into the sparkling reception area with weapons raised.

The French soldiers entered the building with overwhelming speed, capturing dozens of terrified Foundation employees as they moved from room to room. It would only be a matter of minutes before the soldiers reached the blast door leading to the elevator shaft down to the bunker.

The camera angle switched to Avenue Joseph Bouvard. Dozens of French tanks and military trucks rolled down the block, American military vehicles not far behind. All headed straight for the Foundation for Human Advancement.

Van Ness removed the napkin from the collar of his shirt and calmly pushed his plate away. Although this military response was ultimately expected, it still put a damper on his lovely meal.

Let them wage their battle on the streets of Paris. It's of no consequence.

Still, Van Ness shook his head at the stupidity

of it all. By fighting him, America and France were fighting against humanity's very survival.

He rotated his wheelchair away from the desk, powered it out of his office, and rolled through a cavernous warehouse, filled with stocked shelving units that could supply the bunker for years. Freeze-dried food. Medical supplies. Water. Everything required if they needed to hunker down for the impending fallout. He could rule the world indefinitely from inside this nest underneath Paris. The irony was not lost on him. From inside the gates of hell, he could be humanity's savior.

Van Ness navigated his wheelchair into the huge glass dome and drew to a halt next to the central command table.

Edwards gave him a grim nod.

"You look worried, my friend," Van Ness said. "Have we not planned for every possible outcome?"

"I guess so."

"We never guess, my friend."

"I know, Albert. I'm confident."

"Well, sound it then. Let's ready all of our bombs for detonation. Begin with the nests under Washington, Brussels, and Newcastle."

Edwards stared back at him but didn't react.

"Did you not hear me?" Van Ness asked.

"I will get on it right now."

But he remained in his chair, posture stiff, hands dug firmly in his pants pockets. Van Ness had spent enough time in the man's company to know when he harbored doubts. His momentary hesitation gave him away.

He wheeled closer to Edwards, within inches of his chair. Close enough to receive a strong blast of his cologne. He glared into the eyes of the person who had been by his side for two decades. Once again, his number two appeared to be wavering at the wrong time.

"Am I being unclear, my dear friend?" Van Ness said softly.

"Not at all."

"Good. Remember, this faster timeline is their doing, not ours. But rest assured, this was all going to happen, no matter what. Those nests need to be destroyed before it is too late."

Edwards nodded to himself, then rose from his chair and headed over to the consoles. Van Ness empathized with the man. He took no pleasure in the loss of human life. He remembered his first taste of it in the 1960s, when he and his father had purposely trapped a group of cave explorers in Virginia so they could study the creatures' behavior from a distance. It had initially horrified him when those six women had been systematically butchered, but the lessons he learned were invaluable. And now, as the creatures had multiplied and spread around the world faster than he could exterminate them, the stakes had ballooned to unimaginable proportions. So it was only natural that the level of sacrifice would also increase.

Van Ness peered up at the monitors.

The French assault team had cleared the building and made its way into the underground parking lot, prepared to storm the blast door.

He let out a disappointed breath. Despite these

people being his supposed foe, they were just children. The creatures provided the Foundation's only truly intelligent opposition, unlike these prowling imbeciles and their submachine guns.

Van Ness keyed in a code on his wheelchair's control pad and carefully watched the video feed.

In the parking garage a mile above, ten large pipes extended from the walls at regular intervals and blasted methane into the air, quickly filling up the structure.

If you don't learn from history, you are destined to repeat it . . .

A large metal plate embedded in the floor of the parking garage groaned and slowly opened. Hundreds of loud shrieks emanated from below.

The soldiers froze, quickly realizing they had walked straight into a trap. Their radios crackled with the voices of American special forces warning them not to advance without them, but it was too late.

The lights in the parking garage cut out.

Van Ness watched the now dark video feed with a look of sad satisfaction.

Only the frantic muzzle flashes on the screen confirmed the creatures were eliminating the minor irritation that had dared to confront him. The weapons fire grew less and less, until eventually . . . nothing. At least they had died before the methane levels had grown and an explosion had taken them. Actually, he wondered, which was worse? Torn to shreds or burned to death? He couldn't decide. Both had their downsides, but the outcome remained the same.

Van Ness casually checked his watch, impressed by how fast problems got solved. When he had first tested it with disobedient employees, it had taken at least twenty seconds longer, and they weren't even armed. The creatures were growing more efficient, a quality he'd extract from them to ensure humanity's future.

He pressed his control pad again.

Back on the monitor, the lights in the parking lot blasted back to life.

Creatures scampered back into the dark void before Van Ness closed the metal plate once again.

Corpses lay strewn on the ground, most torn to shreds.

One soldier remained alive, missing both legs, bleeding out quickly, crawling desperately toward nothing. It reminded him of his father's story about the mercy he showed that injured German boy so many years ago, when he put a bullet through his brain.

There would be no such mercy for this soldier.

On another screen, more military vehicles and tanks surrounded the Foundation building and soldiers poured in through the entrances. Van Ness briefly worried if the sheer weight of numbers might eventually count against him. But he quickly reminded himself of the fail-safes he had set in place for such contingencies. Although he hated the loss, he anticipated that he'd soon have to level the whole building, leaving the subterranean lair safer from future assaults.

Not that he expected any after today.

With all the nuclear bombs ready to go, the major powers would be scrambling to take care of themselves. Nobody would be able to coordinate a response against him, and, more important, the world's largest nests would be destroyed simultaneously.

They'd curse his name, maybe. But they'd praise his actions . . . when they finally were able to wrap their petty minds around them.

His father's words echoed through his head.

Don't let our dream die . . .

Van Ness switched his focus back to Edwards. "My friend, let me know when we're ready to destroy the next three nests."

"Yes, Albert," Edwards replied.

"Then I want you to bring *every* bomb online."

CHAPTER TWENTY-SIX

Diego Munoz crouched behind a rock in the brightly lit cavern. His heart hammered against his chest. His sweat-drenched T-shirt hugged his body. He held his laser by his side, prepared to fire at human or creature. It wasn't easy to accept he might have only seconds left as a living, breathing person, but that's exactly what he faced.

The faint sound of gunfire crackled somewhere above the cavern, and the shrieks of creatures below provided a continuous sound track to their journey. Directly ahead, the Foundation lackeys in the huge glass dome didn't seem particularly distracted by the ceiling-mounted lasers spinning on their turrets and firing. They looked more like the subservient people who worked in a drug factory . . . or the MTA's head office. Low-level employees who never realized how close they were to organized crime or corporate oppression. Those at the top had it good. Those at the bottom took all the risk and did the grunt work.

Munoz peered at the thick glass structure and

brightly lit elevator shaft. It was awe-inspiring in a dramatic and nefarious way. The organization's tech capabilities clearly stretched way beyond just weapons. But, of course, instead of being used for the greater good, they were used to prop up Van Ness' insanity.

Conspiracy theories were one thing. He had lived much of his adult life focused on the minutiae of events, poring over documents and videos and grainy photos to try to understand the truth of things, to dig into rumor and myth and scratch away at what the establishment told the world, to know what really happened.

Now, though, there was no scratching anymore. This *was* reality, fully exposed before him. And it was horrifying.

But it also meant that, for the first time, he wasn't just on the sidelines, commenting on message boards and participating in the research of the esoteric and arcane. Now, Diego was a participant—was an actor on a stage that he always half believed was just that: a farcical play that filled his spare time. There was no more spare time—the Foundation's control of the creatures, not to mention its arsenal of nuclear weapons, made that the irrefutable truth. And with the chaos unfolding all around them, there was one more truth that hit Diego as he crouched meters away from possible death.

We are the only ones who can alter this course.

Bowcut and Cafferty scrambled from behind another big boulder and dove to his sides. Munoz mentally counted until a laser beam zipped overhead and slammed into the rock face behind them.

"You've got three seconds before it shoots," he whispered loudly.

Bowcut elbowed him in the ribs. "I'm guessing that's not the first time you've said that."

"Funny," Diego replied.

"That's him!" Cafferty blurted out.

"Van Ness?" Bowcut asked.

Cafferty rose to spring forward, but Munoz grabbed him by the shoulder and dragged him back. Cafferty gave him a stern look of protest, which Diego firmly responded to with a shake of the head.

"We need a plan, Tom."

Cafferty was about to argue, but after a deep breath, he nodded. Now wasn't the time for a reckless charge. With a small sigh of relief, Diego dropped lower and peered around the side of their cover position toward the operations center.

A thin man with gray hair, dressed in an immaculately tailored suit, powered a wheelchair across the operations center floor. He pointed at a couple of members of the Foundation, then glared at a vast console of winking lights.

They needed to get closer, but a head-on assault wasn't going to work.

"We need to keep leapfrogging from rock to rock," Munoz said.

"Definitely," Bowcut agreed.

"Let's go."

Diego lurched forward at a crouching run and skidded behind another rock.

Seconds later, one of the lasers fired, blasting the wall behind him. The turret swung back to face the center of the cavern. Bowcut and Cafferty followed his route and once again dove by his sides.

Another scorching set of twin beams zipped overhead.

Munoz figured they had around eight of these minidashes to make, the last being the longest, meaning they'd be exposed for longer than three seconds. The other risk was that someone in the operations center would notice the laser was firing at positions that were slowly advancing toward the loading bay.

These were simply risks they had to take.

He rose again and dashed to the next boulder. The operations center loomed closer and closer.

The sound of a creature's shriek resonated through his body.

Close.

Very close.

Munoz twisted to his right.

Glinting eyes peered at him from inside a cave. A tail whipped out and slammed into the ground inches from his leg. Loose stones blasted against his body. He aimed his laser and fired. The beam punctured through a creature's face and rocketed into the darkness beyond.

They had to do this faster. They were sitting ducks out in the open and sitting ducks hiding in the shadows.

Bowcut and Cafferty dropped to his sides once more, and the lasers deployed again. Diego waited a moment and sprinted for the next piece of cover. He dropped to the rocky ground and sucked in a deep breath of the thick, stale air.

A few more runs avoiding the advanced weaponry got them to within one sprint of the loading dock. They took a chance to catch their breath before the final, longest dash. The dome was fifty yards to their left. Munoz thought at least one member of the Foundation would see them, but all appeared focused on the consoles and overhead screens.

The worst thing was that Albert Van Ness was tantalizingly close. Munoz could see the man moving about, every so often mouthing what were probably orders to the men and women in the command center. It would be the easiest thing to take a shot at him, but Diego guessed his laser couldn't pierce the dome's glass wall—surely that's a contingency he'd have considered. And bullets would almost certainly be accounted for, because that glass had to be strong enough to resist attacks by the creatures. Either way, to risk shooting at Van Ness would be to give away their position, and that would be the end no matter what.

"This is it," Cafferty said. "Guys, just in case . . . it's been an honor."

"It *is* an honor," Bowcut said, her eyes focused on the loading bay. "We're not dying today, Tom."

She pushed a rock the size of a large beach ball off the edge of the cavern and thrust forward, charging across the rocky ground with all her might.

A twin set of lasers blasted the falling rock to pieces, then quickly zeroed in on her sprinting for the dock.

Munoz tensed. Bowcut still had twenty yards to cover.

She threw herself toward the smooth concrete floor just as the lasers fired. The beams missed her by inches as she rolled under the cover of the bay. She then edged back toward the metal door on the right side, out of the dome's view. A worker inside the lair briefly glanced up from his workstation to look at the laser fire, before continuing his work. She was safe.

The laser turret rotated back to face the center of the cavern again.

The shrieks from inside the cavern slowly died out and became eerily quiet.

"Uh-oh," Diego said.

"We have to go now!" Cafferty shouted. Diego was in complete agreement.

The men bolted out from behind a boulder and ran with all their might.

Munoz focused on planting his boots on the flat areas of the cavern. One trip or stumble would mean the end. He powered forward, aware that a weapon was currently sweeping down toward him.

Cafferty accelerated a few yards ahead. His fitness regimen had served him well. He scrambled inside the loading bay and glanced back at his struggling team member. While Diego was in decent shape, he had certainly taken a few semesters at the school of doughnuts. He winced, expecting a beam to slice through him at any second.

Suddenly, a powerful unseen force dragged at Diego's feet, as if he were running in thick mud. The look of concern on Cafferty's and Bowcut's faces told him the same thing.

"Diego, fight it!" Cafferty screamed.

"I . . . can't . . . move!" he yelled back, coming to a halt against his will.

"*Fight!*"

It was no use.

The focused telekinetic powers of the creatures were simply too strong. Diego's feet slipped on the loose gravel and he hit the ground hard, face-first.

The force pulled his body backward, dragging him toward a tucked-away cave where undoubtedly dozens of creatures waited for their prey.

He clawed at anything to stop himself.

"Diego! *No!*"

The laser homed in on Munoz's struggle.

"Help me!" he screamed.

A cacophony of perfectly mimicked "help me's" bellowed back at him from the abyss below.

The laser prepared to fire.

Bowcut whipped a strobe grenade off her belt, activated it, and threw it full force right at the cave Munoz was being dragged into.

The strobe flew into the dark mouth and light exploded from the device.

Shrieks of pain filled Munoz's ears, only to diminish as the creatures disappeared deeper into the caves, and the telekinetic grip on him instantly released.

The laser fired.

Now free, Munoz rolled out of the way just as a scorching hot laser blast destroyed the very ground he was just on a fraction of a second earlier. He prepared to scramble again, but the scattering of other creatures gave the lasers a new target, and they blasted away at the monsters as they fled.

Munoz used this distraction, leaping to his feet

and sprinting. After what felt like an eternity of exposure, he dove into Bowcut's waiting arms in the loading dock.

He was safe.

"Who taught you to throw like that?" he asked, catching his breath.

"Wouldn't you like to know?" she replied cheekily.

Cafferty offered a hand and hauled Munoz to his feet. "Very glad you're alive, buddy," he said. "Now let's finish this."

Munoz nodded. Swallowed hard. Knew he'd just avoided death by a split second and Bowcut's quick thinking. But he *had* escaped with his life, and that gave him a sense of hope.

For the first time in a while, he felt like maybe they could survive this.

Don't get cocky, he thought.

The team silently maneuvered past assorted forklifts and mechanical equipment in the direction of one of the complex's entrances.

This activity was far more in his comfort zone.

Munoz hit an access button on the entrance wall, and a sturdy door slowly opened with an electric grind. The sound echoed around the silent loading dock. He raised his laser, resting his finger lightly on the trigger. Next, he mentally prepared himself for the prospect of killing a person—something he hadn't done since slicing Agent Samuels into two pieces in the New York subway system, and something he didn't relish ever having to do again.

A brightly lit whitewashed corridor lay ahead, wide enough to drive a car down. The team entered slowly, carefully.

Munoz peered his head through the door and scanned the ceiling for security cameras. He couldn't locate any. That didn't mean they weren't already being watched, though.

Time would tell.

They slipped through the door one by one into a cool, air-conditioned atmosphere. It was a welcome relief, though only a minor one.

My only real relief will come when we finish our mission.

If we finish it at all . . .

He led the way in the direction of a service elevator not far ahead. This would take them up into the dome itself, assuming he had memorized the schematics correctly. He moved forward with purpose, taking a left turn at the end. They entered a darkened warehouse-style area filled with crates and densely packed industrial shelving units.

The sound of footsteps came at them from the far end of the warehouse. Not fast or aggressive, but nevertheless closing in on their location down the central walkway.

Two armed men appeared out of the shadows in the distance, walking casually.

The team ducked behind a stack of pallets to avoid detection.

"Avoid fighting until it's absolutely necessary," Bowcut whispered. "If they don't know we're here already, let's try to keep it that way."

Cafferty nodded. "Looks like a routine guard rotation. Diego, any other way to get to that elevator?"

Munoz combed through the lair's layout in his mind. He remembered smaller storage rooms to their left, with a secondary passage that led toward the dome on the other side. He nodded and silently crept in that direction, keeping plenty of distance between the team and the Foundation guards. Bowcut and Cafferty silently followed.

He led them to a door at the side of the warehouse and gently lowered the handle. It opened and Bowcut slipped inside first, weapon raised. A moment later, she ducked back out. "Clear."

Cafferty followed her in.

Munoz entered last and quietly closed the entrance. The hairs on his arms prickled at the extreme drop in temperature. He turned to see the other two just standing there glued to the spot, staring straight ahead, mouths open.

This was no storage room.

On both sides of the room were ten floor-to-ceiling metal chambers with glass fronts covered in frost. Each let out a quiet hum and had thick cables running from them to steel trays on the ground.

Bowcut advanced to the nearest one. "What the hell?"

Cafferty walked to her side. He scraped a thin layer of ice off the glass window, revealing the face of what looked like a cross between a creature and a human, suspended in liquid animation. The deathly still face had one set of razor-sharp teeth, gray skin, and black eyes.

It looked just like the thing that had attacked them in the De Jong building.

Cafferty stumbled back. "Jesus Christ," he murmured.

<u>**CHAPTER TWENTY-SEVEN**</u>

At first, Bowcut couldn't believe her eyes. But she regained her composure quickly, moving along to the next cryochamber and swiping away the frost. Inside, another creature-human hybrid floated inside thick fluid. Blacker than the previous one, but equally as repulsive. Its claws appeared more like fingers, and its chest muscles appeared more human in form.

"He's crossbreeding human and creature," Cafferty uttered. "He claims he wants to eradicate them, but then he does this. Just when I thought it couldn't get any worse."

"That sick motherfucker," Munoz said. "They've taken it way past what we've already seen."

Cafferty nodded, lost in thought.

Bowcut moved along to the sixth cryochamber and palmed away the frost. This seven-foot genetic freak appeared very much like the one she had lasered, and it had a black box screwed into the top of its head, which begged the question: Had the Foundation done more than just merge the two species?

Had it advanced this new monster's capabilities even further?

She moved along and cleared the next chamber's glass.

This creature was six feet tall, had pale gray skin, and looked even more nightmarish. Almost human. It had rippling muscles and a shorter serrated tail. And wisps of hair on its head.

Cafferty and Munoz followed her to the next chamber. She cleared the glass and took a sharp intake of breath. More human, but with creature characteristics. The floating monstrosity had pale green skin and small male reproductive organs and was built like a heavyweight boxer.

Bowcut moved to the final cryochamber. Her hand trembled as she wiped away the frost. She dreaded seeing the next stage in the Foundation's development, but the chamber was empty.

"What the hell?" Munoz asked. "Where is it?"

"I'm guessing this is the one that attacked us on the roof of the De Jong building," Cafferty said. Bowcut wasn't so sure, but she also knew that wondering about this empty chamber—or any of these grotesque experiments—wouldn't save London or the world. She checked her watch. They still had a few hours before the detonation.

"Which way from here?" she asked impatiently.

Munoz motioned his head toward the far end of the room. "Straight out of there and take a right. That's where we'll find the elevator leading up to the dome."

Bowcut headed past the rest of the cryochambers. She had no further desire to see the contents.

She reached the end and pushed down the door's metal bar. It punched open a few inches and she peered into a brightly lit passage that rose into the distance. Steel support girders wrapped around the walls and ceiling.

No footsteps came from above or below.

Bowcut sprung out and swung her aim in either direction. No guards to be seen. That in itself didn't feel right.

Where is everyone?

Munoz and Cafferty joined her in the passage. All three advanced toward the elevator, moving at pace, aiming in all directions, but knowing speed was more important than caution at this point.

A distant boom thundered from above, at the top of the cavern.

She instinctively ducked. The two men pressed themselves against the wall as dust dropped from the ceiling.

They stood frozen, glancing at each other.

No further explosions came.

"What the hell was that?" Munoz gasped.

"Sounds like the cavalry is trying to take the building above and aren't just using guns anymore."

"Or they're getting blown up in the process," Bowcut replied.

"Do you think they'll be able to help?"

"They are helping," Bowcut said. "They're distracting Van Ness. Other than that, though . . . there's no way they'll be able to get down here in time."

"We knew it would come down to us," Cafferty said. "Let's get this done."

They briskly climbed a set of stairs that led into

a huge room that was a cross between a hospital operating room and an IT research facility. White shiny walls. At least fifty work benches covered in medical equipment, computers, machines she didn't recognize. Movement caught her eye on the right side. Various forms of lizards in glass cages.

But her focus was drawn to the central operating table. A pregnant woman lay unconscious, a mask over her face. Tubes extended from various parts of her naked body. She looked to be in her midtwenties. Blond hair. Perhaps of European origin. Bowcut had no idea, though the life support machine by the woman's side showed her vital signs as consistent.

Two men in white coats stood over her, oblivious to the team's incursion. This wasn't worth negotiating. She zeroed in on one of them and fired. A puff of red mist shot from the back of his head. His colleague dropped his chart and turned. Before he could move, she pumped two rounds in his chest.

The thought of what the Foundation was putting this woman through made Bowcut shudder. Just like the creatures experimenting on those pregnant women underneath New York, Van Ness was doing the same exact thing in some twisted crossbreeding race against time.

Cafferty and Munoz followed her to the table, sweeping their aim in every direction. At the organs in metal dishes. The severed limbs of humans and creatures with electrodes attached, in traction. The specimens of baby hybrids in gallon-sized glass jars. Bowcut passed blood hanging from several IV stands. The whole place felt like a research facility from hell.

A sense of trepidation consumed Bowcut as she neared the operating table. Something prodded internally up from the woman's stomach. It moved back and forth, like a mini shark fin.

Bowcut grabbed the ultrasound wand from a cart next to the table and placed it on the woman's stomach. On the monitor, an image formed of the fetus inside the womb. It looked almost like a human baby, apart from the claws, one of which repeatedly scraped the edges of her womb from the inside.

"Just when you thought this can't get any more fucked up . . ." Diego muttered.

"Leave it for now," Cafferty said in a firm voice. "There's only one way we can stop this madness."

But Bowcut couldn't bring herself to leave this innocent woman who had been subjected to this horror. She had seen some twisted stuff in her time, battling drug dealers in the Bronx, but the Foundation had consistently topped any of those experiences. Yet she wasn't sure she could just end this woman's life—if she had the right, let alone the strength.

It gnawed on her soul, as she saw the Foundation's vision of the future for the nightmare it was.

"Sarah," Cafferty said, snapping her out of her darkness. "We can only save her by ending Van Ness."

She took a deep breath and turned away, disgusted. Tom was right.

The team approached the elevator, and Bowcut hit the button.

The doors instantly parted with a confident pneumatic hiss. The large industrial elevator was similar in size to one found in a hospital, big enough to fit several patients on gurneys, or several creatures . . .

They wasted no time entering.

Bowcut steeled herself, perhaps her last chance to take a moment before the fight. This elevator would take them straight up to Van Ness' lair, inside the dome itself. Adrenaline pumped through her body. She gripped the laser tightly with her shaking hands. It wasn't fear—she had passed that point with the Foundation a long time ago. It was the nervous anticipation she had always felt before heading into action.

And the idea of confronting Van Ness and his men.

The elevator closed and they began their short ascent.

Odd classical music started playing through a speaker on the wall.

Munoz frowned and mouthed, "What the f—"

Suddenly, the car jerked to an abrupt halt, cutting off his sentence.

Everyone tensed and aimed their lasers toward the door.

It didn't open.

The music's volume increased to the crescendo.

Any moment now.

Something creaked on the roof.

Before Bowcut had a chance to aim upward, a hybrid creature—similar to the one on that rooftop in London, but even more human in form—exploded through the elevator's ceiling tiles and landed between them on its powerful gray legs. This nightmare creation had an electronic box screwed into its head, just like the previous one she had slain, which meant it was being controlled by Van Ness.

The three recoiled in shock, and she had no time to process this information.

The hybrid instantly batted the laser from Bowcut's hand. Then it crashed a fist into her guts, knocking the wind out of her. She doubled over and took a rapid wheezing breath.

Munoz spun to aim.

The hybrid moved at lightning speed, faster than any of them could think. It ripped the weapon from his grip and smashed it against his head. Munoz's back crashed against the side of the car and he slumped to the ground, unconscious. Blood oozed from the gash in his head.

Cafferty was the only one left standing, wide-eyed with panic etched across his face. He aimed to fire his weapon, but the hybrid lifted Bowcut in the air with terrifying ease and hurled her at him. They both hit the ground hard.

Bowcut ignored the wince-inducing pain from her right shoulder and grunted as she went for the laser on the floor.

As she lifted the weapon, the hybrid sliced its hand down faster than humanly possible, cutting the barrel of the laser gun right in half, rendering it useless.

It slammed its heavy foot on Bowcut's back, and she couldn't move from underneath the crushing weight.

Cafferty tried to crawl across the floor to reach his laser.

The hybrid kicked it clear and crashed its fist into

his face. Speckles of blood sprayed the wall. Cafferty slumped back to a sitting position, dazed. It leaned toward him and pinned him against the wall by his throat.

Bowcut attempted to free herself with every ounce of strength in her body. It couldn't end like this. Not when they had come so close. Every time she moved, though, the pressure on her back increased, until she feared this monster would snap her spine.

Munoz moaned, though he still appeared unconscious.

The hybrid stood in a crouching position, letting out quiet guttural breaths. It had beaten them in a matter of seconds. They were still alive, but she wondered for how long.

Cafferty tried to pry the hybrid's fingers off his throat, to no effect.

Bowcut glanced up at her friend. His face reddened by the second and his eyes bulged. He had only moments left.

A heartbeat later, the elevator smoothly resumed its ascent, and the classical music continued, a sound track to their misery.

The elevator bumped to a gentle halt and a bell let out a polite chime.

The doors opened.

Flanked by four burly guards, Albert Van Ness sat in his electric wheelchair in a marble corridor, staring at the scene. He arched an eyebrow, amused. "Greetings, all. You're right on time."

"I'll kill you, Van Ness," Cafferty gasped.

"You must be the industrious Sarah Bowcut," Van Ness replied smugly, ignoring Cafferty. He turned his attention to Diego, still unconscious on the floor. "And I'm assuming the sleeping one is former gang member Diego Munoz. I believe he's the one who killed my employee Kevin Samuels, am I right? He and I will have to discuss that later."

Van Ness gestured to the guards.

"I'm sure you won't mind if my men assist your colleagues first, will you, Mr. Cafferty?" Van Ness said to the choking man.

Two guards strode over to Bowcut. The pressure of the hybrid's foot on her back decreased when they bent down and grabbed her by the arms. They hauled her up and marched her out of the elevator and down the marble hallway.

As she passed Van Ness and his piercing gaze, she kept a straight face despite the agonizing pain in her ribs and back. She had planned on looking into his eyes today, though never like this. Not as his defeated opponent, ready to suffer whatever fate he had in store for them.

The other two guards dragged the unconscious Munoz by the legs toward the operations center.

"All right, I think that's quite enough," Van Ness said, hitting a button on his control pad.

The hybrid released its grip on Cafferty's neck and he slumped back against the wall, gasping for air, coughing.

Van Ness leaned forward in his chair. "We've both been looking forward to this moment for quite some time, Thomas."

Cafferty slowly raised his head and locked eyes with Van Ness, and the two of them glared at each other.

"So . . . shall we begin?" Van Ness asked.

CHAPTER TWENTY-EIGHT

Let's begin with this," Cafferty said, standing up and rubbing his aching throat. "Where the hell is my wife?"

"Ellen, yes. Lovely to finally meet her," Van Ness replied. "You shall see her soon, Thomas, don't worry. And I must apologize for you getting caught in the middle of my mission in New York City. But rest assured, millions of creatures lost their lives that day, and humanity is safer for it."

Anger welled up inside Cafferty, only exacerbating the throbbing in his temples. His eye had swollen half shut after the genetic monstrosity had punched him in the face. The hybrid now hovered behind Cafferty, hand firmly on his shoulder, poised to strike him down in the blink of an eye. He could feel the creature's hot, acrid breath on his neck.

But the creature paled in comparison to the bigger monster he faced. The larger menace to the world, sitting before him in a wheelchair with a slight grin plastered across his bitter, wrinkled face.

The man he had vowed to end, who now had him at his mercy. His wife at his mercy. His friends at his mercy.

The world at his mercy.

The desperateness and seriousness of the situation made him shudder. He couldn't figure a way out.

"I must say, it does encourage me that after all you and Ellen have been through—infidelity, New York City, London—your marriage has not only survived, it seems to have thrived. Admirable," Van Ness said. "Or foolish. I must confess, I've never been married. I always thought it a distraction from my true purpose. I used to believe most humans were the worst thing to have ever walked this planet . . . until my father discovered these creatures, that is."

"Your true purpose? To hold the world hostage? To kill millions of innocent people?"

"Not the innocent. Those who need to be held accountable for the past."

"The past?" Cafferty asked.

"How quickly you Americans and British forget leaving my homeland in ruins, countless families torn apart, raping us of our wealth, our very history."

"Is *that* what this is about?" Cafferty asked incredulously. "Some twisted revenge for World War II?"

"Kindly don't forget World War I as well," Van Ness replied. "And butchering my mother, and countless other mothers, with the firestorm you created in Dresden. You seem to forget that history is written by the winners. Did you seriously think your war crimes would go unpunished in perpetuity? No, no . . . it's time to start over."

"So all that talk about saving humanity?"

"Is true. Just a certain part of humanity. The purest kind. Have you ever observed a butterfly in nature?" Van Ness asked. "People make the mistake of thinking they brainlessly fly from place to place. The truth is they have meticulously planned flight patterns. They follow the path needed to survive. The opposite behavior of you and your team and your egotistical regimes. The Allies' direction of travel has always been, and will always be, aimless, blinded by greed and bloated self-worth. Allied to stupidity."

"You're fucking insane," Cafferty said.

Irritated, Van Ness replied, "Language, Mr. Cafferty. Please. You are not an uncivilized opponent. Don't pretend to be."

"*Uncivilized?* You're talking about ending civilization!"

"I'm talking about raising up the only civilization that can propel humanity forward."

Cafferty couldn't listen to this much more. Even now, he could not stop thinking about strangling Van Ness. Shoving his wheelchair back so it slammed against the ground, then locking his hands around the lunatic's neck and delivering to him what Cafferty had suffered from the hybrid. Only with a more satisfying ending.

Right now, nothing would give him greater pleasure than to watch the life drain from this asshole's face. It's what he had dreamed about ever since he had walked away from the destroyed remains of the Z Train in one piece.

"No, this is not just about revenge," Van Ness continued. "No, no. Not just that."

Van Ness looked past Cafferty, lost in his own thoughts.

"I haven't been lying to you all. It's always been about defeating these creatures. Saving humanity that is worthy of being saved. But I might as well let them do my bidding first, right? To, as you say in English, kill two birds with one stone?

"No, this is about so much more than even just revenge or preservation. It's about my purpose, my . . ."

Van Ness turned back and gazed at Cafferty.

"For you and I, hasn't it always been about obsession? Legacy? Men like you and I do not stop. Am I incorrect?"

The words hit Cafferty hard.

Because . . .

Van Ness was right.

It was Tom's obsession with legacy that ruined his marriage, his obsession with the Z Train that set off a chain reaction that led to its destruction, his obsession with Van Ness that led to his wife being captured. Cafferty would not stop. He did not know how to.

The look on Cafferty's face told Van Ness everything he needed to know. A satisfied, understanding smile came across Van Ness' face.

"You're . . . not wrong, Albert," Cafferty said. "But you understand what that means for you and me, right?"

"Yes," Van Ness said, slowly nodding. "One of us must live."

"And one of us must die."

The men stared at each other intensely.

Cafferty saw the equal obsession. The equal motivation.

"Luckily for me, that outcome seems well determined, no? So enough conversation," Van Ness said. "Shall we commence with securing my legacy?"

CHAPTER TWENTY-NINE

Tom watched as Van Ness spun his wheelchair toward the glass dome. The hybrid maintained its unbreakable grip on Cafferty, shoving him down the hallway to the operations center.

Every step gave him a deeper sinking feeling. Van Ness wanted Cafferty to watch the next few hours unfold. What was in store for Ellen—or had already been done—sent a chill down Cafferty's spine. Van Ness had proven himself a showman, on top of a callous dictator and cold-blooded murderer.

Whatever he has planned next . . .

Van Ness approached Edwards in the middle of the operations center, Cafferty close behind, held in the powerful clutches of the hybrid. It seemed almost unbelievable to be here, in Van Ness' lair.

"Not so unlike your Visitors' Pavilion in New York City," Van Ness said proudly. "The difference is your Pavilion sits in ruins at the bottom of the Hudson River. This headquarters, this vision, will go down for centuries as the beating heart of humanity's victory."

Cafferty looked up at the various monitors that showed the Foundation's destruction of his country. Headlines scrolled across the CNN news feed of nuclear strikes in South Dakota and Nebraska and the panic ensuing in London. He struggled to believe it had actually happened. The lives lost. The potential nuclear fallout across the United States.

Van Ness is winning . . .

Bowcut and Munoz rested on their knees in front of him with pistols jammed against the backs of their heads. At least Diego had regained consciousness. Sarah attempted to look around. A guard twisted her head back toward the screens.

Cafferty glowered at Van Ness. "You're destroying the world."

"No, Thomas. I'm preserving it in the best way I know how—by creating the world as it *should* be."

"Nests fully destroyed in South Dakota and Nebraska, sir," Edwards chimed in. "The other bombs are coming online now."

"Other bombs?" Cafferty interjected.

Edwards motioned to a map with red dots under all major U.S. and UK cities. "Washington, Los Angeles, Chicago, Houston, Atlanta, Philadelphia, Boston, Manchester, Newcastle, Birmingham, Edinburgh, Dublin—"

"Enough!" Cafferty shouted. "Stop this madness, Van Ness!"

"But it must be done," Van Ness replied without emotion. "The nests under those cities *must* be destroyed. Or the creatures will rise, I assure you."

It became clear to Cafferty that Van Ness' personal vendetta was not Foundation policy. He just wasn't sure if that mattered—if there were nests under those cities, these fanatics would surely be okay with destroying them regardless.

Still, Cafferty scanned the operations center for an empathetic face, anyone who would realize the madness of this situation and help him. All he needed was one person to come to their senses and flip. Yet he found only grim expressions. With the London device due to go off in a few hours and devices already detonated in the United States, those expressions were soon to be reflected by billions of people around the world, as they saw their friends and family murdered and their own lives descend into chaos from a never-ending nuclear winter.

The world was going to be covered in literal darkness, even as the Foundation claimed it was eliminating exactly that.

Rapid laser fire from outside the thick glass dome caught Cafferty's attention. In the cavern, the creatures seemed to be stirring themselves into a frenzy, as if they could sense the coming apocalypse for their brethren.

Inside, he felt a similar frenzy and despaired at the fact that there was absolutely nothing he could do about it now.

He was going to witness the end of the world.

VAN NESS OBSERVED HOW TOM SEEMED TO COLLAPSE, THE hybrid's grip the only thing holding him up. He detested the creature standing there, even as he appreciated its power and purpose. This, he thought, was the only use for these things: as powerful tools to be utilized by those who knew what they were capable of.

Namely, himself.

The thought was a satisfying one, knowing he was one step closer to victory. To seeing his father's dream realized. To seeing those who had broken something in Otto Van Ness broken themselves. To seeing his family's legacy—even as he sat here in a wheelchair—made whole.

"If there is an organizational structure to these nests," he mused, "if these creatures do communicate with each other . . ."

He stared out the glass.

". . . they will remember this day for a long time."

"Kill the asshole if you get the chance," Munoz blurted out.

A guard slapped Diego on the side of the head with his gun, and he winced in pain.

Van Ness bristled at the language. His patience had almost expired with Munoz and Bowcut. They weren't necessary anymore. They were just Cafferty's foot soldiers, after all. It was one thing for the generals to still talk, but the cannon fodder? He caressed the laser pistol, tucked into the side of his chair, and considered whether to kill them before or after the main event.

No, I want them all to see this. They chose their side and would surely have shown me no mercy. Cafferty's humiliation needs to be witnessed by his entire team. They need to realize how much of a fool the man they were following is.

They would live to see the world *and* the creatures die.

And then he would kill them personally.

Smiling tightly, Van Ness turned back to Tom.

"Shall we all check on your wife, Mr. Cafferty?"

CHAPTER THIRTY

Van Ness hit a button on his control pad, and the back wall of the operations center parted smoothly, revealing a glass wall behind it.

Cafferty attempted to break free of the hybrid creature, but the clawed hand held firm.

"Let him see," Van Ness said.

The creature released its grip on Cafferty but followed closely behind. Cafferty sprinted for the glass wall, which looked down on a sterile all-white room, kind of like the view of an indoor racquetball court from above, but with nothing quite so mundane happening below.

His eyes widened in disbelief.

"What . . . have . . . you . . . *done*?" Cafferty cried out.

Through the one-way glass, down below, a terrified Ellen Cafferty stood strapped to a steel pole. Several loops of rope had been wound around the front of her orange coveralls. On the opposite side of the room, just out of attacking distance, a snarling creature was strapped to another pole with graphene restraints. The jet-black creature was massive and powerful, with formidable claws, tail, teeth. Saliva dripped from its mouth as its primal instinct overwhelmed its senses—an instinct to break free from its chains and to kill humans on sight. It roared at Ellen and lashed its tail, slamming the ground by her shoes, even as it furiously clawed at its own restraints and screeched in agony at the low-level light that was cast on its body.

Halfway between Ellen and the creature, a single laser gun lay on the ground.

"You twisted fuck!" Cafferty shouted, spinning rapidly and lunging with all his might at Van Ness. With lightning-fast speed, the hybrid creature caught him, its claws digging deep into his arms, sending blood pouring down his arms and immediately stopping his attack. The hybrid pushed Cafferty's torso back against the glass, spinning him around and pinning him there to watch.

The armed guards forced Bowcut and Munoz to the glass as well.

"One must live, and one must die," Van Ness commented. "Isn't that what we just said, Thomas?"

Cafferty continued to fight, twisting his body back and forth, only digging the hybrid's claws deeper into his own flesh.

"I take no pleasure in this, I assure you," Van Ness said. "But you must learn that grief feels much like fear."

Cafferty's head twisted around. "I already thought the creatures had killed her once. I lost friends in the tunnels under New York. Seen death on a personal scale, and just saw death on a massive scale. Do you think I don't know what grief and fear feel like? Go to hell."

Cafferty scanned the Foundation workers who sat at the operations center's workstations. All twenty staffers had fallen silent, mesmerized by the drama unfolding.

"Have you all lost your minds?" Cafferty shouted at them. *"Have you?"*

Their faces stared blankly at him, careful not to betray Van Ness in any way. He couldn't understand how so many had bought into this demented plot. The world stood on the cusp of destruction and they sat there, passively watching.

"Your protestations to my employees are worthless, Mr. Mayor," Van Ness said. "They understand the importance of this mission, and they are down here because their belief is as strong as mine. Your guilt will not work on them—there is nothing for any of us to feel guilty about.

"Besides, this is your doing," he continued. "This began the day you stood in front of the press in New York City, declaring your intent to hunt me down. To let the creatures win.

"Remember that?"

Of course he remembered that day. That was when he, Ellen, Diego, and Sarah created the David M. North Memorial Foundation to expose Van Ness for the monster he was. He had thought it was a purpose that would be lauded and remembered. That all now seemed like a distant memory. Insignificant, even, compared to the rapid escalation of the last two days.

"What was it you said?" Van Ness asked. "'*I promise you this—I will never stop . . .*' Do you wish you had stopped now, Thomas?"

Cafferty's eyes burned with hatred, but the words also fueled him. He *wouldn't* stop until his dying breath. The problem was he expected that would come soon, and his last thoughts would be about his own failure.

Just then, Cafferty noticed the slightest look on Edwards' face as he listened to Van Ness speak. It was a fleeting moment, but it almost resembled . . . doubt. The sickly looking number two shifted uncomfortably in his chair.

A high-pitched shriek grabbed Cafferty's attention. He spun back and faced the glass. Below, Ellen rocked her shoulders frantically back and forth. The creature tore at its constraints.

Cafferty banged on the glass desperately, but his wife could neither hear nor see the operations center above. It was no use.

A rope finally slipped off Ellen's right shoulder, and she freed her arm. She quickly tried to slip from the remainder of the restraints before the creature got loose and tore her to shreds. The twisted competition grew more and more desperate.

"This is going to be close, don't you think, my friend?" Van Ness asked Edwards.

Edwards didn't reply.

Ellen had almost freed herself. She uncoiled the rope from around her body. The creature gnawed at the last few threads of graphene. Both appeared seconds from freedom. Seconds from an attack.

Van Ness leaned forward in his chair. "I hadn't

expected it to be such a tight contest, though it does bring a mild level of excitement, yes?"

"Mild excitement?" Cafferty snapped. "You asshole, that's my wife!"

"Facing what all of humanity would be up against if you had your way, Thomas."

The creature ripped the last pieces of restraint free with its three sets of teeth. Ellen wriggled loose from the rope. For a heartbeat, they stared at each other, both free of the steel poles.

Cafferty held his breath.

Ellen jumped forward and rolled onto the ground toward the laser. The creature's tail whipped over her head and slammed into the wall, tearing a gouge in the solid rock. Roaring in frustration, it lunged at her with all its might, but in missing, it had given her the extra second she needed.

She grabbed the laser and fired.

A red-hot beam sliced right through the creature's chest. Thick yellow blood sprayed the pristine white room and spattered across Ellen's face. The shrieking creature toppled backward, its torso hanging to the side, attached only by its left rib cage.

Ellen scrambled away, then fired another beam at the dying creature, instantly carving its limbs to pieces. She slumped back against the wall, heaving, tears streaming down her face.

Cafferty, too, welled up with tears.

Thank God . . .

"Very good, very good indeed!" Van Ness began to clap. "What a show!"

In the background behind Van Ness, Cafferty noticed a distinct look of disgust on Edwards' face.

Once again, he wondered if he had a potential ally. Maybe. But then again, *any* normal person would find such a display revolting.

And any normal person would have seen the Foundation as reprehensible a long time ago.

Back inside the room, Ellen now stood, still breathing heavily. She wiped the creature's blood from her face and silently began to gesticulate at the one-way glass above, obviously assuming Van Ness was watching.

Intrigued, Van Ness hit a button on the wall and a speaker activated.

"—ck you, Van Ness! You failed! FUCK! YOU!" Ellen shouted, filling the operations center with her defiance.

Seizing the opportunity, Cafferty yelled out, "*Ellen!*"

Van Ness quickly switched off the speaker, but Ellen's eyes had gone wide, clearly having recognized her husband's voice in that moment.

"It's a shame. At least before, she would have died without unnecessary hope. Ah, well." Van Ness turned his attention to Edwards. "My friend, will you please have Mrs. Cafferty disposed of now? The incinerator will do. Same goes for our friends Bowcut and Munoz afterward."

Edwards nodded and motioned to the guards in the corner. They quickly left the operations center.

"As for you, Thomas, I believe everyone deserves a second chance. A rematch between you and my hybrid creature here. Perhaps you'll fair better than you did in the elevator. But that is the third act.

First, the show must continue." Van Ness turned toward the workers manning their stations. "Status?"

"Mr. Van Ness," a female staff member called from the console, "the bombs are coming online and will be ready for detonation in less than one minute."

Cafferty looked at all the pulsing red lights on the screens indicating the location of Van Ness' nuclear bombs.

"My God," Cafferty said.

"No, not God," he replied. "Albert Van Ness."

CHAPTER THIRTY-ONE

The overhead screens showed dusk falling on several American cities. The dark streets of London were mostly deserted, besides the gridlock on the highways as hundreds of thousands tried to escape the city. Most would not make it out of the bomb radius in time . . . and those who did would almost certainly be driving toward another bomb anyway.

Cafferty remained under the hybrid's powerful grip, unable to break free in any way. Ellen stood below him in the fighting area, laser in hand, back pressed against the wall, thankfully still alive with the creature's torn-open corpse by her boots.

At least he hadn't had to see his wife torn apart by the creature. He was so proud of her, the way she had acted, and his heart swelled at how brave she was. But then it squeezed tight when he realized what Van Ness had just sent his men to do. Her bravery just meant she had delayed her death a little longer.

He deflated once more, knowing he wouldn't even be able to display the courage Ellen just had.

MUNOZ EYED THE TABLET-LIKE PANEL ON VAN NESS' WHEEL-chair. He used it to control the creature and seemingly everything else in the operations center. It looked like it was activated by the German's palm print, though, which meant that even if Diego could snag it, it would be of little use without Van Ness' hand. If he had time, of course, he could probably figure it out. But he didn't have time.

None of them had time.

BOWCUT AND CAFFERTY STARED WIDE-EYED AT THE WORLD map displaying the nuclear devices coming online. Cafferty reckoned there were at least thirty bombs, though he'd lost count. The majority were located in the United States, the United Kingdom, Canada, Australia, and New Zealand, with a few spread around western Europe. He couldn't even dream of the devastation that would shatter parts of the globe. The millions of lives lost.

Cafferty looked up at the other monitors in the operations center. On-screen, news channels were covering the devastation in Lincoln and Rapid City. The drone footage was shocking. Both cities flattened, reduced to ashes and flames. It looked like the seventh circle of hell. Nothing remained except carnage and death. The radiation would take years to dissipate, rendering both cities uninhabitable for generations. In nearby cities like Deadwood and Sundance, the footage was even more heartbreaking: children's faces burned, skin boiling from the spreading radiation; people blinded by the nuclear flash, wandering the streets aimlessly, covered in ash, their skin literally smoking.

"Jesus . . ." Bowcut whispered.

Tears poured down Cafferty's face at the senselessness of it all. Once more he looked toward Edwards. The man stood there, staring at the screens as well, a nauseated look ghosting across his face.

Van Ness circled around the command table in Cafferty's direction. The rubber wheels squeaked as he advanced. The bombs coming online had sparked a look of satisfaction in his eyes. Edwards followed with a grim expression, and his shoes clacked on the polished stone surface. When Edwards neared, Cafferty noticed sweat beading his brow, despite the coolness of the operations center, and dark rings circled his beady eyes.

"Now for the final act, Thomas," Van Ness said. "The vision my father had dreamed about. Destroying millions of creatures and avenging the Fatherland's defeat all at once."

Munoz attempted to say something then, but the guard elbowed him in the sternum, knocking the wind out of him.

Edwards grimaced and took a half step forward, then froze. Munoz could tell something was going on with the man, something that was at odds with Van Ness. That much was clear, but Munoz quickly dismissed the notion. A savior wasn't going to appear.

"I wasn't addressing you, Mr. Munoz," Van Ness snapped at him. "You are not part of my plan."

Suddenly, a large creature smashed into the glass dome of the operations center, and everyone—including Van Ness—jumped from the shock. The enormous jet-black creature banged its head repeatedly against the impenetrable glass, shaking the dome itself. Moments later, a second creature crashed into the glass, and Cafferty instinctively backed away.

Van Ness laughed. "Looks like they're not fond of what I'm doing."

The turrets quickly spun and homed in on the creatures hanging on the glass dome.

"Please excuse my crassness, but on this one rare occasion, it feels justified," Van Ness said. "*Fuck 'em.*"

The laser guns sliced through the creatures, and their torn-open torsos fell lifelessly into the cavern below.

Cafferty stared through the transparent dome at the cavern. He could still barely believe that Van Ness had stationed his headquarters right in the middle of an active creatures' nest, similar in size to the football-stadium-sized one in New York. Even worse, Cafferty could tell the creatures were in a state of frenzy, darting back and forth in the shadows, desperately avoiding the lasers and brilliant beams of light. The lasers now fired nonstop, increasing their bursts dramatically in frequency, turrets spinning constantly to battle the creatures. It was almost as if the monsters knew what was coming.

But how's that possible?

Van Ness snapped his fingers.

The hybrid twisted Cafferty's head toward the German. Resistance was futile against the brute strength, but Cafferty held his head low.

"Chin up," Van Ness ordered. "This will all be over soon."

Van Ness pulled a gold-tipped swagger stick from the side of his chair. He prodded the end under Cafferty's jaw and forced it upward.

"Why don't we begin the countdown now?"

Cafferty looked at the time on the screens: 11:17 P.M.

"It's not midnight yet!" Cafferty said angrily, watching the news coverage of the gridlocked roads out of London. "Give them more time to evacuate, goddamn it!"

"War does not have the luxury of time," Van Ness replied. "Mr. Cafferty, I'd like to bestow on you the honor of pressing the button to begin the sixty-second countdown till detonation. Our new history will regard you as the man who exterminated millions of creatures and helped save humanity. I won't make you thank me for the honor."

A glint appeared in Cafferty's eye. Van Ness had finally revealed himself, like every sleezy politician he had encountered in his career as mayor. Cafferty finally knew exactly what his adversary wanted, and he'd be damned if he gave it to him. Van Ness wouldn't stop until he achieved the ultimate humiliation of the mayor. Pressing the button was it.

Let's teach him how New Yorkers deal with assholes . . .

"So, Thomas," Van Ness continued. "Please hit the button, if you will."

"Albert . . ." Cafferty said, emotionless and calm. "Please excuse my crassness, but on this *one rare occasion*, it feels justified. Go fuck yourself."

Diego belly-laughed, only to be struck in the sternum again by the guard.

"Press the button, Mr. Mayor," Van Ness repeated sternly.

"Go fuck yourself, Albert."

"*Press* the button, Cafferty!" Van Ness said, losing his temper.

"Go *fuck* yourself, Al."

"PRESS THE GODDAMN BUTTON!" Van Ness screamed, veins bulging in his temple.

"GO. FUCK. YOURSELF."

Seething, Van Ness shrugged at him. "It's no matter. If you don't want to do it, I'll make you do it."

"You can't."

"Really?"

Van Ness banged new commands into his control pad. Munoz spied the device out of the corner of his eye, studying how the Foundation's leader was navigating through the system. The control pad beeped with new orders.

The hybrid creature squeezed Cafferty's neck on command, choking off his oxygen supply. It clutched his forearm and forced his hand downward toward the execute button on the console. As Cafferty's face turned beet red and the veins bulged in his temples, he fought with all his might to keep his hand away from the button.

Fight, Tom, fight!

The hybrid was too strong. Cafferty's arm lowered toward the button against his will. He closed his fingers into a fist as an act of defiance.

"You *will* press that button, even if I have to tear your fingers off!" Van Ness screamed.

One by one, the creature forcibly uncurled Cafferty's fingers, nearly ripping the digits off his body. It straightened his index finger to press the button.

It's no use . . . The creature is too strong . . .

"This mission . . . my mission . . . cannot be stopped, Mr. Mayor. *You* cannot stop me!" Van Ness shouted.

"Your mission? You mean your sick, twisted quest for revenge?!" Bowcut shouted, trying to break free from the guards.

"You're damn right I want revenge!" Van Ness screamed back at her, fury in his eyes. "I'VE HAD ENOUGH!"

Van Ness raised his arm over his head, clutched his hand into a fist, and slammed down as hard as he could toward the detonation button.

Suddenly, a razor-sharp creature's claw sliced Van Ness' hand off at the wrist, a fraction of a moment before his fist could detonate the nuclear bombs. The severed appendage hit the ground with a loud thud.

Blood pumped out from the radial artery in Van Ness' wrist in rhythmic intervals. He raised the stump of his arm in front of his face with a look of openmouthed horror. He looked upward to see who his attacker was.

Allen Edwards stood in front of him with a blood-soaked creature's claw in his hand, the one he kept in his suit jacket pocket at all times.

Van Ness' piercing scream reverberated around the glass dome.

CHAPTER THIRTY-TWO

Van Ness' scream died out, leaving his gasping breaths as the only sound in the operations center. Blood had soaked the forearm of his suit jacket and stained the left side of his chair, and it dripped from the spokes of his wheelchair.

Munoz couldn't believe his eyes.

Everyone in the immediate vicinity had frozen. The guards. The operations staff manning the consoles. Even the hybrid creature, who maintained Cafferty in a tight headlock to the point where his face had started to turn purple.

Outside, creatures threw themselves at the glass dome in increasing numbers. Perhaps hundreds, all forced into the light for reasons he didn't understand. Lashing their tails against the wall. Raking the thick graphene glass with their claws. The powerful turrets groaned against the creatures' telekinetic attempts to stop them. Red-hot laser beams sliced the monsters apart as fast as possible to defend the command center from the sudden onslaught.

This unnerving, soundless spectacle sent a shiver down Munoz's spine. Even if they somehow managed to survive the Foundation, which he doubted, he guessed it wouldn't be long before the creatures figured out a way to tear them all to shreds.

The razor-sharp claw—now dripping with Van Ness' blood—hung by Edwards' side.

"I'm so very sorry, Albert," Edwards said, peering down at his frantic boss, who desperately tried to wrap his necktie around his severed wrist as a makeshift tourniquet.

Having completed the knot and slowed the bleeding, the old German glared up at his number two. "Why, Allen?" he spat.

"Because this was never supposed to be about *revenge*."

"It's part of our mission! Part of your damned twenty years of loyalty!" Van Ness fired back.

"It was part of *your* mission. The Foundation exists to save humanity from these horrid creatures. On that, I still stand with you. But this private war . . . this *vendetta* . . . is solely yours. And I cannot allow it to continue. I'm sorry, Albert."

"I understand, my dear friend. I am so very sorry, too."

Edwards looked confused. "What do you—"

Suddenly, a laser beam sliced a hole through Edwards' forehead, and his eyes widened in shock. Slowly, the laser beam moved downward, slicing his face in half. Edwards' lifeless body crashed to the ground in an instant, blood pouring out of his neck, hot viscera filling the room with its stench.

Munoz traced the laser back to its source—a small weapon clutched in Van Ness' remaining hand, by his right side.

Seizing the moment of terror, Bowcut slammed her elbow hard into one of her guards' guts, instantly knocking the wind out of him. The burly man hunched over, only to be met by her knee smashing into his face, breaking his nose. He crumbled to the ground.

The guard watching over Munoz swung his gun around to fire at Bowcut, but she had anticipated that and was predictably faster, blocking his arm as he pulled the trigger, sending a bullet ricocheting off the impervious glass dome. The bullet careened off the walls until it lodged itself into the back of a worker's skull at the central command station. His head crashed against a keyboard. Blood spilled across the workstation.

Bowcut's fist landed squarely in the guard's face. He staggered to the side, freeing Munoz momentarily.

Van Ness raised the laser weapon to slice a beam through Munoz and Bowcut, but Cafferty swung his leg and kicked the gun from the German's hand before he had a chance to fire.

The hybrid creature immediately tossed Cafferty like a rag doll against the wall. He hit shoulder first and slammed into the ground, wincing in agony.

Bowcut charged the hybrid and crashed into it with all her might. The creature barreled back into Van Ness' wheelchair, knocking his control tablet to the ground.

Munoz, sensing his opportunity, scrambled to his

feet as the hybrid swung a right hook at the side of Bowcut's head. Its fist connected with a dull thud, and she stumbled backward.

Four more guards rushed into the operations center, weapons drawn.

We're outnumbered, Diego thought. *And outgunned. Come on, Diego. Think of a way out of this.*

From the ground, Cafferty kicked a rolling chair at the first guard, tripping the man up. He followed it up with a bone-crunching elbow to the man's jaw.

The guard hit the stone floor like a bag of bricks. His gun flew from his hand and skidded away, coming to a rest next to the recovering Bowcut.

"Kill them all!" Van Ness shouted, reaching down for the control pad.

Munoz leaped for the device, snatched it and the severed hand, and quickly backed away. Amid the confusion, he pressed the cold index finger on the home button and the screen flashed to life. Then he started navigating through every application.

"Diego! Turn 'em off!" Cafferty yelled.

No shit, Tom.

"On it, boss!" he shouted back, finding the commands to take the bombs offline one at a time. He executed the order for the thermonuclear weapon underneath Manhattan to deactivate, then quickly deactivated London.

New York City safe. London safe.

Just thirty more cities to go . . .

Van Ness looked up at the monitors and saw the red circles around those cities blink off, one by one.

"Stop him!" Van Ness shouted at the three remaining armed men on their feet.

One of them aimed at Munoz, but Cafferty tackled him to the ground just as he pulled the trigger.

The bullet zipped past Munoz's head and slammed into a server.

Stay focused, Diego!

But he momentarily couldn't take his eyes off the ensuing death match. Bowcut had grabbed the loose gun on the floor. She spun on her knee toward a guard and pumped two rounds into his chest. He toppled backward and crashed against the ground.

The remaining guard fired at Bowcut. She screamed and collapsed to both knees after a round tore through her ankle. The man spun to face the unarmed Munoz and advanced with a sneering grin.

The guard had clearly underestimated Sarah, though. Munoz looked beyond him at her regaining her composure in a matter of seconds and retaking aim.

Bowcut fired twice, hitting the guard in his back with a centered mass. He face-planted on the ground right in front of Munoz's boot. Diego rammed his heel into the man's jaw, hard and fast. A second kick to his temple knocked him out, in case the bullets hadn't done the job.

Munoz returned his focus back to the tablet and deactivated two more bombs.

Washington, D.C., safe. Sydney safe.

Fast, heavy footsteps pounded the stone.

Three more guards entered the operations center and sprinted toward the fight. Workers at their stations scrambled away from the chaos, ducking for cover to avoid stray bullets.

All the while, the creatures were slamming against the glass.

Bowcut spun and fired rapidly, taking one guard out, but missing the other two before they were upon her. One kicked her in the face, sending her flying backward, smacking her skull against the ground. Meanwhile, Cafferty wrestled on the ground with the guard he had tackled, trying to gain the upper hand.

Van Ness stared at the overhead screens with a look of horror. Munoz glanced up at him every time he took another thermonuclear device offline.

Atlanta safe. Los Angeles safe.

Van Ness roared in anger. He spun his electric wheelchair in the direction of the central command station computer.

"Tom," Munoz yelled. "He's gonna set off the bombs!"

Cafferty caught Van Ness' actions in the corner of his eye as he wrestled with the guard. He finally spun the guard on his back, gaining the upper hand. He raised his fist to drive it home, but as he swung downward someone grabbed his arm midair.

Or rather, something.

The hybrid creature had caught Cafferty's punch and was lifting him off the ground by his neck, slamming him hard against the wall. For the second time today the air was being choked out of him, as he watched Bowcut fight for her life and Munoz frantically try to deactivate more nuclear bombs. All of his senses were heightened, even as his pulse pounded in his ears.

Nobody else was coming to help end this madness.

Millions—billions—of lives depended on the three of them.

The cost of failure had never weighed more heavily on his shoulders.

This really is it.

Death or glory for a final time.

Van Ness approached the side of the central command station and pushed the dead worker's head off the desk. The body slid to the ground, leaving a streak of blood across the keys and the execute button.

Two more pulsing red lights stopped on the overhead screen. *Manchester and Dublin safe.* Munoz, reliable as ever, continued to deactivate bombs. But he wasn't fast enough—some bombs would go off if nobody could free themselves to stop the crazy old man.

"Sarah, stop Van Ness!" Cafferty rasped.

Bowcut tried to free herself from the two guards who were overpowering her, but it was no use. Cafferty knew she couldn't reach Van Ness in time. She gave him a look of desperation. He returned the expression while attempting to wrestle away the hybrid's powerful arms.

Six more black-uniformed guards raced toward the operations center. Their footsteps hammered closer, echoing around the ceiling and walls.

Gasping for air that wouldn't come, Cafferty saw the enemy racing directly toward him. But he also noticed that the creatures had stopped attacking the glass dome and the turrets had stopped firing. It had become still in the nest outside.

Cafferty kicked the creature with all his might, but still nothing worked. He hung there, choking.

We're out of options. It's over.

His vision fogged and darkness began to overwhelm him. Van Ness smiled up at him from the command desk's control panel.

We lost.

Suddenly, a laser blast swept across the room from left to right, cutting through all six guards at chest level. Twelve severed arms dropped to the ground. Weapons clattered next to them. The momentum of the men initially carried them forward a step, until the upper halves of their bodies separated from their torsos.

All of them simultaneously collapsed.

Blood and guts spilled across the polished stone floor in every direction.

A fraction of a second later, another laser beam sliced the hybrid creature's arm right off, freeing Cafferty from its clutches. He fell to the ground, gasping for air.

The creature spun to face its attacker just as another laser beam sliced through it diagonally. It slid apart and crashed to the ground in front of Cafferty.

He looked up at his savior.

ELLEN STOOD, TAKING IN THE CARNAGE SHE'D JUST UNLEASHED. The two guards Edwards had sent for her seemed to have not taken into account the fact that she still had the laser Van Ness had left in the room—probably because no one had expected her to win.

Their mistake. She had grown tired of being underestimated. There was nothing she would not do to ensure the safety of her son. She had to survive so that David could live, and she'd be damned if a group of fanatics was going to get in her way.

They gave her the weapon, and her instinct to protect her young—coupled with the training Bowcut had insisted on—was being put to deadly use.

She rapidly cut down the guards on Bowcut with precision. When no more Foundation soldiers remained, she rushed to her husband's side.

"Tom, are you all right?" she said, clutching his face.

Cafferty struggled to gain his voice through his bruised neck. "Stop . . . Van Ness . . ." he growled.

Ellen whipped her head around. The old German raised his remaining hand, ready to slam down the execute button.

"You've lost, Cafferty," Van Ness shouted. He swung his fist downward.

"*No!*" Tom screamed. Ellen tried to bring the laser up but knew she'd be too late.

Less than an inch from the button, however, Van Ness' hand froze midair. His eyebrows furled, and he seemed to be concentrating hard to bring his hand down onto the button.

Nothing.

His arm wouldn't move, and it shook, as if he was fighting an invisible force. A look of confusion spread across his face. For the first time, Cafferty witnessed a new emotion on Van Ness' face.

Fear.

Van Ness' eyes bulged. His backside jerked up a few inches out of the wheelchair. The sight paralyzed Ellen, and though her gun was up, she didn't fire. She noticed as Tom scrambled to his feet and knew he was wondering the same thing she was:

What the hell is happening?

Van Ness' body lifted into a standing position, seemingly on its own, as if his disabilities had suddenly vanished.

"What the . . . ?" Ellen muttered, watching the bizarre scene unfold in front of her. All eyes in the operations center were glued to the strange spectacle, except for Munoz's, as he continued to deactivate more bombs.

Terrified, Van Ness rapidly looked in all directions, until focusing beyond the glass dome at the cavern. And then she understood.

"The creatures . . ." Cafferty said.

The entire nest of creatures had focused their telekinetic power to target Van Ness directly.

Seconds later, Van Ness' frail, upright body slammed into the glass dome's internal wall with tremendous force. He tried to push himself away from the glass with his right hand and his bloody stump, but collapsed against it, like he was being crushed by an ultrapowerful magnet. His screaming face pressed against the glass so forcefully that blood began to run out the corners of his eyes and his nostrils. His head was locked against the glass, unable to turn in any way, facing right at Tom. He glared at Cafferty as drops of blood streamed down his face and dribbled from his chin.

"Help . . . me," Van Ness pleaded in anguish. "Hit the damned pedal by my chair. Launch the super-weapon."

Ellen looked over at Tom, who was watching indifferently, betraying no emotion on his face. But she knew her husband. No matter how much he hated Van Ness, how much he wanted the man dead (just as she did), Tom wasn't a monster. He wasn't someone who could easily kill someone or watch someone—even a person as evil as Van Ness—die without feeling the loss of life. Yet she also understood he didn't want to show Van Ness he actually cared that he was witnessing the bastard's final, pain-filled moments, because she felt the same way.

She took his hand.

He looked down at it, as if unsure of what he was seeing. Then he looked into her eyes.

"Tom . . . stop this," she said softly.

He looked at her, incredulous.

"It's over."

"It's not over, Ellen. All the lives lost because of this asshole . . ."

There was pain in his eyes as he struggled between all he had gone through and all he still wanted to do. She squeezed his hand.

"Van Ness started it. And I'm going to finish it."

"There's already so much blood here," Ellen replied. "You don't need to put any more on your hands."

He turned back to look at Van Ness, and she saw his eyes go rapt by the sight. She watched, too.

It was gruesome. The glass remained impervious. Van Ness' body and internal organs were not.

His intestines were being pulled toward the edges of his skin, arteries and veins shifting inside his body as if a powerful vacuum wanted to suck everything out. As if the creatures wanted to tear every atom of Albert Van Ness apart.

He'd be dead in a matter of moments.

Van Ness' screams grew in intensity. Blood trickled out of his ears, down his chest.

Ellen turned to her husband. Only she could break the former mayor's gaze from what he most wanted in life—the death of this monster. He turned to look at her.

"Tom . . . stop this," she pleaded.

"No!" He was shocked at her suggestion, and it pained her that maybe he *was* too far gone. "Ellen, no. He—"

"He'll pay for his crimes, we'll make sure of it," she said quietly, cutting him off. "But Tom, not like this. This isn't who I married. This isn't David's father."

They gazed into each other's eyes, all the love and hope she had ever felt trying to melt the ice she saw staring back at her. Somewhere in there—behind the bruises and pain and fear—was her husband.

She hoped.

"Show me . . . show *him* . . . you're better than this."

Cafferty's mind thought back to when he almost lost Ellen because of his obsession with the Z train.

He was about to lose her again.

That's not going to happen.

And as Van Ness was about to be torn apart, Cafferty slammed his foot down on the pedal to launch the superweapon.

In the cavern—now darkened from creatures attacking and taking out the globes—a shimmering cloud puffed out over the dome and spread in the stale air. Seconds later, the glint of a strobe arced into the center of the thousands of foil pieces, then activated.

Spears of light shot to every dark cave, crevice, and corner. Millions of refractions, lighting the place up to the point where Cafferty squinted and shielded his eyes from the intense glare.

Intense rays punched against the clusters of creatures. Faint shrieks emanated through the glass as they scattered and fled toward the nearest caves. It brought back memories of activating the IMAX in the Visitors' Pavilion, only thousands of times more brilliant.

Released from the creatures' telekinetic grip, Van Ness slid down the glass wall and lay prone on the ground. He struggled to push himself onto his back with his remaining hand, and the fire returned to his bloodied eyes.

Cafferty strode over to him. Not letting him die was fair enough, but he wasn't going to be denied this next move. He hunched next to the old German.

"Mr. Van Ness . . ." Cafferty said, drawing back his fist. "New York sends its regards."

Cafferty smashed his fist into Van Ness' face, knocking him unconscious.

It's over.

CHAPTER THIRTY-THREE

THREE MONTHS LATER

Tom Cafferty stood behind a lectern in front of the United Nations General Assembly. Representatives from every nation packed the semi-circular rows of desks to his front. Organized in alphabetical order. Each with equal rights in this room. The secretary-general and president sat to his rear, in front of the vast gold wall with the huge UN logo emblazoned at its center.

The secretary-general had given a speech detailing how the French president and key members of his team had been arrested in connection with the Foundation. He had also described how multinational teams had raided sites across the globe to finally shut down Van Ness' operation. If this, coupled with the two nuclear detonations in America and the hosts of dormant bombs under other cities, wasn't enough to compel the world to act, Cafferty wasn't sure what would.

He had been introduced as the man who had

saved millions of lives, and the standing ovation was only just dying down after two minutes. The overwhelming sense of satisfaction brought a tear to his eye. The achievements of his team, against all odds, and his personal vindication. He looked to his left, where President Brogan, Ellen, Diego, and Sarah stood. All smiling. All here to back him. His wife cradled David in her arms, and she gave Cafferty her "you got this" nod.

He cast his mind back to the blue room in City Hall. That was the day he started this mission, though he never expected it would lead here. He was now a major player on the international stage after taking down Van Ness and the high-level politicians who had conspired against humanity.

But that just meant there was more work to do.

The last of the claps faded.

Cafferty cleared his throat and leaned toward his mic. "Ladies and gentlemen, I stand before you today thankful to be alive. Thankful that my family is alive, that my team is alive, and so, *so* many more survived that day. And my heart remains broken for all those who perished at the hands of an enemy they didn't know existed, both human and monster—although it wasn't always clear where those lines were drawn the last few days. And that is part of the problem we still face.

"Which is why I'm here. I'm here to tell you that it is the dawn of a new day on this planet. I'm here to tell you about a new path forward, a new shared responsibility, a new common mission.

"I'm here to tell you all that there is only one thing that should matter to any of us now."

Cafferty looked back at Ellen, and she gave him a supporting nod.

"Ladies and gentlemen, we are a world of different nations. Different peoples and cultures and religions. We have different dreams and beliefs and ideas about how the world should work. All of that is wonderful . . . but it can also be our undoing. Because of those differences, we allowed the Foundation for Human Advancement to further divide us, to use our differences against us.

"Happily, I'm here to tell you that with the Foundation for Human Advancement no longer a threat, we have a chance to examine those differences. To examine them . . . and *forget them*. Because they are nothing compared to the threat we still face.

"Citizens of the world, I'm here to tell you that the crimes of Albert Van Ness pale in comparison to what these creatures"—and with a touch of a button on the podium, images of the creatures filled the screens behind Tom, causing gasps to ripple through the chamber—"are capable of. I'm here to tell you it is them versus us.

"I'm here to tell you that if we don't find a way to fight them that doesn't require destroying the earth to do so, we might not have a world left where humanity—all of humanity—is safe."

He stood back as he waited for the translators to finish spreading his word. Slowly, the faces looked back at him . . . and he sensed a growing indifference in the room. Almost unbelievably so. After what the world had just been through, his presence—his call to action—was being met by this?

Do these people not get it?

For a lingering moment, he felt some of the frustration Van Ness had voiced. To be met by such silence. *Is this why Van Ness had taken things into his own hands? Is that what I'm going to have to do, too?*

He cast the thought to the back of his mind, assuring himself that he was nothing like that monster.

Yet now doubts lingered . . .

He pressed on.

"You have seen the evidence. And there can be no doubt that the creatures exist. The world has a new common enemy, an enemy that does not discriminate based on nationality, creed, or race. An enemy that does not care about borders, or respect elections, or differentiate between men, women, and children. An enemy that is climbing closer and closer to the surface of the earth. An enemy that outnumbers us, is evolving rapidly, *understands* our actions . . . and is hell-bent on revenge."

Cafferty knew his last sentence would evoke a reaction. The leaders of various nations began murmuring in the assembly hall finally. He waited for them to die down before continuing.

"That doesn't mean we are without hope. My team—the David M. North Foundation—has the know-how to take them down. We will partner with any and all of you to end this global scourge once and for all. No blackmailing, no infiltration into your administrations, and no weapons of mass destruction. We are here to help all of humanity. I urge you to take us up on our offer."

A warm ripple of applause followed his words. Cafferty paused to take a sip of water to moisten his parched throat. He had made big speeches before, but never anything of this gravity. Millions, if not billions, of eyes were on him. He knew this speech was being broadcast around the globe. He imagined his face on screens across the world—in living rooms, in bars, and on pretty much any device that could stream or receive a television signal. He had to make this count.

"This is not a time to rest," Cafferty continued. "A stain on the world has been removed. But now, with him gone, it is up to us to act as one and to win the war against the creatures."

Cafferty grimly eyed the dignitaries again.

"Let me be absolutely clear with you: humanity is at a crossroads. If we take the wrong direction, we will end up as a forgotten chapter in this planet's history. If we take the right road, we'll flourish for another thousand years to come. The David M. North Foundation is ready to show you the way."

There was scattered, light clapping throughout the hall. Cafferty's brow furrowed, and he wondered how they could be so nonchalant about what he was telling them. He wondered if they thought this was a battle that was already won.

They don't get it.

He walked off the dais.

DAVID'S HEAD SHIFTED ON ELLEN'S SHOULDER, AND SHE gently readjusted him on her hip and rubbed his back.

"Tom did well up there," President Brogan said. "Are you coming to our meeting tomorrow?"

"He's hired some fresh blood to do my old job.

The David North Foundation is expanding fast, but it's about time I spent some quality time with my son."

"Completely understand." Brogan turned to Bowcut and Munoz. "What about you two? Besides the White House reception, we've hardly had time to speak."

"Stuff to do, Madam President," Munoz said. "Besides, you don't want a bottom-feeder like me bringing down the class of the Oval Office. It's been nice to meet you, but that's not my scene."

"Same here," Bowcut added. "These official occasions don't suit me, though I promised to show my face for Tom. That said, something tells me we'll meet again, Madam President."

"I'm sure we will. Thanks again. Your country is grateful."

"I think we're all grateful the rest of those bombs didn't go off," Bowcut replied. "Just remember, none of us want medals. We're happy to let Tom be the face of the Foundation, because it lets Diego and me get our work done."

"Not a problem. There are other ways to express our gratitude."

"Just a thanks will do," Munoz replied. "And maybe a break on our taxes."

Brogan smiled but made no promises.

"Worth a shot," he muttered.

With that, he and Bowcut headed off and slipped behind a curtain. Both unassuming, both heroes. Neither wanted any public credit.

Pride swelled inside Ellen as she watched her

team leave. She and Brogan turned their attention back to the stage.

As Ellen watched her husband walking toward her, his eyes lit with resolution, the nagging feeling she had felt during the speech had finally formed into a conclusion.

Tom had sounded like . . . Van Ness. Granted, the two men both had obsessive personalities, but had different goals. Except now the madman's goals were her husband's. Tom had stepped in to fill the void, and his rhetoric was frighteningly similar. She wondered if this was how the Foundation for Human Advancement had begun before Van Ness warped its mission.

"How did I do?" Cafferty asked.

"Great, though I don't see you having much free time going forward."

"I'll always have time for you and David." Cafferty grabbed the toddler from her arms and lifted him into the air. "Isn't that right, buddy?"

"I hope it's true, Tom, for all of our sakes."

The secretary-general's assistant came over. Tom handed David back to his wife and let himself be ushered away.

Ellen understood the drive behind her husband's mission. She believed in it, too. But every time she had encountered his unwavering determination, it had led him to dangerous places for different reasons. They had been lucky before, because he had been able to find his way back. This time, though, she worried he might go too far. She thought of how quickly he had given David back to her. How easily he had left them here, by themselves, as he went off to save the world.

The thing was, the world now knew the threat. He could always step back—Diego was in a better position to explain how the technology worked; Sarah could train others in the tactics to actually fight the creatures. He could be with his family, having done enough to atone for whatever mistakes he felt were his from New York.

But Tom being Tom, she knew he wouldn't.

She feared that next time, their family might end up paying the price.

CAFFERTY STRODE INTO THE SECRETARY-GENERAL'S PRIVATE office. The walnut desk and bookcases and the sumptuous leather chairs surprised him. He had expected something more somber in the UN building.

The secretary-general sat snug in a leather chair. He was a Tunisian with gray hair and light brown skin, and he encouraged Cafferty toward the opposite chair. A glass table sat between the two with a bottle of whiskey and two glasses.

Cafferty sat down, loosened his tie, and poured himself a generous measure. He needed it after making that speech. An internal pressure valve had been released, and he wanted to relax. He took a sip, but then put the glass down.

He couldn't relax just yet.

"We received your request this morning," the secretary-general said. "I have to say, Tom, it came as a bit of a surprise."

Cafferty's eyes narrowed. "A surprise? We need

to dramatically scale up our resources to win this fight. The money to enable my foundation to do this is hardly an unreasonable price, Secretary-General."

"This is similar to what Albert Van—"

"With all due respect, sir," Cafferty replied, cutting the man off, "do not compare me to him again."

"Tom, I didn't mean it like that."

"I'll be totally transparent, and the world governments will see where every penny goes. Don't worry about that part, Secretary-General. But rest assured, any complacency now on all our parts will cost lives. That's a risk I'm simply not prepared to take. Are you, sir?"

The men eyed each other. The secretary-general didn't answer immediately. Instead, he scrutinized Cafferty's face, which transformed from relaxed to irritated.

"Speak to your team," Cafferty said in a firm tone. "Let me know your answer by tomorrow afternoon."

Cafferty downed the whiskey and rose to his feet. This meeting was over. His terms had been made clear, and he still had plenty of individual countries to deal with.

The world stands on the brink, now more than ever.

CHAPTER THIRTY-FOUR

Somewhere in the middle of the Atlantic Ocean, waves crashed hard against all sides of a strange-looking metal rig. The anchored steel structure resembled a much, much smaller oil rig, but the only things on the platform were a helipad and an unusual concrete box, no bigger than a car garage. Carved into each side of the concrete box were four small, circular portholes with steel bars running through them. The portholes were unusually low to the ground, resulting in a constant barrage of sea spray splashing into the concrete cell.

The silhouette of a lone figure peered through the bars of a porthole, as the rig swayed slightly in the swell. The figure turned away from the ocean and returned to the dark confines of the concrete box.

The only things in the depressing room were a toilet, a sparse bed, a barely adequate half bath, and an old tube television, volume turned off.

On the TV set, Tom Cafferty addressed the UN General Assembly.

The glow from the TV lit up a small portion of

the room just in front of it, and the silhouetted figure watched the screen. As Cafferty spoke, the figure clenched his right hand slowly into a fist.

The pictures were annoying, but equally as laughable and pathetic.

When the speech finished, the TV screen in the prison cell returned to endless static, illuminating the grizzled expression of an old man sitting in a wheelchair in the middle of the room. A gray beard covered his tired face, with deep wrinkles around his bloodshot eyes. Vomit caked his prison jumpsuit from the relentless rocking of the ocean rig.

If these fools think they can win this war without me, they'll soon learn what only I know.

The man stared at the static, motionless.

The world will come begging on their knees, desperately asking me for help.

The prisoner fought back the vomit, but it was no use. It dribbled down his jumpsuit, adding a new layer onto the old.

And I will help save them . . .

Under one condition . . .

If Thomas Cafferty is dead.

ACKNOWLEDGMENTS

The success of *Awakened* is due in large part to our amazing fans—thank you for always supporting Sal, Joe, Q, and myself. You truly are the best fans in the world. Huge thanks to my tireless, talented, charming friend and coauthor, Darren Wearmouth. Thanks to David Pomerico from Harper Voyager, Lisa Sharkey and the entire team from HarperCollins, and Karen Davies and the team from Harper360 for being the best in the business. Thanks to Susan, Carsen, Joseph, Nicole, and Chá—my fantastic colleagues and friends—for helping make all this creativity possible. Thanks to Jack Rovner and Dexter Scott from Vector Management, Nick Nuciforo and Brandi Bowles from UTA, Danny Passman from GTRB, Phil Sarna and Mitch Pearlstein from PSBM, and Elena Stokes and the team from Wunderkind PR. Our team is truly the best!

Mom and Dad (and my entire family)—love you

all. Thanks for always being so supportive. Jiggy—sorry for chapter 1. Spear—you're to blame for all this.

—JAMES S. MURRAY

I'm proud of how this book turned out after James' and my long hours of riffing, writing, editing, and shots of Jameson. He's a great guy to work with and I deeply value our partnership. I'd also like to thank three other people. First, Paul Lucas from Janklow & Nesbit, who works tirelessly on my behalf. Second, David Pomerico from Harper Voyager. I've already said in the *Awakened* acknowledgments what David brings to the party, but his patience and understanding are also two admirable traits he possesses. Third, a person who shall remain nameless but who provided a constant source of motivation. Lastly, and most importantly, a huge thanks to you for reading *The Brink*.

—DARREN WEARMOUTH